Dear Reader,

When I attended my twenty-year high school reunion, I really didn't know what to expect. After graduation I had moved across country and over the years I'd lost touch with most of my classmates. I have to admit I was nervous. Would we recognize each other? Would talking be awkward?

Despite my worry, I was delighted to find that walking into my high school was like being swept back in time, and even though many years had passed, my old friends were surprisingly the same. Even though we'd aged, when we spoke to each other, our distinct personalities still came through. Memories came rushing back and so did our familiar chatter and laughter. Our connection remained despite our individual life journeys.

Some say that our oldest friends are our best friends. I think in some aspects this is true. Maybe it's the shared experiences in those formative, sometimes tumultuous, years of growing up that create such a bond that lasts a lifetime. Or maybe it's just the comfort of knowing someone who has seen the real you though bad-hair years and braces. Whatever creates the connection, I am grateful that it exists.

In *Unlocking the Truth*, Anne Gibson has a chance to visit some of her high school classmates. I hope you enjoy reading Anne's adventure as she digs into the past to find clues to solve a mystery that could damage one or all of them.

Many blessings to you,
Kelly Ann Riley
writing as Emily Thomas

Unlocking *the* Truth

Secrets of the
BLUE HILL LIBRARY

EMILY THOMAS

Guideposts

New York

Secrets of the Blue Hill Library is a trademark of Guideposts.

Published by Guideposts
16 East 34th Street
New York, New York 10016
Guideposts.org

Cover and interior design by Müllerhaus
Cover illustration by Rob Fiore, represented by Artworks Illustration
Typeset by Aptara, Inc.

Printed and bound in the United States of America
10 9 8 7 6 5 4 3 2 1

CHAPTER ONE

Overnight, autumn had splashed brilliant hues of yellow and orange on the trees lining the streets of Blue Hill, Pennsylvania. From her kitchen window, Anne Gibson had an excellent view of the rolling hills. She took a deep breath of contentment. She enjoyed the peaceful Monday morning routine as her two children readied for school. The smell of brewing coffee signaled a fresh day with a clean slate to fill spending time with her family and working on the house and library she'd come to love.

"Mom!" A resounding crash sounded below and footsteps pounded on the stairs. Anne nearly dropped her coffee mug as their big brown dog burst into the kitchen. Paws flailed on the polished wood floor as he slid into Anne's knees. With an *oomph*, she caught the animal.

Her nine-year-old son, Ben, skidded to a stop behind him. "Sorry, Mom."

Anne tugged on Hershey's collar, making him sit. "What happened? Are you okay?"

"I went to feed Hershey on the back porch, and he almost knocked me over getting into the house. I think he wanted to see you."

"*Hmm.*" Anne suspected that, although Hershey had a nice doghouse and run in the backyard, he considered himself a member of their family with equal rights to the house.

"What was that crash?"

Ben's hazel eyes widened. "Oh, uh, you know those books that were in the hall?"

"Yeah?" Anne had stacked several piles of books outside the Reference Room while she'd put another coat of paint on a shelf. She still had a number of items on her To Do list before she had the library just how she wanted it.

"They all tipped over," Ben said. "I can go pick them up if you want."

Anne sighed. She usually locked the door between their living quarters and the second-floor library area. She shouldn't have left it open this morning when she'd returned a book to the Fiction Room that she'd read last night. "You won't have time for breakfast if you do. I'll take care of them later. Take Hershey back downstairs and then wash your hands. Hurry, okay?"

Ben grabbed Hershey's collar and pulled the reluctant Lab out of the second-floor living area and down the back stairs. Anne smiled as she turned to the sink to wash her hands. She hadn't wanted to take in a pet so soon after moving back to Blue Hill from New York. They had experienced so many changes since her husband had passed away, but Ben had wanted a dog so badly. Shortly after their move to Blue Hill he'd helped a stray dog find its rightful owners and continued to beg for one of his own. He'd even written up a signed contract of commitment to take care of a dog. Anne had been so impressed with the maturity and responsibility her son showed, she took him to the Blue Hill Humane Society and he picked out Hershey.

"Liddie, sweetheart, you need to come eat." Anne poked her head in her daughter's room. Her five-year-old sat on the bed surrounded by discarded clothing. "Why did you change clothes?"

She rubbed her neck. "The shirt itched me."

"Itched you?" Anne picked up the long-sleeved blouse they'd just bought. She felt the collar between her fingers. "Well, it is a little stiff. We'll just wash it again and then it should be okay. If you're going to wear short sleeves, you need to take a warm sweater or sweatshirt. It's going to get colder this afternoon."

Liddie nodded and rubbed her neck again.

"Let me see." Anne lifted Liddie's soft brown hair and examined her neck. The pink skin did look slightly irritated. Poor baby.

"Mom! The toast is burning!" Ben yelled.

Anne dashed back to the kitchen as the smoke alarm went off. She had been using Aunt Edie's old toaster, which was almost as much of an antique as the house itself.

Charcoal slices smoldered. Anne grabbed a potholder and snatched up the bread slices, threw them in the sink, and turned the water on. Ben coughed as he climbed on a chair and poked the smoke alarm button until it stopped.

Anne pushed the window up, letting in the crisp air. The sound of barking rushed into the room. Hershey was chasing a squirrel around the backyard.

"Stop that, Hershey! Let the squirrel alone!" Anne yelled. Hershey paid no heed, but the squirrel leapt on the hundred-year-old oak, chattering all the while.

"Do you want me to go down and tell Hershey to stop barking?" Ben asked.

Anne glanced at the clock. They were officially behind schedule. So much for her peaceful start to the day. "Let's just eat. He'll stop soon." At least she hoped so. "Did you wash your hands?"

"Oh! I forgot." Ben headed for the bathroom.

Anne quickly spooned up the oatmeal from the stove into bowls, sprinkled on some raisins, swirled a little honey on top, and placed them on the table for the kids.

"Liddie," she called. "Come eat."

Anne eyed the ancient toaster, wondering if she dared trust it again. The more modern model she'd brought from New York was broken. Besides, the old silver 1950s toaster reminded her of pleasant summer breakfasts with Aunt Edie. She tucked in another two slices and kept an eye on them as she finished the lunches. She placed sandwiches and grapes into the lunch boxes, Liddie's Tinker Bell and Ben's Spider-Man, and clicked them shut.

"Mom." Ben returned to the kitchen. "The faucet is dripping again."

Anne suppressed a groan. "I'll see if I can get it fixed." She spread peanut butter on the toast. Liddie still hadn't made an appearance.

"Liddie, honey. Please hurry. You'll be late!"

Liddie shuffled into the room. She'd changed shirts yet again. The soft blue, long-sleeved T-shirt was wrinkled, but Anne wasn't going to send her back to pick out something else. Liddie scooted onto her chair.

"Let's say the blessing. I think it's your turn, Liddie," Ann said as she took her children's hands.

Liddie shook her head, surprising Anne. Usually Liddie liked to say the blessing and offered to say one even if her brother got chosen instead.

"Ben?" She turned to her son, who fidgeted in his seat.

Ben bowed his head. "Dear Lord, thanks for this day and please bless the food. Please help me on my math quiz today. And please help Hershey stay out of trouble. Amen."

"Amen." Anne glanced at Liddie, who poured milk on her oatmeal and dug in. At least she was eating. Anne supposed her little girl was tired from the church picnic yesterday. The children played hide-and-seek for hours. Her rambunctious kindergartener could run as fast as the boys in her class and did a good job keeping up with her brother too.

Anne passed the milk to Ben. "I didn't know you had a math quiz today."

Ben shrugged. "I forgot about it until last night."

"Are you ready for it?" Anne asked. As a fourth grader, Ben often had homework, and Anne wanted him to establish good study habits.

He shrugged. "Maybe."

There wasn't time to pursue the subject of trying your best versus just thinking maybe, so Anne filed it away for future discussion. There was so much more to parenting than she'd ever imagined, and she hadn't expected to be doing it alone.

Talk was minimal as they quickly ate their food. It wasn't Anne's idea of a relaxed breakfast, but they'd get to school on time if they left soon. She sent the kids off to brush their teeth and get something warm to wear. Then they descended down the two flights to the first floor, which housed the main library.

Liddie picked up something by the front door.

"What is it?" Anne asked, pulling a long, navy sweater over her T-shirt and jeans.

Liddie shrugged and handed over a medium-sized manila envelope. Anne tossed it on the checkout desk and hustled the children through the door.

Crisp air greeted them as they crossed the wide porch to the sidewalk. The temperature had taken on a chill after a gorgeous fall day yesterday in the park. Their feet crunched through the piles of leaves.

Raking leaves would make a good job for Ben. Anne had spent many hours doing the same when she'd grown up in Blue Hill. When she was young, she would leap in the piles her father had spent hours raking up. Her dad, bless his heart, had never complained. One time he dove right in with her and buried her in the brightly colored pile.

"What are you smiling at?" Ben asked as they reached the car and Anne was helping Liddie into her booster seat.

"Just remembering how fun raking leaves was with your grandpa. We're going to have to get started on our yard soon."

Ben made a face, but Liddie looked up. "I want to rake leaves. Please?"

"We'll have plenty of opportunities." Anne waved to a neighbor as they drove down the street. She quickly found a parking spot at the Blue Hill Elementary School, a tall, three-story brick building that was at least seventy years old. She had attended here when the building used to house the high school. A few years ago, a new high school had been built and this one was remodeled and converted to an elementary school. Ben separated himself from them as soon as they left the car. He had spied Ryan Slater and ran off with a "Bye, Mom!" flung over his shoulder.

Liddie stuck close and seemed to drag her feet when they reached her kindergarten room. Usually she charged right in.

"You okay, Liddie?" Anne automatically placed her palm on the child's forehead. No fever. "Are you tired?"

Liddie shrugged and slunk into the noisy room full of kindergartners.

"See you later, sweetie." Anne gave her a quick kiss on the top of her head, reluctant to leave when Liddie seemed so out of sorts.

"Liddie!" Suzy, a little blonde girl waved. Liddie waved back and ran over to the table where Suzy was playing with lumps of brightly colored clay.

Anne turned back down the hall with relief, thinking again that her daughter was just tired from her busy weekend. She drove toward home with a prayer that her children would have a good day.

When she reached home, she checked on Hershey, who was snoozing in the sun. She climbed the stairs, pausing on the second floor to look at the toppled stacks of books. They'd all have to be sorted again. She pushed them back against the wall and continued to their apartment.

After cleaning up their breakfast mess, she checked on the bathroom faucet. It did have a slow leak. She wondered if she could ask Alex over to fix it. Or maybe he could refer her to someone who wouldn't charge too much. She grabbed the kitchen phone and dialed. Alex's voice mail answered.

Since Alex Ochs, her high school boyfriend, had done renovations on the house, she knew the brief message she left wouldn't be a surprise. And since he now owned a contracting business and had been raising Ryan, his late sister's ten-year-old son and Ben's best friend, she hoped he'd be able to fit the small request from a friend into his schedule.

Anne brewed herself another cup of coffee and went downstairs to the library's checkout desk. She had a few minutes before opening the library to the public and decided to go through the stack of mail that had gathered since last Friday.

Anne took a sip from her mug and sorted through envelopes, separating out the bills, a magazine, the manila envelope, and a card from her mother. Even though her mother was proficient with e-mail and on Facebook, she still sent cards and notes through the mail at least monthly. She slipped out a pretty, flowery card. Tucked inside was a photo of her father on the greens standing by a shiny blue golf cart. On the back of the photo her mother had written, "Dad's new toy."

Anne smiled, glad her parents were enjoying life in Florida, where they'd retired five years before. Her father had been able to take an early retirement from his position in the finance division of a steel manufacturer thanks to his company's buy-out offer.

Her mother's note was short and sweet saying how much she missed Anne and the kids and hoped they'd be up for the holidays.

Anne set the photo aside to show Liddie and Ben when they got home from school.

She picked up the manila envelope next and slit open the flap. She pulled out an article that appeared to have been clipped from a newspaper. A black and white picture topped the page and a headline read:

Secrets and Betrayal in Blue Hill

Anne examined the photo, which seemed familiar. Was that the Blue Hill High School gym? A dense crowd of teenagers danced beneath hundreds of streamers hanging from the tall ceiling. In the background a banner stating "Homecoming Dance" was tacked on the wall above the band.

She read the opening sentence.

The night was supposed to be a celebration, but treachery delivered a blow that would change people's lives forever.

Anne quickly scanned the column and gasped.

The article was about her!

CHAPTER TWO

A knock on the library door startled Anne, and she dropped the news article as if it burned her fingers. She glanced at the clock. One minute past opening time. She hurried to the door and unlocked it.

"Hello, Mrs. Gibson." Kelsey, a red-headed college student who frequented the library to study, strolled inside carrying a bulky green backpack.

"Got lots of homework?" Anne asked.

"Yep. English paper due, and the teacher says we can't use all Internet references. We have to use some books. Imagine that."

Anne smiled. "Imagine that. Do you need help finding anything?"

"Nah. I got it." Kelsey hitched her backpack higher and headed to the Nonfiction Room.

Anne picked up the article again. No byline. The page was typeset like a regular newspaper but with no identifying byline or reference to a publication.

Was this some kind of joke? Anne flipped the envelope over. No return address. She looked closely at the stamp in the corner. No postmark. The envelope hadn't even been mailed. With the library patrons coming and going, anyone could have dropped it off.

The night was supposed to be a celebration, but treachery delivered a blow that would change people's lives forever. It all started innocently enough at Blue Hill High School. The homecoming weekend was the highlight of the fall season. The homecoming committee planned for weeks to make the night perfect. Jennifer Bruin was on the decorating committee, and her innovative ideas transformed Blue Hill High into a magical underwater scene.

Excited students arrived for the game and dance afterward, not knowing they were mingling with six traitors whose thoughtless actions that night would start a domino effect that landed others in harm's way.

Anne Gibson arrived, appearing sweet and innocent as Blue Hill's homecoming queen, but looks can be deceiving. She was escorted by Alex Ochs, honor student, class vice-president and homecoming king in a chariot of sorts, a 1950s custom convertible. Their self-centered behavior that night caused them to abandon a friend in need.

Jennifer Bruin attended the dance with Michael Banks. Talk floated around the high school that they were dating. However, no one could discern their affection for each other that night. Jennifer's constant criticism drove Michael away, causing his actions to directly impact another, causing pain and suffering.

Kevin Kutcher—

The door opened. Betty Warring and her sister, Nellie Brown, walked in. Betty thumped forward, leaning on her cane. She got around pretty well, or as she joked, she could make good progress if there wasn't any wind. The elderly sisters lived together and took turns reading biographies out loud to each other. They were determined to make their way through the library's biography section. Today they were returning *The Black Count*.

Anne shoved the envelope on top of the article and forced a smile. "How did you like the real story of the Count of Monte Cristo?"

Betty leaned against the counter. "I found him quite intriguing, but Nellie said she liked the novel by his son Alexandre Dumas better."

"Now, now, what I actually said is that I can see why Alex would use his father as the basis for a hero. I found the novel *The Count of Monte Cristo* more of an adventure," Nellie said as Anne checked the book in.

Betty shrugged. "Same thing."

Nellie sniffed. "Not really. We're comparing fiction with nonfiction and..."

Normally Anne joined in their lengthy discussions, but she was having trouble concentrating today. She let them happily prattle on as her mind wandered back to the article.

Who would write an article about her? And what self-centered behavior was the author referring to? She'd gone to homecoming with Alex. They'd been elected homecoming king and queen. It had been one of the most exciting but nerve-racking nights of high school. Alex had dressed in a dark tux and looked so handsome when he picked her up. He'd given her a wrist corsage of lilacs, one of her favorite flowers. They'd borrowed Aunt Edie's old convertible and—

"Anne?" Betty tapped her cane on the floor.

Anne shook herself out of deep thought. "I'm sorry. What were you saying?"

"You were far away, weren't you?" Nellie said with a knowing smile. "Such a sweet expression."

Anne's cheeks warmed. She wasn't being a professional librarian at the moment, daydreaming about a teenage date. She cleared her throat. "So, are you ready for the next biography? Who's up next?"

"I'll have to check what comes after *The Black Count*," Betty said.

Nellie rolled her eyes. Betty liked going down the shelf from A–Z, whereas Nellie preferred being spontaneous and picked out whatever appealed to her at the moment.

Betty leaned on her cane and started off for the biography section located in the History Room.

Anne waited until they seemed occupied and went back to reading.

Kevin Kutcher, high school newspaper photographer and reporter, was assigned to record the evening's event, but he let everyone down. He had a gift for sniffing out stories and seeking justice, except when it really mattered.

Heather Ellison, a gifted flutist and school flirt, danced with several partners. She had empathy for those around her. So how could she miss the opportunity to help one person at the dance who needed her the most? Her actions could've prevented a miscarriage of justice.

Six Suspects. One crime. Justice never served. Retribution never made. The guilty party has a week to confess or this article will be sent the next morning to the Blue Hill Gazette *and the police department. May justice be served.*

A chill started behind Anne's knees and shot to her hairline. Who had sent this? And what crime were they referring to? This was just bizarre.

Wendy Pyle, Anne's occasional assistant, burst in the door, out of breath and radiating her usual enthusiasm for life. Her chin-length bobbed black hair was ruffled, and her blue eyes sparkled. "Hey, sorry I'm a little late. I had to start a load of dishes since I didn't have time last night."

She stuffed her denim purse behind the counter. "The kids had such a good time yesterday at the picnic," Wendy said referring to her seven children ranging in ages from four to fourteen.

"Ben and Liddie did too," Anne said. "Liddie had a hard time getting going this morning."

"Mine too. Ethan and Jacob were cranky," Wendy said, referring to her four-year-old twins, "but the picnic was worth it. Such fun. We may be able to squeeze one more in if we get Indian summer. You know, next time I think I'm going to suggest we pick a theme for the potluck. Maybe we could all bring Crock-Pots of soup and various breads or sandwich fixings, or do a Thanksgiving thing with turkey sandwiches, cranberry salad, and corn on the cob. What do you think?"

"Both sound great," Anne said. Wendy was usually bursting with ideas for the library, and so it was no surprise she'd take on a church event. Sometimes her multiple insistent suggestions could get aggravating, but she kept Anne on her toes. Anne was starting to really appreciate the energetic woman.

"I think I'll talk to Dorothy then," Wendy said, smoothing her hair. "She's supposed to be the social event organizer, although I'm not sure organization is a gift of hers."

"You might want to give her a break. She doesn't have seven children and experience like you."

Wendy pealed with laughter at Anne's teasing. "So true. If I didn't stay super organized, I'd be overrun." She stuck her hands on her hips. "What needs to be done around here?"

"Nothing much yet. I was going to head upstairs to put the books back in the Reference Room. There's a college student in nonfiction doing research, and Betty and Nellie are in the biographies."

Wendy grinned. "Are they arguing over which biography to pick?"

"I think so. They've been in there quite a while."

"You know, I once suggested that they could check out two books at a time and each read one, but they looked at me like I'd grown horns."

"I think they enjoy reading together."

"And arguing. I'll go see if I can referee." Wendy marched across the front entryway into the History Room.

Anne tucked the article in the envelope. She wasn't ready to share it with anyone until she found out who sent it and why. She gathered up the two books in the return basket and headed for the stairs.

She shelved a novel in the Fiction Room. The airy light-colored paint on the walls gave the room an aura of whimsy and fantasy.

She then returned the Dr. Seuss book to the bright, cheerful Children's Room with its three sunny yellow walls. She'd chosen chalkboard paint for the fourth wall so the children could draw pictures on it. The wood floor shone under colorful rugs complemented by the natural wood finish of bookshelves and small tables and chairs. Anne returned to the hall and looked at the books that had been displaced by Hershey. Luckily he'd only knocked two stacks together so it wouldn't take long to return them to order. She picked up an armload and went into the Reference Room. As she knelt down and began replacing books, her mind wandered back over the years.

Aunt Edie had been so excited that Anne was chosen homecoming queen that she insisted she and Alex borrow her old two-seater convertible. That way they could sit on the back and wave to the crowd during halftime.

The parade had been a blur of noise and color with people in the stands waving and shouting. She'd been so nervous when they'd started around the field. Alex, sensing her jitters, had reached down and squeezed her hand. That was the type of friend Alex had been. Intuitive and kind. She managed to wave, and her comfort level grew until she was having a blast.

The homecoming dance was held in the gymnasium, where Anne and Alex had joined their group of friends. The Moonlit Reef theme with blue decor matched her aqua dress and Alex's blue bowtie perfectly.

The gym had been warm, and after a couple of dances with Alex, they had gone to the refreshment table. As Anne recalled the evening, memories flooded back. The gym had been decorated in an underwater theme with glittery green streamers hanging from the ceiling resembling seaweed. She remembered she'd been nibbling on a seashell-shaped sugar cookie and sipping the blue raspberry punch when she spied Jennifer Bruin across the dance floor. Jen had her arms crossed over her chest. A scowl marred her pretty face.

Jennifer and she were in homeroom together and had been friends since grade school. Tall, with long, curly auburn hair, lots of freckles, and pretty green eyes, Jennifer had attracted the attention of Michael Banks, one of the football team's star players. Michael Banks was a fullback, and his height and muscle bulk always made Anne feel tiny when standing next to him. He'd asked Jen to the dance, but for some reason they weren't getting along. Jennifer had grown more agitated as the evening went on until she eventually told Anne she was going to break up with him. She asked for a ride home, but Anne and Eric had come in the convertible, and there wasn't enough room for all of them.

Anne smiled at the memory. Jennifer and Michael actually had been going out for only a month, but it seemed forever in teenage time. Despite that night, Jennifer and Michael hadn't broken up. In fact, they married after Michael joined the Blue Hill police department fourteen years ago. Now they had three children.

She couldn't remember when Jennifer had left the dance. Right after they finished talking, Anne discovered Alex dancing a slow dance with Melissa Armstrong, of all people! Pretty, popular Melissa had always liked Alex, and Anne had been relieved that Alex didn't pay any attention to Melissa's hints at wanting to go out. But then they were dancing!

Even now Anne felt that twinge of jealousy that almost ruined her evening.

Anne stuck another book on the shelf and went out to the hall to grab the next stack. She thought about what the author had said about Heather. School flirt? The petite, dark-haired beauty danced several dances with different football players, but she didn't think Heather had seemed overly flirtatious with anyone like the author had implied. She was just a bright, vivacious girl who played the flute in the marching band and got to know the team. She couldn't remember if Heather had stuck around at the dance long after that or not.

Heather had worked on the school newspaper with Anne and Kevin Kutcher. The article said Kevin was there taking photographs, which would make sense. She'd heard that Heather was now a teacher at the high school, but she didn't know what had become of Kevin.

Her memory of the rest of the evening was hazy except for that crystal-clear image of Alex explaining he had only danced with Melissa to be friendly.

So…Michael, Jennifer, Kevin, Heather, Alex, and she were considered suspects by the author of the article. Obviously the author had to have been at the dance to know such details about them. But what had happened? And who had been involved? She racked her brain. Other than her tiff with Alex over Melissa, she didn't think she'd done anything wrong that night.

Regardless of the circumstances, the author's threat had been very clear. If Anne didn't find out who wrote the article and what the crime was within seven days, she and her high school friends might find themselves in real trouble.

CHAPTER THREE

A nne lifted the lid on her printer/copy machine and placed the fake news article on the glass. The main floor of the library was quiet. A few patrons moved around the stacks.

Wendy had helped the sisters decide on a Bill Cosby biography as their next pick. Although Betty wanted a more historic selection, she agreed to Cosby since she used to enjoy his TV show.

Kelsey had checked out a book on the Appalachian Mountains and another on mining, and she remarked again on how she could get the same information online. Anne had merely smiled, thankful there were still books one could hold and put on a shelf.

Upstairs in the Children's Room, Wendy conducted one of the weekly story times they offered. Although reading to the children was one of Anne's favorite perks of the job, she was glad Wendy wanted to do it this morning. Anne's mind kept wandering to the mystery of the fake news article.

The machine spit out the copy, and Anne put the original article back in the envelope. Taking a highlighter to the copy, she marked the suspects in the article:

Anne Gibson
Alex Ochs
Michael Banks
Jennifer Bruin

Heather Ellison
Kevin Kutcher

They'd been typical teenagers, so why the six of them, out of hundreds of others who'd gone to Blue Hill High? What was the connection? And who could've done something so bad it would follow them for nearly two decades?

The author referred to treachery. Was that overdramatized? Surely if something so horrendous had happened back then she would have heard about it. Of course there had been drama and misunderstandings sometimes, but nothing life-changing. She thought about her own behavior. She hadn't been involved in any crimes, but had she done something inadvertently to hurt someone?

The library phone rang and she picked it up. "Blue Hill Library. Anne Gibson."

"This is Flores Sanchez, the elementary school nurse. This isn't an emergency, but we have a situation with Liddie."

Anne's heart rate immediately went into overdrive anyway. She gripped the phone harder. "What happened?"

"I see from her records that her immunizations are all up to date, so I'm thinking this is some sort of rash. I think it best if you get her over to the medical clinic to see the doctor."

"Of course. I'll be right there." She hung up the phone as Wendy came down the stairs with two parents and four children. Anne drew Wendy aside and explained the situation.

"No problem. I'll take care of things here," Wendy said. "It's probably nothing serious. She seemed fine yesterday at the picnic."

Anne knew Wendy was trying to comfort her, but her stomach would never unclench until she made sure her baby was okay. She grabbed her purse, jumped in her car, and headed for the school.

After finding a parking place in the crowded lot and checking in at the main office, Anne headed for the nurse's room. At her knock, a female voice beckoned her in.

The large room held a small desk, several chairs along the wall, and a cot. Liddie sat in one of the chairs by the desk. Her hands were clenched in her lap, her head bowed.

Flores Sanchez wore a white lab coat. "You must be Liddie's mom." She rose from behind the desk. "Liddie couldn't stop scratching in class, and her teacher grew concerned."

Flores lifted the hair off of Liddie's neck. Tiny raised bumps dotted the area that had been slightly red that morning. "She says she was playing in the woods yesterday, so I'm thinking it may be poison ivy. Looks like it's spreading on her arms too."

Annie knelt beside Liddie. Her poor baby. "My son was out in the woods yesterday too."

Flores sighed. "We better get him in here then. What's his name?"

"Ben. He's in fourth grade."

"I'll be back in a few minutes." The nurse went out the door.

Anne smoothed Liddie's hair. "How you doing?"

Tears pooled in her brown eyes. "It itches. The nurse said not to scratch, but I want to."

"Just hold on. We're going to get help for that." She told Liddie about the note from Grandma and about Grandpa's new golf cart, trying to distract her.

The door opened and Flores came in, trailed by Ben. "I'm afraid he has a rash too. He says it's hard to sit still."

Ben turned and lifted his shirt. An angry rash covered the lower half of his back.

"Oh dear," Anne said, getting up. "I'll take them over to the clinic."

Flores nodded. "Let me know what they say."

Anne led her children out the door, and when they got outside Ben grinned. "I got out of my math quiz."

Anne sighed. "Does your back itch badly?"

"Oh yeah." He rubbed his hand on his shirt.

Anne got her keys out of her purse. "Why didn't you tell me about it this morning?"

He shrugged. "It wasn't bad. Not like now."

They piled in the car and drove over to the Blue Hill Medical Clinic. The squat building that housed the urgent care facility had once been a bank when Anne lived in Blue Hill. Ivy crept up the faded brick walls and wound around the corner pillars. After parking in the back lot, Anne ushered the kids up the cracked white steps and pulled open one of the double black doors. The outside of the building had an aged look about it, but the inside was modern and sterile with blinding white walls and flooring.

Anne filled out the paperwork in the crowded waiting area. The clinic was run by a rotation of four doctors and two nurse practitioners. Since they hadn't visited before, Anne left the section on doctor or nurse practitioner preference blank. After a half hour they were shown to the busy back area, where the nurse weighed Ben and Liddie and measured their height before leaving them in a small exam room. Liddie climbed up on the exam table, and Ben took a seat in one of the two green vinyl-backed chairs. Cartoons played on a television on the wall.

After several minutes, a man of medium height with tight curly brown hair came in the door. He adjusted his round glasses as he smiled at Anne. "Well, hello. Long time no see."

"Hello." Who was this man? She glanced at his name tag. Dr. Anthony Shields.

"Tony," he said. "I was a grade behind you at Blue Hill High." He held up his hand as she was about to apologize. "It's okay, not a lot of people from school recognize me. I left after graduation and only moved back here two years ago."

"Oh, I remember! You ran the tech club. So nice to see you again." Anne smiled, thinking how much he had grown. Tony had been short for his age and hung out with the nerdy crowd. Some of the more popular kids liked to tease him, and one time the guys locked him in the janitor's closet for three hours. Anne had never participated in any of the teasing or pranks, but she hadn't gone out of her way to befriend him either.

"I just recently moved back too," she added.

He nodded. "The library. I thought that was an excellent use of the old house. My wife and I bought a 1940s fixer-upper."

"Is she from here?"

"No, Yvonne is from Michigan." He washed his hands at the tiny sink in the corner. "Met her at medical school. We're expecting our first next January."

"Congratulations. I'm happy for you, Tony."

He dried his hands and turned to Libby. "So, little lady, let me take a look at you first." He checked the rash on her neck. "When did this start?"

Guilt swamped Anne. "She was complaining this morning that her shirt collar bothered her. I should've known something more serious was going on."

"Don't feel bad. It looks like poison ivy, and the rash sometimes doesn't appear for a day or two." He washed his hands again and then took a look at Ben.

"Okay, young man, how did you get poison ivy on your back?"

Ben shrugged. "I don't know. We were just playing hide-and-seek like we always do."

"Did you get flat on the ground to hide?" Tony asked with a wink at Anne. "Roll?"

"Well, sure."

"Crawl along?" He made motions with his arms.

Ben grinned and nodded.

"Well, it looks like both of you must've hidden in a patch of poison ivy sometime yesterday. I'm afraid you're going to be uncomfortable for a few days."

"Bummer." Ben reached to scratch, then snatched his hand away.

Tony pulled a prescription pad out of a drawer. "I'm going to recommend a steroid shot to help ease the symptoms and a prescription for some anti-itch cream. Also, you can give them an over-the-counter antihistamine at bedtime." He paused in writing and looked at Anne. "They probably should stay home from school for a few days."

"Really?" Ben's smile returned.

"Is it contagious?" Anne asked.

"Not usually, except in bad cases where the urushiol oil is still on the skin and someone else comes in contact with it. Then yes, there is a chance of spreading it. Best to be cautious. Did they have showers last night?"

Anne nodded. "An hour or so after we got home."

"I'd suggest taking another one right away and washing with lots of soap. Don't use very hot water. That will open the pores and might make it worse. Later, after the oil is gone, hot showers may ease some of the itching. Also, if you had any pets with you in the woods, they need a bath so you don't come in contact with any oil still on their fur."

"Hershey played with us," Liddie said.

"I assume Hershey is your dog?" He looked at Liddie, who nodded. "Then I suggest he gets a bath. Wash any clothes you wore out there at least a couple times too."

"Okay," Anne said a little faintly. Who would've thought that a fun day at the park would result in this?

"Here's the prescription for the cream and a note to get them an excused absence from school." He tore the top two pages off his pad and handed it to Anne. "What I'm really concerned about is that the rash is spreading to their faces."

He pointed to a bump rising on Ben's chin. Anne examined Liddie and noticed a curved red line on her cheekbone.

"They have to be extremely careful. If they scratch the rash it can leave scars." He put his hands on his hips and eyed both kids. "No scratching. It will be hard, but you must try your best, okay?"

Liddie nodded, her eyes wide.

"Okay," Ben said with a sigh.

Tony turned to Anne. "If it spreads close to their eyes, then come back in right away. If not, come back at the end of the week."

"Thank you, Tony."

He paused in the doorway and smiled. "Nice seeing you, Anne. Welcome home."

Liddie jumped off the table and gripped Anne's arm. "Did he say shot?" Her voice quavered.

"I know you don't like them, but it'll help."

"Don't be a baby," Ben said, leaning back in his chair.

Liddie lifted her chin and glared at her brother. "I'm not!"

A nurse in pink scrubs strolled in with two syringes. "I'm Sandy. I'm going to give you your steroid." She smiled and looked from Ben to Liddie. "Okay, who's first?"

"He is." Liddie pointed at Ben.

Ben's face paled a little, but he held out his arm.

Sandy dabbed alcohol on his skin. "This will be quick." She gave the shot so fast that Ben blinked, startled.

"Is it over?" he said.

"Yup. Fastest shot giver in the East." She stepped over to Liddie, who gripped Anne's hand and squeezed her eyes shut. Liddie jumped when the shot went in, but Anne was relieved she didn't even make a sound.

"You both were so brave." Sandy dropped the syringes in the red box on the wall. "Can they have a lollipop?" she asked, and Anne nodded.

Sandy whipped two lollipops out of her pocket and gave them to the kids. "Okay, you guys can go wait out front." They followed her to the counter, where the secretary was putting their information into the computer.

Wendy came through the door with another nurse. Four of her brood followed her. "Anne!"

"Poison ivy too?" Anne asked.

Wendy nodded. "And there are more kids at school who have it. I put a note on the library door that we will be closed for a while. Hope that was okay?"

"Fine by me. I'm heading home in a few minutes."

Wendy turned and went on down the hall and into a room. Anne opened her purse to pay her deductible and realized she'd stuck the copy of the article in there when she'd been in a hurry to leave home. She spied Tony writing in a chart at the nursing station behind her.

"Wait here," she said to the kids and sidled up to the counter where he was. "I know this is a weird question, but were you at homecoming? I guess that would've been your junior year."

"The year you were homecoming queen?" Tony grinned.

Anne cheeks warmed and she nodded.

"No it wasn't our thing. You know, the geek squad? My buddies and I went to a movie." Tony lowered his voice in a loud, teasing whisper. "Actually we couldn't get dates and didn't feel like standing on the sidelines. Why?"

Anne lifted her shoulder in a shrug. "I was just trying to remember some things about that weekend."

"Good luck with that." He shut the chart and stood. "I prefer to forget high school." He gave her another smile and walked down the hall.

* * *

"Can I help?" Ben called from the back porch.

Anne wrestled with Hershey's leash. "No, you stay there. I don't want you getting exposed to any more poison ivy."

After leaving the medical clinic, they'd stopped at the pharmacy to get the prescription cream. Once home, Anne had sent the kids straight for the showers. She threw their clothes from the picnic and school into the washing machine in the basement. Then she re-opened the library and worked in between checking on the kids and putting cream on their growing rashes.

Wendy called and said she wouldn't be back for the rest of the day. Her kids were covered in rashes too. By the time Anne attended to the last patron and closed up the library, she was dragging her feet. Luckily she had frozen chicken stew in the freezer. She dumped the stew in a casserole dish and shoved it in the oven. Then she went out to the backyard to tackle the dog, literally.

"Hershey, calm down." She'd managed to hose him down despite his dancing around at the end of the leash. Hershey liked water, but he didn't care for the soap bottle.

"Start at his head," Ben instructed from where he sat on the steps with Liddie.

Anne gripped the shampoo bottle harder. The problem was getting the dog to hold his head still. He flapped his ears, spraying her with water as she squirted shampoo over the dog's back.

"Don't forget to do his belly," Ben said.

Anne scrubbed the dog down with her gloved hands and was reaching for the hose to rinse him when Hershey gave a mighty shake, splattering suds and dirty water over Anne from head to toe.

"Having fun?" a deep voice asked from the backyard gate where Alex Ochs stood with his nephew, Ryan.

"Oh yeah. It's been a party," Anne said with a grimace. She waved her arms trying to fling off the suds. She could feel them in her hair too, sliding down to her neck.

"Hershey got into the poison ivy too," Ben said to Ryan.

"Oh yeah. I got a little too." Ryan held up his hand and showed Ben and Liddie.

Alex set his toolbox on the steps. "I came to fix the faucet."

Hershey shook again, and Anne screeched.

Ben stood and yelled, "Stop that, Hershey! Bad dog!"

Liddie giggled. "Mom looks funny!"

Anne looked down at her soaked clothes and then at Alex. They both burst into laughter.

Alex came down the steps and caught the dog's leash. "Why don't you go clean up? I'll finish the dog's bath."

Anne bit her lower lip. "I don't want you to get exposed to the poison ivy too."

"Doesn't bother me now," Alex said, reeling in the dog. "I think I got exposed too much as a kid and built up immunity."

"Okay, if you don't mind. Thanks! Why don't you two stay for supper? It's the least I can do. I have stew already in the oven." Anne stepped onto the porch and shed her tennis shoes. "I need to talk to you about something."

"I need to talk to you too," Alex said, his tone serious.

Wondering what was up, Anne padded into the house and went quickly upstairs. She showered and changed into some fresh jeans and a long-sleeved shirt. She found a pair of deck shoes and headed into the kitchen.

Anne looked out the window to see Alex toweling off Hershey. She took the article out of her purse and put it on the counter so she could discuss it with Alex after dinner. She popped some biscuits in the oven, and by the time Alex and the kids came upstairs, dinner was ready.

"Smells great," Alex said. He washed his hands at the kitchen sink, and Anne sent the kids to the bathroom to wash up. She dished up the bowls of stew and took the pan of biscuits out of the oven and set them on the counter. She was getting a platter out to put them on when she heard footsteps running and laughter.

"Sounds like they got distracted," Alex said with a smile as he wiped his hands on a towel.

"Sounds like it." Anne went to the stairs and called, "Time to eat." She turned to find that Alex had put the platter of biscuits on the table. She smiled her thanks as the boys and Liddie found their seats. Ben and Ryan kept a conversation going about a video game that was being released soon, but Liddie squirmed in her chair and picked at her food. Anne felt so sorry for her. She looked miserable.

Anne asked Alex how his work was going, and they talked briefly about some of his contracting projects, but the conversation lagged some as if Alex was distracted.

"This is really good, Anne," Alex said as he scraped up the last drop. "Thank you."

Anne smiled. "You're welcome, and thanks for washing the dog. Do you want seconds on the stew?"

"Uh, no. I think I'll check that leaking faucet." He shoved back his chair and carried his dishes to the sink. He grabbed his toolbox and headed to the bathroom.

Anne got up to take her dish to the sink. "Liddie, do you need more medicine?"

She nodded. "It itches. Bad."

By the time Anne got Liddie slathered with more cream and sent the kids off to watch a favorite TV show, Alex had finished in the bathroom.

"The faucet should be fine now," he said, avoiding Anne's gaze.

"Thanks again," Anne said, puzzled. What was with him? "I don't know what I'd do without you and all the work you've done around here."

Alex stared at her, a strange look in his brown eyes. He reached into his back pocket and pulled out a folded sheet of paper.

"What are you doing, Anne? Why are stirring up the past?"

"What are you talking about?" She took the paper from him and unfolded it. Her stomach dropped. It was an article identical to hers, complete with the warning at the bottom.

Alex ran his hand through his brown hair. "I can't believe you would do something like this after all these years."

"Do what?" she asked, confused. "You think I wrote this?"

CHAPTER FOUR

Anne held up her copy of the article. "I didn't write this. Why would you think that?"

"I saw your copy on the counter over there. It was all marked up as if you were working on it, and I just assumed that you were upset with me that night over Melissa. You used to write for the newspaper and—" A flush rose up his neck, and he sat heavily on the kitchen chair. "I'm a dunce. Sorry."

Anne continued to stare at him, her heart twisting. Granted, they hadn't spent time together since their high school days, but was that any reason not to trust her? Even for a moment?

"I thought maybe it was a prank or joke to get me to remember that night."

"I wouldn't joke like that. I wouldn't hurt my friends."

"Okay, it was a stupid assumption on my part."

Anne agreed, but she held her tongue. His assumption hurt her, but it also reminded her that their friendship couldn't just pick up from where they'd left off in high school. She'd hurt his feelings by breaking it off from him when she went to college. Her ambition propelled her away from Blue Hill to college, and then she'd met Eric.

"I'm sorry," he said.

"It's okay. I was shocked when I got the article too. I guess I can understand the confusion when you saw it here." It would take time to rebuild trust with Alex on a grown-up level.

She forced a smile, picked up her copy of the article, and sat down opposite Alex at the table. "So, at least we know that the article didn't come from either one of us. Do you have any idea of what crime was committed that night?"

Alex shook his head. "I don't remember anything like that. I had a good time."

"I did too. Except for graduation, it was the highlight of my senior year." Anne smiled.

"Your dad put a scare into me when I came to pick you up by inviting me in and asking my intentions with his daughter."

"He did? I don't remember that." She and Alex had been out on several friendly dates before the prom. They'd known each other for most of their lives.

"It was when you were still upstairs. He looked so stern. I almost ran back out the door."

"You're kidding," Anne said. "What did you say?"

"I stammered around and said something like, 'taking you to the prom and bringing you home safely.'"

Anne burst out laughing. "I'm glad he didn't scare you away." Her father liked to joke. And at the time, it would have been mortifying to her if she'd known.

Anne got a magnifying glass out of a drawer and held it over the article's photo. Could there be a clue in there? "It's grainy, but I think that's Michael leaning against the wall." She pointed to a tall, broad-shouldered boy. "That means Jennifer is probably way over here." She traced her finger across the photo to the table holding a punch bowl. "There!"

"How did you know that?" Alex asked.

"They were having an argument. Jen was going to break up with him."

"That obviously didn't happen since they were together the rest of senior year. They got engaged shortly after you left for college."

"I think they must've patched it up on the way home. I'm surprised they are still living in Blue Hill. Jennifer always talked about wanting to live in a big city. New York, Boston, or Chicago, those were all high on her list. Maybe even Los Angeles."

"Well, Blue Hill is a world away from any of those," Alex said. "And I'm glad about it."

Anne looked away. Alex had wanted Anne to stay in Blue Hill. That's what they'd argued about when they graduated. But Anne had wanted a bigger life experience. She had been thrilled living in Brooklyn with Eric. She never would have come back here if it weren't for the terrible circumstances she found herself in and Aunt Edie's kindness.

Anne glanced at the article. "According to the author, we were being self-centered and took the convertible."

Alex rubbed the back of his neck. "Well, if we had carpooled, I wouldn't have locked the keys in your Aunt Edie's convertible and she wouldn't have had to come help us out."

"It was okay," Anne assured him. "She couldn't have been that miffed about it since she treated us to ice cream."

Alex smiled. "I didn't realize until then how much fun Aunt Edie could be."

"I think she really enjoyed being at the ice cream parlor," Anne said, remembering Aunt Edie's smile as she scooped up her hot fudge sundae amid the throng of high schoolers that migrated over to Coffee Joe's after the dance. She'd left before Alex was done eating, departing with a wink for Anne.

Anne sighed and turned her focus back on the photo. "Heather was mentioned in the article. She was at the dance, but I don't remember when she left." She spotted a blurry figure of someone by the girl's locker room. "There. Maybe that's her."

Alex took the magnifying glass and studied the spot where Anne pointed. "Could be."

"I heard she's a teacher at the high school. Maybe she knows something about that night. I could try to catch up with her, as well as Jen and Michael."

"Okay, so now where is Kevin?" He scanned the photo. "I don't see him."

"The article indicates he was supposed to be there taking photos, so maybe he took this one."

"Lots of kids were snapping photos though."

"That's true," Anne said. Even her father had snuck in the door and taken some video footage of the dance with his new camcorder. She sighed. "He could've just been out of sight when this one was taken, but I wonder what it means 'he let everyone down.'"

"Maybe he wasn't there. I don't remember seeing him," Alex said.

"Me either." Anne had never been close friends with Kevin. He'd just been part of the newspaper staff and hung out with the same friends. "What ever happened to Kevin after graduation? Did he get into medical school? He used to want to be a doctor."

"I lost track of him. His folks recently downsized and moved into an apartment. I know because I did some remodeling for the new homeowners. Maybe Michael or one of the others knows where he is."

"Okay. That leaves you and me," Anne said.

"Where were we when this was taken?"

"I'm over here." Anne pointed near the punch table, where only half of her face was visible. "And you were here." She pointed to him on the dance floor with Melissa, mostly obscured by other dancers.

Alex leaned closer. "Are you sure that's me?"

"I think so, because that's Melissa."

"Hey, I only danced with Melissa because she asked me. I was only trying to be friendly."

Anne stared at him. "I think those were the exact words you used that night."

Alex propped his chin on his hand. "And you had that same look on your face, and then you stomped off."

"I didn't stomp off," Anne said aghast and then realized he was teasing. "At least I didn't *stomp*. I was wearing four-inch heels." Anne burst into laughter.

Alex laughed with her. "You still could move pretty fast."

"My feet were sore afterward, but those shoes were perfect for my dress."

"Yes. Priorities. Must have the right shoes," Alex said with a grin.

Anne laughed, marveling at the memory of how important clothing was to her at that time. Now with the rushed life of being a single parent, being comfortable took on a whole new priority.

Anyway, as she recalled, Alex had followed her outside, and that's when they'd discovered the keys were locked in the convertible. By the time Aunt Edie came and they'd gone for ice cream, Anne had forgiven him. It also made her realize that she had cared for him a little more than she'd thought.

"I'm sorry I acted jealous. I didn't know what to say."

"I'm sorry I gave you cause."

They smiled at each other. She was glad to have her friend back in her life, even if he didn't trust her totally just yet.

She looked down at the article between them. Anne recognized the majority of them if not able to recall all their names. Most of the high school had been at the football game and dance.

"I keep thinking that the author has to be someone we know. Someone at the dance. Someone who is around here now."

"Can you think of anything we could've done to hurt someone?" Alex asked.

"Not as seriously as the person is implying." Anne tapped her finger on the table, thinking. "Maybe he or she is exaggerating. You remember how it was back then. The smallest slight could be blown way out of proportion."

Alex rubbed the back of his neck again. "But why didn't the writer just come out and say what happened?"

"We need a plan," Anne decided and reached in the drawer and got a pen and pad. She felt Alex's frustration, and she'd feel more in control if she had a plan.

"I'll contact Michael, Jen, and Heather. It'd be nice to talk to them after all these years anyway." She jotted it down on her notepad. "Since Michael is a policeman, maybe he can dig up something from that night. Any crimes committed or incidences."

"I'll ask around to see if anyone knows where Kevin is."

"And I can run by the *Blue Hill Gazette* office and see what news they have for that night. It'd help to have the yearbook too. Mine is packed around here someplace. The section on homecoming might hold a clue or at least help me remember names." She tapped the pen on the paper.

"I'll look for mine," Alex said. "It's most likely shoved on a shelf in my den. I hope this is just a bad practical joke, but I agree we need to look into it." Alex sighed. "I'd hate to think that one of our friends might get hurt somehow because someone is out for revenge."

Anne felt a chill tickle her neck. "I hope it doesn't come to that either."

Alex shoved his chair back. "Time to get Ryan home to bed."

Anne walked Alex and Ryan to the back staircase that led outside and started the kids' bedtime routine. Ben was old enough to get ready for bed on his own, so Anne just popped in to his room to say prayers with him. He looked miserable trying to find a comfortable position in the bed.

"Ben, wake me up if you need more medicine, okay?" Anne said and gingerly kissed him on top of his forehead where there was no rash. Since he was older, she allowed him to leave his light on for a half hour and read if he liked, but when she left he was just staring at the ceiling.

"Mommy, I don't want this nightie, I want my Hello Kitty pajamas." Liddie tugged at her nightgown.

"Honey, the Hello Kitty pajamas are in the wash, and besides, they are long-sleeved and might rub your rash.

"But I don't want this one."

"Liddie, stop fussing."

She flung herself backward on the bed, arms crossed with a big pout on her lips.

Anne sighed and decided to ignore the behavior. Liddie usually wasn't this difficult. It had to be the unsettling day and itchiness.

Anne sat on the edge of the bed and picked up the storybook about the adventures of a little missionary girl in Africa, which they had been making their way through. "Should we see what Martha is up to today?"

"No."

"Okay, you can go to sleep." Anne stood and started toward the door.

"Mommy, where are you going?" Liddie wailed.

"To bed."

"But you haven't read to me yet," Liddie said, blinking as if she was going to cry.

Lord, grant me patience.

Anne settled back down and read the story of how Martha disobeyed her mother and got lost in the jungle. By the time Anne reached the part of the story where Martha was rescued by the family dog, Liddie had fallen asleep. They hadn't even said their prayers yet. Anne whispered a prayer for Liddie and then went to make sure the house was secured for the night.

After a shower, she climbed into her own bed and plumped up the pillows against the headboard. She'd brought the fake article and a notebook with her to do a little brainstorming.

Opening to a fresh page, she wrote the names of everyone mentioned in the article and looked for connections between all of them. They were all a part of the same church youth group. In addition, Anne, Heather, and Kevin had worked on the school newspaper together. And Alex, Michael, and Kevin had played basketball together.

Anne sighed as she thought about her classmates. Could she have said or done anything that might have hurt someone else? There were the usual teen misunderstandings and pettiness, but she certainly didn't think she'd done anything criminally wrong that night.

She read over the article again. The warning was clear. Unless the person came forward, the article would be sent to the newspaper and the police. She needed to find out what actually happened that night.

She laid her head back and closed her eyes. *Lord, please help me find out what happened before someone's life or reputation is ruined.*

* * *

"Mommy!" Liddie called in a high-pitched voice.

Anne hurried into Liddie's bedroom. Her precious little girl was sitting up in bed, her eyes squinty, her hair tousled about her red face. The poison ivy rash, beneath a few pale streaks left by the cream, had spread and was beginning to blister and seep.

"Good morning, sweetie," Anne said with forced pleasantness, trying to hide her alarm at Liddie's appearance. "How are you feeling?"

She whimpered and rubbed her sleeves. "Itchy."

"Try not to touch it, sweetie." Anne sat on the bed and carefully smoothed Liddie's hair back. Some of the hair stuck to the rash and Liddie winced. "I'll get the medicine."

She headed to the bathroom, stopping by Ben's room. He was still asleep, but the rash on his neck looked angry too. She quickly backed out, hoping he'd be able to sleep for a while longer.

She grabbed the tube of prescription cream and returned to Liddie's room. She used a cotton ball to dab the medicine all over the itchy red spots.

"Does that feel better?"

Liddie nodded. "A little."

Anne plumped up Liddie's pillow against the headboard. "Why don't you just rest here while I go make breakfast? Do you want some scrambled eggs?"

Liddie made a face. "I'm not very hungry."

"How about pancakes with applesauce?" Anne suggested. Pancakes and applesauce was one of Liddie's favorite meals, usually reserved for the weekend since it took a little extra time to prepare.

"Okay," Liddie said without enthusiasm, attesting to how miserable she must feel.

Anne hurried to the kitchen and quickly got out a box of pancake mix and the electric griddle. She plugged in the griddle and was adding water to the mix in a bowl when Ben shuffled into the kitchen. His cheeks were bright as if sunburned.

"Pancakes? Yum."

Anne smiled at her son. "I'm glad to see you have an appetite. How are you doing?"

He yawned. "It was hard to sleep. My back is itchy."

Anne set the stirring spoon down. "Let me see."

He turned and lifted his pajama top. Ben's lower back above his belt line was streaked with red bumps. The doctor had said it could take a couple days before the entire rash surfaced.

"Oh boy, you really did roll in it," Anne said grabbing the medicine off the table. With fresh cotton balls, she swiped cream gently along his lower back just under his shirt hem.

Ben shivered. "That's cold!"

"Sorry, but hopefully it will dry up the rash and make you feel better." She spread the cream gently. The griddle was starting to smoke, and she handed the tube to Ben. "Can you put this on your neck and cheeks?"

She rushed over and poured out pancake batter on the griddle.

"Do I have to stay home?" Ben asked.

"The doctor thought it was best," Anne said. There was no way he could sit comfortably with the rash on his back.

"I'm going to miss soccer practice."

"It should only be for a day or two. I'll get your school books and assignments so you can work on them here." Anne flipped the pancakes and turned to help him finish applying the cream. The rash wasn't oozing as much as Liddie's was, but not all the tiny blisters had burst yet. She hoped the cream would dry them out. She sent him off to change into something clean and comfortable, then she returned to finishing the pancakes.

The phone rang. "Good morning, Anne," Wendy said. "How are the kids?"

"Itchy. Liddie is miserable. How are your children?"

"Miserable too. I'm afraid I won't be able to come in to help in the library today. I better stick around here since they can't go to school. I hope that doesn't inconvenience you. I can try to come later this afternoon." Her voice sounded stressed, and Anne rushed to reassure her.

"As much as I appreciate your being here, I'll be fine," Anne said, although she was hoping to get out and do some research on the article this afternoon. "There are some advantages to living above the library. The kids will be within earshot. And I'm going to call Remi and Bella and see if they can come in." Twins Remi and Bella Miller were high school grads sitting out a semester before entering college. They usually only came in Monday, Wednesday, and Friday mornings, but maybe they'd make an exception. They also had watched Liddie and Ben a couple times for Anne.

"Good idea," Wendy said, sounding relieved. "Hopefully everyone will be feeling better tomorrow."

"Hopefully," Anne agreed. They chatted a bit about what needed to be done in the library while Anne cooked up the rest of the pancakes. By the time she finished and said good-bye to Wendy, Liddie had wandered out and sat at the table. Anne fixed up the pancakes the way Liddie liked them with syrup and applesauce. Ben preferred butter and syrup.

After breakfast, Anne got them settled in the living room with a nature DVD and called the school office to inform them that Ben and Liddie wouldn't be in. The office clerk was sympathetic and told Anne she'd get in touch with the teachers.

Anne went downstairs to the library and unlocked the front door. She stepped out on the porch and gazed at the clouds rolling overhead, casting a gloomy pall over the day. Anne caught the scent of impending rain as she gathered up the returned books.

Anne decided to work on the fall display while several patrons browsed the bookshelves. The effort of taping colorful silk autumn leaves along the rack containing fall-themed books reminded her of the preparations in the gym before the homecoming dance. Her friend Jennifer, who had a flare for decorating, had helped design the theme in the gym.

Anne smiled at the memory of Jen's enthusiasm. Her ideas were sometimes a bit too radical for their small, conservative high school, but she added a fresh twist of ideas to many of their events. Anne remembered it was Jen who had taken fabric, dipped it in a special glue with glitter, and created a shimmering cascade of seaweed that had hung from the gym ceiling.

And now Jennifer was on the list of suspects in the article.

Anne went back to the desk behind the counter and pulled out the local phone book. Michael and Jennifer's phone number was listed. She checked out a patron and then dialed the number.

"Yo!" a cheerful female voice answered.

"Hello, Jen?"

"You got her."

"This is Anne Summers Gibson and—"

"Oh, Anne!" Jen said with a squeal. "I'd heard you were back in town. I've been meaning to call you for weeks and weeks, but the kids keep me running crazy. How are you?"

"I have kids too, so I understand," Anne said, thinking of her two miserable babies upstairs. "I'm doing great. I've been busy setting up the library."

"I saw something about the library in the paper and planned to bring the kids over. I think it's wonderful that Aunt Edie left you her place. We had such fun playing hide-and-seek there and playing dress-up with the old clothes in the attic."

"We did have fun." Anne smiled at the memories. When she and Jen were kids, Aunt Edie would let them come over and have the run of the house.

"So what's shakin'?"

"Actually, Jen, I'm calling about something that happened yesterday. I got a strange piece of mail and — "

"You too?" Jennifer exclaimed. "Isn't it weird? Someone is making up stories about us. Michael thinks it's just a prank, but it worries me a little."

"I hope that's all it is too. I was hoping you might remember something about that night that I don't."

"I know! Let's get together to compare notes. I have an appointment over lunch, but why don't you come over for coffee later this afternoon? We can catch up and talk about the article."

"I'd love to." Anne explained about the kids and poison ivy. "I'll call if I can't get away."

"No problem. But the kids get home about half past three. Just warning you that the insanity level will go up along with the noise here," Jen said with a giggle.

Anne replied she wouldn't mind at all but would try to get over there around two. She hung up the phone with a smile.

Although living in Blue Hill hadn't been in her plans back in high school, it felt good being home. There had been a huge emptiness in her New York home after Eric passed away. Every room held a memory of him, which was comforting and painful at the same time. She hadn't wanted to leave, yet coming home had its benefits such as reconnecting with old friends like Alex and Jen. She had no regrets for the life she had created far away from here, but it was fun feeling essences of the old Anne, the teenager, with the excitement of having her adult life just beginning.

She picked up the article, studying it again. She just hoped those memories didn't cover any secrets that ruined someone's life.

CHAPTER FIVE

Anne parked in front of a cute 1940s cottage with a white picket fence, a postage-stamp-sized lawn, and flower boxes at the windows. She double-checked the number on the mailbox. 125 Brown Robin Lane. This was the place.

She quickly checked her appearance in the rearview mirror. She'd been in such a rush to leave the house, she hadn't had a chance to even comb her hair since this morning. Bella and Remi had been available after all, and as soon as they arrived, she'd raced upstairs and made Ben and Liddie chicken noodle soup and applied more medicine to their poor skin. Liddie whined that she didn't want Anne to leave but soon got distracted when Bella came upstairs and offered to play Candy Land with her.

Anne smoothed a brown strand back into her low ponytail and wished she'd taken the time to trade her large-framed glasses for her contacts.

She got out of the car and opened the picket gate. The tiny house was charming but so unlike her flamboyant friend. Jen had been ultramodern in her style, at least as a teenager growing up in a small town. During sleepovers, Jen had talked about the sleek condo she'd have in downtown New York, Boston, or another big city. Interesting how paths changed, just like Anne's had. Now, here she was back in Blue Hill.

"Anne!" a woman with auburn, short-spiked hair flew out the door and wrapped her thin arms around Anne for a quick hug. Except for a few laugh lines by her green eyes and a couple pounds around her middle, Jennifer was the spitting image of her high school version.

"You're looking good, girlfriend!" Jen's gaze swept over Anne, making her feel a little self-conscious in her T-shirt, jeans, and tennis shoes compared to Jen's black slacks, burgundy peasant shirt with big sleeves, and knee-high boots.

"So are you."

Jen twirled. "Not bad for a mother of three, huh?" She giggled. "Hard to believe it's been more than fifteen years." She stepped back and let Anne enter. The hardwood floors in the living area were finished in a rich cherry hue. Overstuffed modern couches flanked the stone fireplace. Anne was impressed how Jen had combined her contemporary flair with small touches of history in the old house.

"Your house is so lovely."

"Thanks. I hated it at first." Jen glanced around with a sigh.

"Why? This is a great part of town."

"Oh, it wasn't the house. Just that it was located here in Blue Hill. Remember how I wanted to live in a big city? I'm so envious that you got to live in New York! Do you miss it?"

Anne nodded. "I do, but it was time to change directions."

"Well, I got sidetracked. I inherited the house from my grandmother. Michael and I were all set to move to Chicago, where he had a job offer, when she got sick with cancer and my mother couldn't handle it, being frail herself. So we stuck around to help out for a month and that became two, then three. Finally when Granny passed away and left us the house, Michael had a job on the force here and then the kids came, and well, here we are." She sat down on the other end of the comfortable couch.

"So you have two kids?" Jen asked.

"Ben and Liddie. Nine and five." She pulled her cell phone out of her purse and showed Jen a photo she'd taken at the church picnic.

Jen picked up a frame from the side table and handed it to Anne. "Mia is in first grade this year. She's my baby. Jed is thirteen going on twenty-one. Tim is my quiet one and he's eleven."

Anne studied the photo of the three children standing in front of a Christmas tree. The tallest boy had Michael's curly dark hair. Jed and Mia had their mother's auburn hair. Jed barely cracked a smile, but Mia grinned for the camera, revealing a small dimple in her cheek like Jen's.

Anne handed the photo back with a smile. "They're so cute, Jen."

"And a handful, especially Mia. Takes after me, I'm afraid. Always into mischief." Jen laughed. "I even dragged you into some of my pranks. Which I always thought were harmless until—" She glanced down at the coffee table at a paper that looked like the article Anne had received. "I've been racking my brain over what I could've done to be accused of a crime. I can think of lots of things I probably should and shouldn't have done in high school, but nothing that would be considered a crime by any normal person."

"Me too," Anne agreed as she pulled her copy out of her purse. Delving into high school memories had brought back regrettable incidents to her mind, like not trying harder to befriend a shy new girl who joined midsemester. Anne had been swamped with school paper duties and schoolwork. The girl dropped out of school after a month. Later, Anne learned the poor girl's parents had been going through a divorce, and she chose to go live with her grandmother in another town because she didn't fit in at Blue Hill High. Anne felt terrible for not getting to know her.

Then there was also the time she maneuvered out of a lab assignment with Jason Little because he could be obnoxious. Always cracking jokes. Anne later realized, looking back, that Jason was just covering for being insecure and needing friends.

"I've been trying to compile a list of possibilities," Anne said, focusing back on the task at hand. "Like you said, I can't think of anything serious that happened. But maybe it was related to something earlier. Is there anyone who might hold a grudge and is dramatizing the whole thing?"

"Well, there was Tina Dressler and Mindy what's-her-name. I can't think of her last name now. They never liked me."

Anne had a sudden flash of memory of the girls' steamy locker room after PE class. "Maybe it had to do with your super-gluing their shoes to the floor while they were in the shower."

"Maybe," Jen said with a small smile. "But then it wasn't as malicious as what they did to spread the rumor around school that I had mono from hanging with the football crowd. And to think I hadn't even kissed a boy yet, not even Michael."

"And how would you know it would rip the bottom off Tina's shoes?" Anne said, remembering what Jen had said to the gym teacher.

"Exactly, and who knew that Converse shoes cost so much? I got my gym shoes at Kmart," Jennifer said. "But anyway, the rumor she started caused a fight between Michael and me before the homecoming dance. Andy Dickerson had mono and couldn't play in the homecoming game. Michael had the nerve to believe Tina."

"Is that why you weren't getting along at the dance?"

"Oh, you remember that, do you?" Jen asked with a sheepish grin.

"Women never forget anything when it comes to romance and all that icky kind of stuff," a male voice said from the doorway to the kitchen.

"Michael!" Anne popped up as the broad-shouldered, large man crossed the room. His abundant curly dark hair had receded, leaving a shiny bald spot, but his blue eyes were as sparkly as ever. He gave her a bear hug.

"Little Anna Banana." Michael grinned, calling her the nickname he gave her sophomore year when her mother kept packing bananas in her lunch after she'd read an article that bananas were brain food.

"Mikey!" Anne teased back. "Or should I call you Officer Mikey?"

He squared his shoulders. "That's Officer Banks to you."

"Soon to be Detective Banks," Jen said with a warm smile for her husband.

"We'll see. I'm going to take the exam next spring. Competition for positions is fierce, especially now with budget cuts."

"I think it's terrific that you're going for it," Anne said, delighted for her friend.

"And of course that's also assuming he keeps his record clean." Jen glanced down at the article on the coffee table. "Someone is trying to smear our reputations."

"You worry too much, Jen." Michael picked up the article from the coffee table and settled back in the easy chair.

"Besides, the author doesn't mention who the culprit was or, for that matter, what the crime was," Anne added.

"Sounds like a nutcase to me," Michael said.

"Do you know anyone who might pull something like this?" Anne asked Michael.

"The guys on the football team used to pull pranks, but I can't see any of them going to the trouble to write an article. If they were really angry with me, they'd just come over and get in my face."

"The direct approach." Anne grinned. The football players were a rough and tumble group but basically nice guys. "Okay, so I'm thinking that from the details from the article that the writer had to be at the dance."

"I don't recall anything unusual," Michael said. "But then I was preoccupied." He glanced at his wife. "We were having an argument over nothing."

"Nothing?" Jennifer's pitch rose. "You believed that awful rumor that I had mono, and you wouldn't dance with me."

Michael shook his head. "I never believed you had mono. You accused me of wanting to see other girls all because what's-her-name…"

"Tina."

"…asked me to the dance." Michael gave his head a little shake. "And I said no. And I didn't dance because I have two left feet and look ridiculous."

Jen grinned and looked at Anne. "He still does, but I love him anyway. Sorry. We're being rude and wasting your time."

"Oh, it's fine," Anne said with a deadpan expression. "This just reminds me of old times."

"Score!" Michael said with a booming laugh.

Anne giggled. "I'm teasing. You two weren't that bad. Besides, we were just kids." She pulled out her notebook from her purse. "Now, back to this article. There are six of us mentioned. I was with Alex, and we met my great-aunt Edie afterward and went for ice cream. Heather was at the dance, but I don't remember when she left."

"Ah. Heather," Michael said with a small smile. "She was a pretty little thing in her marching band uniform."

"Do you see what I mean?" Jen rolled her eyes and turned to Anne. "And he wondered why I was upset about Tina."

"I meant that a lot of the guys thought she was cute," Michael said. "Sweetheart, I really only had eyes for you. Still do."

Jen smiled at her husband and turned to Anne. "Heather was upset that night, and I think she left early. I vaguely remember some guy was bugging her." She glanced at her husband.

"Don't look at me. I had my hands full with you."

"So you guys went straight home from the dance?" Anne asked, her pencil poised over her notebook.

Michael glanced at Jen. "I wouldn't say straight home. We sat in the car and talked for a while."

"What time did you get home?" Anne persisted and then smiled. "Sorry, I sound like I'm giving you the third degree."

"You're a soft touch," Michael said. "I just wish we could be more help. If I were doing the questioning, I'd say Jen and I really had no solid alibi. We can only alibi each other, and of course we're biased."

Jen frowned. "Like the article said, we might have been so preoccupied with the quarreling that we didn't notice something was going down."

Anne nodded. "It wouldn't have occurred to me that anything was wrong." And why would the author bring this up now, all these years later? It was very puzzling. Judging from Michael's and Jen's faces they seemed as oblivious as she felt.

Anne glanced back down at her notes. "Back to Heather. Have you talked to her recently?"

"She teaches at the high school," Jen said. "I bump into her occasionally at the grocery store."

"Her last name is Stafford now?" Anne recalled what she had learned from Alex.

"Yep. She married Mark a few years ago," Jen said. "Do you remember him? He was two grades ahead of us and on the drama team at church one year. Tall, skinny, dark, a little geeky but kind of cute."

Anne got an image of a gangly teen with thick, black-rimmed glasses. "I think I remember him. He had braces that he had to wear headgear for...?"

"That's him," Michael said. "Decent guy. He's an optometrist now. If you ever need new glasses, he may give you a small discount if you mention you went to Blue Hill High."

"I'll have to remember that. But…I don't remember him being around our senior year. He would've been in college by then, right?"

"Probably. I don't know how he and Heather ever got together. She was more interested in Jerry Newman."

"Now there was a guy destined for the lockup. What a temper," Michael said. "Great fullback but not always the smartest guy."

Jerry had been a grade behind, and Anne didn't know him well. He'd been in a couple classes with her, but he usually sat at the back and didn't pay much attention. He played football but ran with a different, rougher crowd. "Where's Jerry now?"

"No idea, but I can check. Got busted for a couple DUIs and disorderly conduct when I first joined the force. Either he's kept himself clean or left town."

"Or he's in prison somewhere," Jen said, shaking her head. "Anyway, Heather must've wised up and stopped going after the bad boys like Jerry Newman because Mark seems as nice as they come."

Appearances could be deceiving though. Anne made a note to follow up on Jerry. If he had been at the dance that night, maybe he and Heather got into some kind of trouble. "What about Kevin Kutcher? Did you see him at the dance?"

"Don't recall," Michael said. "The dude left for college and, as far as I know, never came back."

"He hasn't come to any of the high school reunions, just like some other people I know." Jen threw a pointed look at Anne.

Anne bit her lower lip. "I wanted to. It just seemed too far of a drive with little kids and then…I expect I will be here for our twentieth."

"We still have a few years to go before then. Don't make me feel any older than necessary," Jen said with a laugh.

Michael snorted. "You're not old. You're in the prime of life."

"Yeah, right." Jen laughed again and flopped back on the couch.

Anne drew a question mark by Kevin's name. Maybe Heather would know where he was since she had also worked on the newspaper with him.

"You guys have been so great answering all my questions," Anne said. "Let's take this from another angle. Any clue to what crime the writer is referring to?" She looked at Michael. "Is there some way you can check the police records for that night? See if anything occurred?"

"I already thought of that. I ran a quick search but nothing turned up. Not surprising since the station's computer database is being updated. I can check in the hardcopy files in the basement when I get a chance."

"That would be helpful," Anne said. "I appreciate your time with this."

"I still think we're worrying over nothing." Michael heaved himself to his feet. "But we appreciate your looking into it. Let me know if you need anything else. The leaves out front are calling me."

"Yeah, we're just the picture of domesticity here," Jen said, picking up a throw pillow and hugging it close. "Hey, Anne, I was sorry to hear about your husband. I should've called you. It's just—"

Anne placed her hand over Jen's. "I know. It's okay. I wish I had stayed in touch better too. But I'm glad we share such fun memories. No one can take them away."

Jen smiled but still looked wistful. "So true."

Anne stuffed the copy of the article and her notebook into her purse. "Thanks for the coffee and the talk."

"I enjoyed it. I just wish this hadn't been the reason," Jen said. "I guess one way or another we'll find out the truth about that night. Six more days to go."

Anne nodded, although she was determined to uncover the article's author before time ran out.

Jen walked Anne out the door. Michael held a huge rake and was already surrounded by piles of leaves he was moving toward the curb to be picked up.

"Making good progress," Anne said, thinking of the many leaves covering her own yard.

Jen turned to her and gave her a hug. "Let's stay in touch more. I'd love to see the library and maybe we can have lunch sometime soon."

"I'd like that," Anne said. She gave Michael a wave and climbed in her car, glad to have a chance to reconnect with her high school buddies.

The day was still gray, and the chill hung thicker. She turned the car on and cranked up the heater before pulling out into the street. As she headed back downtown, she mulled over her conversation with Jen and Michael.

They claimed nothing happened that night other than their teen angst and quarreling. Michael had said he would check into crimes, which would be helpful if he uncovered anything. Anne still wanted to continue to investigate on her own. After all, the writer didn't say anything illegal had happened. Could a crime mean a crime of the heart? Or perhaps embarrassing someone? But would that constitute ruining someone's life?

If the writer had sent the article to all the accused suspects, the article would have gone to Heather and Kevin. She didn't know where Kevin was, but she knew where to find Heather. She made a left turn and headed for the high school.

* * *

Blue Hill High School was a modern one-story building built a few years ago. Since classes were over for the day, the parking lot had mostly emptied.

She had called home to check on Liddie and Ben. Ben answered and said Liddie had fallen asleep on the couch and he was reading a book. Anne told him she'd be home in an hour.

As she was buzzed into the office, she felt a feeling of nostalgia even though she hadn't attended here. The unique school smell took her back to her school days, and she even felt that twinge of apprehension going into the office. Not that she had ever had to go to the principal's office personally for being in trouble, but she'd known some who had to stand the scrutinizing and, if deserved, punishment of Principal Beckett.

A young woman with short blonde hair and vivid blue eyes sat behind the long, white counter. She looked up with a smile. "Good afternoon."

"Hi! I'm Anne Gibson. I was hoping to see if Heather Ellison, I mean Stafford, is in? I went to school with her."

"I thought you looked familiar." The woman's smile widened. Anne glanced at the woman's name tag. Shelby Truman. "Truman? I knew a Nancy Truman."

"That was my older sister. I was a freshman when your class graduated." She lowered her voice. "I had brunette hair then and it was long, down to my waist. Hardly anyone recognizes me now."

"Well it's nice to meet you again. Is your sister living close by?"

"No, she's in Seattle. A corporate lawyer now. She comes back to visit every couple of years," Shelby said. "Now, what were you saying? You wanted to see Mrs. Stafford?"

"Yes, I was hoping she was still here."

"Well, normally the teachers stick around for a while after school lets out." She glanced at the monitor next to her. "Hold on. Let me check her schedule." She clicked a button. "Oh, she isn't here. She's out at a music teachers' conference. Is there something I can do to help?"

"No, but thanks. I can wait to talk to her later."

"Okay," Shelby said.

Anne turned at the door as a thought struck her. "Does the school still have all those framed class photos on display somewhere? I'd love to see them if so."

"Sure, they're hanging in the hallway down by the cafeteria, but you need a visitor's badge. Even after hours. Although if school were in session, you'd have to be escorted. They're getting really strict." She opened a drawer and extracted a white badge with a clip. The word VISITOR was printed across the front with bold black ink. "Just bring it back when you're done. The office is open until five."

"Oh, and sign in here." She pushed a clipboard over the counter to Anne. "I have to see some sort of identification too."

Anne signed her name and put down her phone number, glad that the school was being so strict but sad that it was necessary. After she showed her driver's license, she clipped on the badge as she went down the vacated halls.

The picture rack was attached to the wall near the cafeteria door. It consisted of frames of senior class portraits dated from the present back to 1890.

She flipped through the revolving display to her graduating year and scanned the faces, wondering who could possibly have written that article.

She found Kevin Kutcher. Thick, dark-blond hair hung over his forehead, and he had intelligent looking green eyes. A small, oblong pink birthmark spotted his jaw. She hadn't known him really well, but they had spent time together on the newspaper. The article said he was supposed to be at the dance taking photographs. Could the photo in the article be one of his? The author could have copied it from anywhere. There had been a couple of pages of the homecoming game and dance in her yearbook, which reminded her that she needed to find it when she got home. Was the photo in the article taken from there? It had been so long since she'd even looked at the yearbook that she couldn't be certain.

She turned her focus back to the class photos. There were Jen and Michael. Jen hadn't changed that much, but back then Michael had a thick mat of curly hair. Her gaze paused over Alex. He had been so cute back then. He was still good-looking but in a more mature way. She glanced at her photo. She had worn her hair longer than shoulder length like it was now. She was wearing glasses in the photo, appearing studious and more serious. She had started wearing contacts in college and still did for special occasions.

She moved on to Heather Ellison, who grinned at the camera with a bright, friendly smile. Her locks, cut in early Jennifer Anniston style, framed her face with delicate features. No wonder boys chased after her. She wondered what had happened that night to make her upset.

Last she looked for Jerry Newman's photo. She flipped back to the class after hers. No Jerry. Had he not graduated? She moved over to where the football teams were displayed. She scanned the faces, but she didn't recognize Jerry. Could be she just didn't remember exactly what he looked like.

Anne returned to the office, where Shelby was standing behind the counter stapling stacks of papers together. "Did you have a nice trip down memory lane?" she asked.

"Yes, thank you." Anne took off the badge and handed it back. Shelby put down a departure time on the clipboard.

"Shelby, is there a way I can find out if someone graduated from the old high school? I didn't see them on the class photos in the hall."

"If they graduated, then they'd be out there even if they didn't have a photo. They'd be listed at the bottom."

"I saw those, but Jerry Newman's name wasn't on it." He was on the football team. He would've been in the class your sister was."

"I remember the name but not much else," Shelby said. "I wasn't into football. But like I said, if he wasn't listed out there then he didn't graduate from here."

She pulled a sweater off the back of the chair and slipped it on. "Did you want to leave a message for Mrs. Stafford? She should be back by Thursday."

"That would be great."

Shelby handed her a pink message pad, and Anne filled it out giving Heather her cell phone.

Anne thanked Shelby and headed out to her car. The wind had kicked up, blowing oak leaves across the pavement. She thought about Michael and his piles of leaves, hoping the wind hadn't ruined all his work. Just like she hoped that the article's author didn't have the power to erroneously undo someone's life.

CHAPTER SIX

I s there anything else Ben or Liddie needs, Nina?" Anne asked to the kind, gray-haired office assistant as she picked up the two textbooks and papers from the counter in the office of Blue Hill Elementary. While Anne had been driving home from the high school, Ben's teacher, Mr. Layton called and said that he'd left more of Ben's school assignments in the office. She'd decided to make a quick stop rather than wait until the next day.

"I don't think so," Nina said, looking down at an open file. "I have a copy of the doctor's note, so I think you're all set. Mr. Layton said to call him if you have questions. He left his number on one of those sheets."

Anne located the phone number on a page of detailed assignments. It looked like Mr. Layton was very organized and Ben wouldn't have any trouble making up missed work.

"I hope Ben and Liddie can come back soon," Nina said.

"I expect they'll be back up to full speed in a few days," Anne replied. "Thanks for everything, Nina."

She left the office and paused in the hallway. She couldn't help but think she preferred this old building to the new, modern high school. Although the school had been remodeled, it still carried the aura of another era and felt so familiar it was as if she had attended here last week rather than so many years ago. In these halls she had giggled with her girlfriends, agonized over test grades, and dreamed about the future. Never would she have imagined that her children would be attending here as elementary students.

She trudged back to the entrance, and as she passed the gym she could hear shoes squeaking and balls dribbling. She peeked in the windows to see a basketball practice. She closed her eyes, imagining what it had looked like during the homecoming dance.

To the right of the entrance had been a booth with blue drapes that were adorned with silvery starfish and sea horse decals. This was where the photographer had taken photos of couples and groups before they entered the main room. She wondered where the photo of her standing beside Alex was. She'd kept it on the mirror in her bedroom. That reminded her that there had to be a record someplace of everyone who had attended, although some people had opted not to get their picture taken that night. Nonetheless, she still wanted to see those photos, if they still existed at all.

She pulled out the article from her purse and held it up so she could look at the photo. The angle of the photo indicated it had been taken inside, possibly along the far wall, facing the scoreboard, which had been covered by the homecoming banner. The photographer had to have gone in through these doors to get the shot.

She still had to talk to Heather at some point. Heather had floated between the newspaper staff and yearbook, and since she now worked for the school, hopefully she'd have a clue to where the photos may have been stored.

Anne hurried home and got there in time to close the library and tidy up. She fixed dinner, did a load of laundry, fed Hershey, bathed Liddie, applied medicine to both her children, and got them comfortable. She granted them a half hour of a favorite Disney show and then had a sudden urge to talk to her mother.

"Hi, Anne. I'm so glad you called. I was just thinking about you and the kids," said Anne's mother from her home in Florida.

"I was thinking about you too. How's everything?" Anne sank down on the couch, exhausted, and leaned back feeling a wave of comfort at the sound of her mother's cheerful voice. Frequent e-mails flew between Blue Hill and Florida, but Anne especially looked forward to their frequent phone chats.

"Everything's good. Your dad is becoming more of a golf addict every weekend, not that I mind. At least he's getting exercise, and I'm getting some peace and quiet in the house." She chuckled. "How are you and my precious grandchildren?"

Anne looked at her two little ones. "I'm fine, but the kids had an encounter with poison ivy on Sunday. They were playing hide-and-seek in the woods, and it looks like they rolled in the stuff. I had to keep them home from school. It's so bad the doctor was afraid they could still spread it, not to mention they would have trouble sitting still in class."

"My poor, poor grandbabies. They must be miserable. You tell them Grandma wishes she were there."

"I will," Anne said, also wishing her mother were with them. "By the way, guess who their doctor was? Anthony Shields; he was in my class in high school. He was really great with the kids."

"Oh yes, I remember people saying that he was going places with his life. A doctor. How wonderful! Glad to hear that Blue Hill is benefiting from his expertise."

"I'm hoping the medicine Tony prescribed will help it clear up quickly. They each got a shot and some anti-itch cream."

"When I was a kid my mother used oatmeal on the rash. You mix it with water to make a poultice and spread it on the rash. Dried it out nicely. Only thing is that it flakes as it dries and can make a mess. Do you remember when I used it on you? You had a terrible case of poison ivy when you were little."

"Really? I just remember getting it on my fingers a couple times and once on my ankle."

"Well I guess you wouldn't remember. You were only three. But you got it in our yard. We had no idea that it was growing by the shed, but you found it. Somehow you got it all over your arms. Drove you crazy for a couple days. I had to duct tape mittens on you to keep you from scratching."

"I'm glad I don't remember then," Anne said with a little laugh.

"You never got it that bad again. I think people get immunity after a while."

Alex had mentioned the same thing. Maybe that was why she hadn't broken out with it after being close to the kids and Hershey. "I might try the oatmeal if the cream doesn't take care of the rash," she said. Ben looked over at her, obviously eavesdropping, and his expression was clear he didn't like that idea.

Anne carried the phone with her out to the kitchen and put the kettle on the stove for a cup of tea. "Mom, do you remember the homecoming dance I went to with Alex?"

"A mother doesn't forget when her daughter was homecoming queen," her mother scolded with a laugh in her voice. "We had such fun picking out a gown for you. I cherish those memories."

"Me too," Anne said with a rising lump in her throat. Oh, they'd had a few rough times during her teens when Anne tried to assert her independence, but now she missed her parents and wished they were still living in Blue Hill. It had been the right decision for them to move to Florida, but there were times Anne wished they were next door.

The kids and she had just seen them in the summer, but the time had flown. No matter where her mother was, however, she knew that she could always count on her being there for her. Her mother had even stayed with her for a time after Eric had passed away when she was still in shock and full of grief. Even her father had helped out by taking care of the details before returning home to Florida. She didn't know what she would've done if her mother hadn't been there, distracting the kids and cooking meals. She shook off the memory and returned her focus on the conversation.

"Do you remember anything unusual happening in town that night?" she asked.

"Unusual? Like what?"

"Like kids pulling a prank of sort or maybe a crime."

"Not that I recall. I mean it was homecoming weekend so things always seemed to get a little nuts." Her voice softened. "I remember how beautiful you were riding around the field with Alex in Edie's car."

"Aunt Edie was so sweet to loan us her convertible," Anne said. Her short reign as "royalty" on the homecoming court had become a family affair, as she and her mother and Aunt Edie had discussed clothes and hair for days beforehand. Her father bought a new video camera and recorded the parade. He'd also lingered outside the gymnasium door and videotaped her going inside to the dance. Her heart gave a little thump of excitement. The video would be another record of people who were at the dance.

"Mom, does Dad still have that video he taped of the homecoming parade and dance?" Anne asked.

"I'm sure he does. You know he doesn't throw anything away, especially something like that."

"Would it be possible to send me a copy?" Anne asked. "Like in the next day or so?"

"Sure, honey. I'll get your dad right on it." Her mother's voice sounded intrigued, but she didn't press.

"I've been talking with some of my old high school friends. Remember Jennifer Bruin?"

"Oh, sure. Didn't she marry a policeman?"

"Yes, she did. Michael Banks. He was in my class too and played on the football team. What about Kevin Kutcher?" Anne asked. "Does his name ring any bells?"

"Doesn't sound familiar, but then you had lots of friends."

"He worked on the school newspaper with me and belonged to our church youth group. Blond hair, green eyes. He wanted to be a doctor like Anthony. It'd be nice to reconnect with him." And maybe useful.

"You didn't ever go out with him, did you?"

"No, but I had a crush on him for a couple weeks," she admitted with a smile. She'd even liked Michael for a little while. He never knew and nothing came of it. Such were fleeting teenage relationships. Jen and I were wondering what had become of him. She said he hadn't been back for any of the high school reunions."

"If he was a doctor, I'd think that he'd be listed somewhere. In private practice or with a hospital."

"Good idea, Mom. I'll have to do a bit of research."

They talked a bit more about the possibility of a trip over the holidays and about her mother's tomato plants. After saying good-bye, Anne realized the conversation had left her feeling more energized. There had been a video. Watching it might spark some memories that she and Alex had forgotten.

"Mom, can we watch a DVD?" Ben asked as their Disney program concluded.

It was only seven thirty, so Anne agreed. They had been inside all day, and Liddie had been napping off and on. They probably wouldn't be sleepy for hours.

She wandered out to the kitchen and decided to whip up a pumpkin cake, one of Liddie's favorites. The poor child had hardly eaten all day.

The smell of pumpkin and cinnamon and nutmeg so reminded Anne of happy times in the fall. Anne's mother enjoyed baking, but Aunt Edie was the one who'd turn baking sessions into a party.

She pulled out her copy of Aunt Edie's pumpkin cake recipe. It was still on the original index card she copied right here in this house. It was stained in the corner from a drop of vanilla but still legible.

She checked the cupboard for all the ingredients. She considered asking Liddie if she wanted to help, but when she peeked into the living room, Liddie was curled up on the couch looking very comfortable. Anne decided she probably shouldn't disturb her, or the itching might start again.

While the cake baked, Anne got out her laptop and brought up some doctor databases that rated physician services. Several sites popped up. She could search by state or nationwide. She tried Dr. Kevin Kutcher, and several physician databases popped up. K. Kutcher was listed as a dermatologist in Maine. She clicked the link and got the statistics on the doctor. A headshot proved it couldn't be Blue Hill's Kevin Kutcher.

Maybe he didn't become a physician after all. She tried the online white pages for the state of Pennsylvania. Two Kevin Kutchers popped up but neither lived close to Blue Hill. The ages listed by their names were several decades older than what Kevin would be. She sighed. He could be in another state or have an unlisted phone number.

The cake still had ten minutes, so she continued to explore online. She typed in Heather's name and "flute" and was pleasantly surprised to see several articles pop up including a link to an old roster of the Pennsylvania State Symphony. She'd been the first chair flutist. Anne remembered that she was good but didn't realize how good. Another article described Heather playing for a Washington, DC, symphony. From what Anne gathered, that had to be quite an accomplishment. She wondered why Heather had given that up to come back to Blue Hill and teach in a school.

Anne pulled the cake out of the oven just as the children's movie ended. Ben and Liddie were drawn into the kitchen by the enticing aroma.

Liddie's eyes widened. "Oh, can we have some? Please?"

Ben leaned closer to the cake. "Looks really, really good."

Anne was about to say they should wait until tomorrow but then figured, what could it hurt? It had been a difficult day for all of them. She cut them each a small slice of warm cake and heated some caramel syrup in the microwave. She drizzled the syrup over the cake slices and then added canned whipped cream. By the time she'd finished fixing her piece, she was convinced that cake was a good idea.

They sat at the table. The overhead lighting cast a cozy glow. Outside the wind rattled the window, but thanks to Alex's weatherizing of the old place, the kitchen stayed warm and free of drafts.

"Grandma said she wishes she could be here with you. She's sorry you're so itchy. She suggested something we can try — putting wet oatmeal on your rash," Anne told the kids. "It's supposed to dry it out."

"Yuck," Ben said with a shake of his head "No way."

Liddie just kept her head down and dug her fork deeper into her cake.

"Grandma said it worked on me when I was a little girl. We might want to try it if the cream doesn't work quickly enough and you're still itchy in the morning," Anne suggested and then changed the topic to the DVD the kids had just watched.

After they'd finished their treat, Anne checked over both of the kids. There were a few more sets of tiny blisters on both of them, but she reminded herself that Tony had said the rash usually erupted twenty-four to forty-eight hours later. Anne was hoping they were reaching the end stage of new eruptions.

She applied the prescription cream and gave them the antihistamine syrup and then sent them off to get ready for bed.

She put their plates in the dishwasher and went upstairs to check on Liddie.

Liddie had changed into a pink nightgown and sat in the middle of her bed. She was scratching her arm.

"Honey—"

Liddie dropped her hand and her eyes brightened with tears. Anne hurried over to her. "I know you're uncomfortable, but if you scratch, you could just make it worse. The medicine should start working soon. I'll get you a cold cloth and see if that helps."

She got a damp washcloth from the bathroom and placed it over the angry crimson skin where Liddie had been scratching, and then she picked up Liddie's book from the nightstand. "Okay, let's see what Martha will be up to tonight." She opened to where she'd left the bookmark.

"*Martha awoke to a bright, sunny day. Heat shimmered over the orange African ground. Her dog—*"

Liddie groaned and shook her head.

"What's wrong?" Anne set the book in her lap. "You don't want me to read?"

Liddie shook her head again.

"Okay, honey. Whatever you want. Let's have a prayer. Do you want to pray? You can stay right there."

Liddie hesitated and then nodded. She clasped her hands together and closed her eyes.

"Dear Jesus, please help Ben, Hershey, and me and everyone who got the bad ivy to get better. Amen." She opened her eyes. "Was that okay?"

"Perfect," Anne said, sending her own prayer up that the kids would heal quickly. Hershey didn't seem to be suffering any ill effects, but she added him to the prayer just the same.

Anne set the bedtime storybook back on the nightstand. "Do you want me to turn the light out now?"

"No."

"Okay, we'll leave it on for a little while. I'll go check on Ben."

"Stay. Please?" She reached out and grabbed Anne's hand. Her little fingers felt hot in Anne's palm. Anne decided that if Liddie and Ben weren't better in the morning, they were going back to the medical clinic first thing.

Anne shifted into a more comfortable position on the edge of the bed and began humming some of Liddie's favorite Sunday school hymns. Just as her eyes eventually closed, Ben came out of the bathroom and peeked in at them. Anne gave him a smile and he tiptoed back to his room.

When Liddie was breathing evenly, Anne turned out the light and quietly left the room. Ben was lying spread-eagle on top of the covers. "I'm hot."

Anne touched his forehead, which was warm but didn't have the sharp, hot feel of a fever. "Do you have chills?"

"Just hot."

Anne got him some cool washcloths and did her best to make him comfortable for the night. By the time she took a shower and got ready for bed, she was exhausted again. She flopped spread-eagle on her bed like Ben had on his and stared at the ceiling.

Lord, I'm grateful that it's only poison ivy and not something worse. And I'm grateful for the life You've given me. Please continue to bless us, and help the kids to get better quickly and let me somehow be able to help my friends.

She was drifting off when Liddie called her. She hurried to her room. Liddie was sitting up in bed, clutching her blankets around her. Her chest heaved and her breath came out in puffs.

"B–bad dream, Mommy."

"Oh, honey, I'm sorry." She wanted to hug her but couldn't touch her without disturbing her rash. She smoothed her hair. "Do you want to talk about it?"

"Bad, bad, bad," Liddie repeated and mumbled something else, but she was too sleepy to make much sense. Anne stayed with Liddie until she seemed calm and slipped back to sleep.

Anne returned to her room only to have Liddie call her again an hour later. Anne repeated the routine of offering comfort and trying to soothe her little girl.

As she was heading back to her room, she spotted light under Ben's door. She pushed the door open. Ben lay on his back, washcloths still covering his arms, reading a book.

"It's almost midnight," Anne said gently.

He looked up, startled. "Oh, hi, Mom. I can't sleep."

"Are the washcloths helping at all?"

"A little."

"Okay, I'm going back to bed. If the itching gets worse, let me know. Try not to stay up too late."

He nodded and turned his attention back to his book.

Anne crawled back under her covers, but she couldn't fall asleep. The old house creaked in places. It was a comforting sound now, unlike when she'd first moved in. It also held secrets. Just like the article.

Her mind raced over the details of the article. What was she missing? If the author was trying to punish them, why hadn't he or she been more specific? And why come forward now? It was clear the author must have been at the homecoming and knew each of them. She felt a chill thinking that one of her classmates might be behind this threat. Who could it be?

She sat up. This was ridiculous. Worrying didn't help the situation. Hadn't she just earlier given her problem to the Lord? Instead of obsessing, she needed to do something like finding her senior yearbook.

She reached over and turned the light back on and padded over to the closet. She had stored a couple boxes in there after the move. She pulled out a box labeled "Eric." She ran her hand over the lid. She'd saved some of the items her late husband had kept on the dresser and in his office. She reached farther into the closet and found an oversized hatbox that had once been Aunt Edie's.

The round, pink hatbox was labeled "Mementos." She'd retrieved it from the storage closet of her Brooklyn apartment when she'd moved to Blue Hill. Except for glancing inside before putting it on the stack for the moving van, she hadn't looked in it for years.

She set it on the bed and undid the tape holding the lid on. At the bottom was a yearbook. To her disappointment it was from her freshman year. Where could the others be? She didn't remember having them in New York.

When she had visited Aunt Edie, sometimes she left things here. Aunt Edie had given her a small antique cedar trunk when she was eight to keep her treasures in, and it had stayed here with the house. She kept it locked with a little silver key that she had added to her charm bracelet.

In the beginning, Anne had stored her dolls and doll clothes in the trunk, and then later she kept things like the papers of the secret club that she, Jennifer, and some other girlfriends had formed. She'd also saved other mementos like the note she'd gotten from Skippy Newton in seventh grade that had a drawing of an eye, the word *like,* and a capital *U* on a napkin. It turned out he'd given it to her on a dare, but she considered it her first love note.

Could her yearbooks be in that chest? She'd always meant to retrieve it someday, but time passed and it hadn't been a priority. The chest was probably still in the attic or perhaps the cellar. Aunt Edie wouldn't have gotten rid of it. Anne hadn't noticed it in the chaos of moving in and the repair work going on. She was tempted to go up and search now but thought better of it. Exploring the cavernous attic in the middle of the night with a friend might have seemed adventurous when she was a teenager, but it didn't hold any appeal right now. Especially by herself.

"Mommy!" Liddie called.

"Coming, sweetheart," Anne called. She wasn't going to get any sleep this way. She spied Aunt Edie's old rocker and a crocheted afghan that she'd put in the corner, and dragged it with her to Liddie's room.

She comforted Liddie again and then went to get her Bible and devotional book and settled in the rocker next to Liddie's bed. She pulled the crocheted afghan over her and hummed softly as she opened the devotional book and turned to the message for that day. The text was Proverbs 3:5 and 6: "Trust in the Lord with all thine heart; and lean not unto thine own understanding. In all thy ways acknowledge him, and he shall direct thy paths."

Perfect. It was just the reminder she needed tonight, and she would remember to seek God's direction as she searched for the person who'd threatened her and her friends.

* * *

Wednesday morning, Anne felt like sandpaper lined her eyelids and a vice gripped her shoulders painfully from dozing in the rocker. But it had been worth it, she decided, as she gazed at Liddie's peaceful face. Liddie had slept through the rest of the night knowing her mother was close by. Anne checked on Ben, and he was resting comfortably too.

The peaceful interlude of the early morning hours ended at breakfast. Liddie and Ben were still extremely uncomfortable and wanting to scratch all the time, despite a fresh layer of anti-itch cream.

Shouldn't the rash be getting better by now? Anne thought crankily while standing guard over the unpredictable toaster. The slice popped up, and while Anne carefully snagged the corner of it, she still managed to burn the tip of her finger. She dropped the toast on a plate.

"Mommy, Ben is being mean."

"I am not!" Ben protested.

Liddie narrowed her eyes at her brother. "Are too."

Anne turned from the refrigerator with the butter in her hand. "What is Ben doing that is bothering you, Liddie?"

"He keeps looking at me!" She pointed her finger at Ben. "See!"

"So?" Ben stuck his tongue out at Liddie as he scratched the back of his neck.

Lord, grant me patience.

"Mommy!" Liddie said in a long whine.

Enough was enough. The bickering wasn't going to stop anytime soon with them being so miserable. They were going back to the medical clinic as soon as the twins, Bella and Remi, got to the library for their normal Wednesday morning shift.

"Ben, if you're finished, why don't you go get dressed? We're going to see the doctor again this morning. Maybe he can do something to make you feel better."

Ben shot a sideways look at Liddie but thankfully didn't continue to argue. He slid back his chair and took his dish to the sink.

"And after you get dressed, can you go down and feed Hershey?" Anne asked, buttering her toast.

"I always do," he muttered as he headed for his bedroom.

Ben was very good at remembering to feed his dog. Anne just meant she wanted him to hurry. They were a sorry group this morning. Eric would have called it a Blooper Day and tried to tease them out of their sour moods. If Aunt Edie were here, she would've just snapped her fingers and put them all to work with house chores. Work cured a multitude of sins, she'd always said, including crankiness.

Anne carried her toast and coffee and sat across from Liddie. The rash on Liddie's face actually looked a bit drier, but there were damp spots on her collar from her neck. The ugly rash on her arms looked the same, though. Liddie scratched the back of her hand and whimpered.

"Sweetie, you're tired, and no wonder with the bad dreams you were having. What was so scary?" Anne asked in an effort to distract her daughter and also get her to talk about her fear in the light of day. She didn't want a repeat of last night.

Liddie dug deeper into her cereal, her head down.

"Liddie, won't you talk to Mommy about it?"

Liddie shook her head.

"Are you sure? You'll feel better."

Her daughter took a spoonful of Cheerios. Anne chewed on her toast and waited. When a couple minutes passed, Anne offered, "Would it be okay if we prayed about it?"

Liddie nodded. "You say it."

Anne bowed her head and prayed, "Dear Lord, thank You for this day You've given us. Please help Liddie and Ben to get better soon and help Liddie with whatever is bothering her. Thank You for being there for us. Amen."

Anne looked up. Liddie opened her eyes but still avoided Anne's gaze. What was troubling her little girl? Could it just be the poison ivy making her miserable? But then, why the bad dreams?

Anne cleaned up their breakfast things and then changed out of her bathrobe into jeans and a blue floral long-sleeved blouse. She tugged on her soft, warm boots. The temperature had dropped during the night, so she also grabbed a soft navy pullover sweater.

She swiped on a bit of mascara and tied her hair back. Her face was exceedingly pale and drawn this morning, so she applied a little rosy blush that she seldom used and powdered concealer on the dark circles under her eyes.

Satisfied that her appearance didn't advertise her lack of sleep and disgruntled mood, she picked up her sweater and purse. As a second thought, she grabbed the folder containing her copy of the article and a notebook from the nightstand. If there was time today, she wanted to stop by the newspaper office and see if she could find any mention of crime during their now-infamous homecoming weekend. The thought of doing something productive to get to the truth behind the article cheered her some.

Remi and Bella were right on time and at the door when Anne hurried downstairs to open the library. As she let them in, a blast of chilly wind swept past her and fluttered the papers on the display board.

"Man, it's cold out there," Bella said, setting her backpack on the floor.

"Winter is coming," Remi half-sang, as she removed her parka and stylish wool cap. "I can't wait for Christmas. My favorite time of the year."

"Well I hope it doesn't come *too* quickly," Anne said with a sigh. "I've been enjoying the pretty fall. Besides" — she smiled at the girls — "if winter really gets here, it means you two will be off to college. I'm going to miss you, although I'm happy for you both and know it will be exciting."

"Yeah," Bella said looking around the library. "Hard to believe we won't be coming here anymore."

Remi shook her head looking disgusted at the melancholy in her twin's voice. "We still have three whole months. That's forever."

Anne smiled, remembering how days seemed to pass so much slower in high school. "I appreciate any time you can put in here."

The girls tucked their coats and bags behind the counter as Anne outlined what needed to be done that morning, which included checking in books and putting them away, pulling a couple of books that Mr. Willow had requested, and assisting patrons if they needed it. They could always call Anne if they needed her.

Liddie and Ben climbed in the back of the car, where Anne double-checked that Liddie was safely in her booster seat. Traffic seemed extra heavy that morning, or maybe it was just that Anne's nerves were stretched thin from lack of sleep. Whatever the case, it seemed to take days to get to the clinic and then a year to get into the exam room.

Dr. Shields wasn't in, and Anne opted to see one of the nurse practitioners on duty to reduce the wait time for one of the other doctors. Georgia Griffin examined the kids' rashes, consulted their charts, and then gave them another shot.

"You should start to feel better soon." The middle-aged nurse with a kind, weathered face tsked in sympathy. "Believe it or not, it's not as serious as it looks. Oh, I know it's terribly uncomfortable, but it could be much worse. At least it hasn't spread to their eyes, and since they're past the forty-eight-hour window, you probably won't see any new eruptions. They'll now go into healing mode. These things must take their course."

She held up a hand to stop Anne's next question and answered it. "And it's different for everybody on how long it takes."

"They want to scratch constantly," Anne said, trying to temper the slight whine in her voice. Maybe she should try to grab a cat nap that afternoon. "Is there anything else we can do?"

Ben grimaced behind the nurse's back and shook his head.

"I'm going to get a prescription for a slightly stronger anti-itch cream with stronger drying properties."

"What about trying home remedies like an oatmeal poultice? My mother used that on me, but I don't think I had it as bad as Liddie or Ben."

"It can't do any harm and might actually help," Georgia said with a small shrug. "Just realize you may wash off the medication, so be careful about the timing. I'd give the new cream at least a day to work. I just wouldn't put anything harsh on their skin right now."

"What would be too harsh?" Anne asked.

"Some people wipe their skin down with bleach after being exposed, and it gets rid of the oil so they don't break out or at least don't break out as badly as they could. But it would be way too harsh and might burn them, especially since they're children. Although, it does seem to work on my brothers who are in the woods a lot."

"Don't worry, we won't try that. Probably just the oatmeal poultice."

The nurse nodded. "Another way to use it is to grind the oatmeal up in a blender and tie it in a cloth pastry bag and put it in a nice hot bath. It's not as messy. Or you can try calamine lotion, although what we're giving is stronger." She glanced out into the hall. "I'll get you the prescription, and you can take care of the final paperwork at the counter."

"Thanks for the suggestions," Anne called after her.

Ben crossed his arms over his chest. "I'm not taking a bath in oatmeal."

"Me either," Liddie piped up and then she looked puzzled. "Why would I take a bath in cereal?"

"It's not like sitting in a bowl of oatmeal. You'd hardly notice it if we did what the nurse said," Anne said. "And if it makes you stop itching it's worth it, right?"

Ben didn't look too sure about that.

"Please watch Liddie. I'm going to go down the hall and pay the bill, so we can get out of here." Anne got in line at the counter to check out.

The long hallway of small exam rooms bustled with activity, and Anne stepped closer to the counter to let nurses, patients, and other medical staff get by.

A tall man wearing a long, white coat with a patch that said Lab Tech pushed a loaded cart out of a room and slid by her. "Excuse me," he said. Anne did a double take. His voice, his bushy, light hair pushed back from a wide forehead, and his green eyes were familiar. She looked at his jaw. There was the strawberry birthmark.

"Kevin?"

"Yes?" He turned so she could see the name tag.

Kevin Kutcher. It was him.

"I'm Anne Summers. Well, my married name is Gibson," she said. "We went to Blue Hill High School together."

His smile widened. "Of course! Anne! I didn't know you were in Blue Hill. Are you visiting or living here?"

"Living here. I have my great-aunt Edie's old place. I was recently talking to Jen and Michael, and we were wondering what had become of you. We had no idea you were back in town."

"That's only because I moved back here about three weeks ago and haven't had a chance to connect with any of the old gang. I'm so glad to have run into you. Say hi to Jen and Michael for me."

"Kevin. Get a move on," a nurse said from a doorway down the hall.

"I've got to go. Maybe we can catch up some time."

Anne nodded. "Listen, Kevin, if you have some time later today, there is something important I'd like to talk to you about. Maybe I could call you if that would be all right."

He glanced at the clock on the wall. "Hey, I have a lunch break in about twenty minutes. Want to meet down the street at Coffee Joe's so we can talk?"

"Sure, if it's not any trouble," Anne said. "I have my kids with me. I hope you don't mind."

He glanced in the room at Liddie and Ben. "No problem. I like kids." He pushed his cart to the room where the nurse still waited with a scowl. Anne hoped she hadn't gotten Kevin in trouble.

Of course, any or all of them might already be in trouble if the author of the article carried out the threat of exposure.

Chapter Seven

I scream, you scream, we all scream for ice cream," Anne sang gaily as she parked their car in front of Coffee Joe's. All this research into her past was bringing back all kinds of memories, including silly ones. Being tired wasn't helping her maintain her grown-up demeanor. And she was feeling giddy about finding Kevin. She'd been searching online all over the country for him, and here he was in Blue Hill.

Liddie giggled. "You're funny, Mommy."

Anne turned in her seat. "Your grandpa used to sing that when the ice cream truck came around the neighborhood."

"What ice cream truck?" Ben said.

"Oh, there used to be a little truck that had ice cream and popsicles painted on the outside. It would play a tune and drive by our house a couple of times a week during the summer when I was about your age. When all the kids in the neighborhood heard the truck coming, they would run out to the curb to buy ice cream."

Ben frowned. "Why isn't there a truck now?"

"I don't know. Good question. There might be, but we just haven't seen it." Anne unbuckled her seat belt. "So, is it too cold for ice cream? Maybe this is more a day for hot cocoa."

"It's never too cold for ice cream." Ben opened his door.

"I want hot cocoa *and* ice cream." Liddie said.

Anne reached over the seat and gave Liddie a high five. "Actually that sounds good. We can get a small cone *and* a small hot cocoa—but only after we eat our lunch."

Ben held the shop door open for Liddie and Anne, reminding Anne of Eric and how he'd been teaching Ben to be a gentleman. Good manners had been important to her sweet husband, and she always felt so special going places with him.

Coffee Joe's was a small shop nestled between a sporting goods store and a health food store. Joe's offered ice cream cones, sandwiches, and a variety of mouth-watering bakery items besides the wide variety of coffee drinks and teas. A counter ran the length of the room where customers could order.

There was only one other customer in the place, and Anne guided Liddie and Ben to one of the small, round metal tables that were scattered around the room.

Joe, the original owner, had retired and his son Joe Jr. now ran it. Right now it looked like a high school student worked behind the counter. Anne decided to let the kids go ahead and eat their lunch while they waited for Kevin. When they'd finished their tuna sandwiches, Anne went back up to the counter and ordered two soft-serve cones, two cocoas, and a mocha latte for herself.

The door opened and Kevin breezed in. He joined Anne at the counter and ordered a caramel mocha latte. "It's great running in to you," he said. "I haven't been to any of the reunions and was wondering who was still around."

"You mentioned you just moved back recently?" Anne asked.

"Yeah, it wasn't something I'd planned on, but my parents have been struggling with some health issues."

"I'm sorry to hear that."

"I figured someone ought to be close by. Luckily the lab here had an opening." He glanced around them. "It's weird being back in Blue Hill. Sometimes I'll be walking down the street, and it feels like I never left. Of course it doesn't help that I'm temporarily living in my old bedroom. Really contributes to the time-warp feeling."

Anne smiled. "I know what you mean. Everything is so familiar, but we're different. We've changed, and we're looking at Blue Hill from grown-up eyes."

Anne's order was ready, and Kevin helped her take ice cream and cocoa over to the kids

He looked at the kids' arms as he set the treats down. "Poison ivy?"

Anne nodded. "They've been really uncomfortable, and they can't go back to school until it heals some."

"That's rough. I used to get it when I was a kid too. My mom would use charcoal powder on it."

"Did that help?"

Kevin grinned. "I don't know if it helped or not, but I think it made her feel like she was doing something helpful. I liked it because I'd use the leftovers to streak black under my eyes to make me look like a football player or soldier, depending on my mood."

"So, was it just you that moved back or do you have a family?" Anne asked. Kevin wasn't wearing a wedding ring, but then since he worked in a lab, he might not be able to wear it to work.

"No. No one right now. I was married for about two minutes, and it just didn't work out."

"Oh, I'm sorry, Kevin."

He shrugged. "Hey, life is too short. No sense in wasting time on anything that wasn't meant to be." He glanced at the kids. Ben was sucking at the bottom of his ice cream cone.

"What about you? I think I heard you say once you weren't going to get married for a long time, if ever, and you would travel the world as a journalist."

"I said that?" Anne asked with a little laugh. She probably did. "I changed my mind about traveling when I met my husband, Eric. He was my whole world, and I'm happy with my career in library science." She lowered her voice. "Eric passed away, and then I was laid off from the library system. Shortly after, my great-aunt left me her house, and it's been partially renovated as the new town library. So that's what brought me back here."

"That's cool about the house, but I'm sorry you went through such a rough time," Kevin said. "You just don't know what life will bring."

"So true," Anne said.

"So, how are Jen and Michael?" he asked.

"Doing well," Anne said. They chatted for a while about their friends. Kevin said he also hadn't seen Heather. Finally, Anne brought her copy of the article out of her purse and placed it on the table.

"Did you get this too?"

Kevin glanced at the sheet. "Yep, and then I threw it away. Didn't take it too seriously. I wasn't even in town that night."

"So you weren't at the homecoming dance?" Anne asked, surprised. That would explain why she hadn't seen him that night.

"I thought Mrs. Earland assigned you to take photos for the paper."

"Did she?" Kevin gave a little shrug. "It was college days at UNC, and I had a last-minute college admission interview. It was a long drive to North Carolina. Anyway, I heard it was a great game. Sorry I missed it."

Anne barely remembered the game, although she thought they had won. "So you did you end up going to UNC?"

"Nope. Decided it wasn't for me." He took a long swallow of his latte.

"Any idea who might've held a grudge against us? Or what crime the writer is referring to?" Anne asked.

He shrugged. "Beats me. Sorry I can't be more help. I figured it was nothing to worry about. The truth always comes out, right? So, why worry?" He shoved back his chair. "I'd better get going. Mom has physical therapy this afternoon."

"I'm so glad we got a chance to visit, Kevin," Anne said. "We'll have to get the old gang together sometime."

"Looking forward to it. I'm available most evenings. Obviously. I have no life here yet. Just let me know when. Here's my cell number." He pulled a pen out of his pocket and jotted it down on a napkin before he left.

Anne lingered over her coffee, waiting for Liddie to finish her ice cream. Kevin had a point about not worrying if she knew she was innocent, but Anne wasn't ready to give up searching for the truth.

Maybe Kevin didn't care what people thought about him, but the library and her job dealt with the public. Even a lie could damage someone's reputation. She certainly wouldn't want to be accused of a crime and have to prove her innocence, especially with the library just starting to show momentum in gaining membership. She didn't need people gossiping that she or any of her old friends might be criminals.

She jotted down what she'd learned from Kevin on the napkin with his phone number, which wasn't much except it did create a conclusion that gave her goose bumps. Since Anne hadn't been in town long and Kevin even a shorter period, the writer of the article must be someone who was watching all of them closely. Very closely.

* * *

As Anne drove down Main Street to the *Blue Hill Gazette*, she couldn't help but check her rearview mirror to see if anyone was following. She knew that she was probably being overly paranoid, but whoever wrote that article had to be someone aware of her current life and the lives of the others mentioned in the article.

Five of them had received the article. She wondered if Heather had gotten a copy. Most likely she did or would find it when she got back in town.

Anne parked the car in front of the newspaper office, a two-story, red-paint dwelling of charming Victorian architecture. A bell rang overhead when she, Liddie, and Ben went inside. As she approached the counter looking for the girl who worked there, the door burst open behind them and a pretty blonde woman swooshed in. She stopped short when she saw Anne. "Hi, Anne!" Grace Hawkins, editor of the *Blue Hill Gazette*, said. "What's up?"

Anne smiled. "I need to access newspapers from seventeen years ago."

Grace's blue eyes widened and she laughed. "Have you got yourself embroiled in yet another mystery?"

Anne waved her hand dismissively. "I don't know if I'd call it a mystery exactly." Grace had helped Anne search microfiche archives of the paper before, and they'd become friends.

"What exactly are you looking for?"

Anne hesitated. If she explained she was looking for a crime that occurred on her homecoming night, then Grace, no doubt, would want to know why. Anne wasn't ready yet to involve anyone who was not directly involved.

Liddie made a whimpering sound and scratched at her cheek. "Mommy, I want to go home."

"Oh, you poor thing." Grace examined Liddie's face. "What is it?" She glanced at Ben. "And you have it too."

"Poison ivy," Anne said. "We were at the clinic earlier."

"That's rough," Grace said with a shake of her head. "So, what was it that you needed? I'll be happy to look for you, so you can get these little ones back home."

"Oh, Grace, I'd appreciate it," Anne said sincerely and put her hand on Liddie's shoulder as Liddie reached to scratch again. "I'm interested in any crimes that were committed seventeen years ago, in the last two weeks of September and possibly the first couple weeks into October," Anne said, deciding not to pinpoint the date of homecoming.

"What kind of crime? Burglary? Jaywalking? Parking tickets?" Anne couldn't help but grin as Grace pressed her for information.

"Whatever you can find," Anne said. "I don't mean to be so cryptic, but I can't really explain right now what this is all about."

"Okay. I understand." Grace sighed. "I'll see what I can find." She took a small notebook out of her purse. "All crimes in the last half of September and early October 1996," she said and jotted the dates down.

"Thanks, Grace. Can you give me a call if you find something? I can drop by to get it later."

"No problem," Grace said and then called out to the kids as they went out the door, "Hope you feel better soon."

Anne ushered the kids back to the car, grateful for Grace's friendship and offer to look through the newspapers for her. Anne could tell by Liddie's fidgeting that she was getting to the breaking point and really needed to get home.

"What are you looking for, Mom?" Ben asked as he buckled himself in.

Anne made sure Liddie was safely buckled in. "I know this sounds strange, but I'm not sure. Something happened when I was in school here that may have upset someone, but they didn't say what it was."

Anne got in front and looked back over the seat. "If I can figure out what happened, then maybe I can find the person who needs help."

"Sounds weird," Ben decided.

"It is." Anne pulled out in traffic. The whole thing was weird, yet it could have serious consequences for someone.

* * *

"Liddie, I wish you'd find something to do," Anne said as she prepared a new novel to be shelved. The library was in a lull mid-afternoon. Preschoolers would be taking their afternoon naps, and it was too soon for the school kids to be out. Two senior citizens had just left, and Liddie was wandering around the fiction section.

"Like what?"

"Well, did you finish those worksheets that your teacher sent?" They'd stopped by the school on their way home. Ben was upstairs working on a math lesson. Anne had started Liddie on some worksheets at one of the tables, but Liddie hadn't spent much time there.

She nodded.

"Can I see?"

Liddie went to the table and then took the sheets over to Anne. Liddie had traced letters *m*, *n*, and *p* and filled out another page of counting exercise that involved ducks, frogs, and butterflies.

"These are good," Anne said. "Now it says you should color the pages." Anne pointed to the crayon symbol.

"I don't have any crayons," Liddie said.

Anne suppressed a sigh. "You know where we keep them. Come on, let's go get some."

They went upstairs to the library's Children's Room. She opened the closet where they kept some pretty plastic baskets that held craft items used for Story Time or after-school activities. Wendy was especially enthusiastic about the children's programs and had started a library camp last summer. Anne missed her friend and her energy. The library seemed extra quiet without her buzzing around. She wondered how Wendy's kids were doing with their poison ivy rashes.

So far, it looked like their trip to the clinic had been worthwhile. Liddie was restless, but at least she wasn't endlessly trying to scratch. Ben had seemed relatively comfortable when he had settled at the kitchen table with his homework. Anne had placed a towel underneath him, hoping it would help to draw off moisture from the rash. Who knew that a game of hide-and-seek could have such consequences?

Anne got a packet of crayons and closed the closet door. Liddie was sitting cross-legged on the floor stacking colorful blocks on the short round table where Anne kept a basket of small toys for her youngest patrons, as well as a trunk full of costumes. Anne gave her a few minutes to play and re-shelved some of the picture books that had been left out.

Footsteps sounded in the hall, and Ryan stopped short in the doorway. His arms were red and blotchy from his exposure in the woods, but otherwise he appeared happy and energetic. "Hi! Is Ben here? I wanted to know if he could come out and play."

Anne straightened from where she'd been shelving books. "Ben's upstairs doing some schoolwork. He'll be glad to see you, I'm sure."

"I rang the doorbell, but he didn't answer."

"He didn't?" Anne said with a twinge of alarm. "Let me go check on him. Liddie, I'll be right back."

Anne took the stairs to their apartment two at a time and rounded the corner into the kitchen. "Ben!" she called.

Ben's face was pressed against his math book on the table. He turned his head and looked at her with bleary eyes. "I think I fell asleep."

"I think you did too." Anne laughed, relieved he was okay.

He blinked several times and stretched his arms over his head. "What's wrong?

"Nothing's wrong. I was just worried because you didn't answer the door when Ryan came by." Anne picked up a sheet of paper that had fallen to the floor.

Ben sat back in his chair and yawned. "Is he still here?"

"He's downstairs and wants to know if you can go outside."

"Can I?" He shoved back his chair, suddenly very alert.

"Did you get your schoolwork done before you fell sleep?"

"I did most of the assignment. I can finish it tonight."

"All right, but put a sweatshirt on," Anne said. "Stay in the yard, okay?"

Ben dashed to his room as Anne went back downstairs. Ryan sat near Liddie looking at a picture book she'd opened on the floor.

"He's coming down." Anne smiled at Ryan. She glanced at his arms. "How's your rash?"

"Not bad. It's going away." He held out his arms, and indeed it appeared that his rash had faded. "Hardly itches at all."

"That's great. I'm glad you're feeling better," Anne said, wishing her children would recover faster.

Ben appeared in the doorway, carrying his sweatshirt. "Let's go out and play with Hershey." The boys left to go downstairs.

Liddie's lips trembled and she looked like she was going to cry.

"Liddie, what's wrong? Did you want to go out with them?" Anne asked.

Liddie shook her head.

"What's bothering you then?" Anne studied her daughter's flushed face, worried.

"I just feel...bad."

"Like you're sick?" Anne felt her forehead, which was cool under her fingers. No fever. "Does your tummy hurt?"

Liddie shook her head again and glanced at the crayons that Anne left on the bookshelf. "I want to color."

"Okay, sweetie. Let's go downstairs."

They returned to the bottom floor, and Liddie colored her school papers for a while. Anne finished labeling the new novel and entered the information in the computer. She shelved it on the new arrivals shelf and worked on another.

Three middle-school students came in looking for references on pioneers for a history project. Anne sent the students off in the right direction and then checked books in and out for other patrons.

At closing time, Anne went to the door with the last patron to lock up. As she said good-bye to Mrs. Jenkins, a car pulled up to the curb and Grace Hawkins jumped out.

Grace waved at Annie with a yellow folder and trotted up the steps. "Hey! I got the information you wanted."

"Already? That's great service. Door-to-door too," Anne teased. She pulled the door open wider. "Come on in. I was just closing up."

"It was a slow news day, and finding these for you gave me something to do. I have the police blotter articles for the last half of September and beginning of October 1996."

"That's great!" Anne hurried back to the counter and opened the folder. She skimmed through the sheets with growing excitement. She looked up and noticed Grace was watching with a curious gleam in her eyes. With effort, Anne casually set the sheets down and closed the folder.

"See anything of value?" Grace asked.

"Not yet, but this is what I needed. Thanks again," Anne said with a smile. "Would you like some coffee or tea? I have pumpkin cake upstairs."

Grace put her hand on her stomach. "Yum. That sounds really good, but actually I have to run. Because it was a slow news day, I'm going to have to cover the agricultural meeting and hope they talk about something interesting. I'm not sure how I'll be able to stand the excitement," she said drily as Liddie wandered over with a sheet in her hand.

"Hi there," Grace said. "It looks like you've been coloring. Can I see?"

Liddie handed over the worksheet. She'd colored some of the ducks purple and others orange. Anne smiled. Ben at Liddie's age had been so concerned about getting it "right" and sticking to reality. His ducks would've been colored brown or white, whatever ducks looked like in the wild. Her daughter's imagination, on the other hand, soared into the land where anything was possible.

"I love your bold choice of colors." Grace smiled. "Keep up the good work."

Liddie beamed. "Thank you." She slipped her hand into Anne's. "I'm hungry."

"We'll make supper soon." Anne squeezed Liddie's hand.

Grace glanced down at the folder on the counter. "Good luck with your research."

"Thanks." Anne was grateful that Grace didn't continue to probe her. If she didn't figure out who was behind the article or someone didn't come forward and confess, Grace would know all about the article next Tuesday anyway.

"Oh, I almost forgot." Grace turned with a snap of her fingers. "Baking soda."

"Baking soda?"

"Yep. I wrote an article a long time ago about natural remedies, and baking soda is supposed to work really well for rashes like that. Put baking soda in the bathtub and soak in it."

"I'll keep that in mind. Thanks." Anne shut the door behind Grace. Her stomach growled. Like Liddie, she was hungry and eager to get on with the evening. She picked up the folder of newspaper articles and headed for the stairs. First she'd make dinner and then scour through the newspaper articles to see if she could find a clue to what crime she or her friends had supposedly committed.

CHAPTER EIGHT

"Fetch, Hershey," Ben yelled and heaved a tennis ball across the backyard. The sleek brown dog streaked across the yard, snatched up the ball, and dashed back to the boy. He dropped the ball at Ben's feet and bounced back on his hind legs, wagging his tail.

Ryan grabbed the ball and tossed it high in the air. Hershey made a flying leap and did a half somersault. The boys laughed, and Hershey barked with glee.

Anne stood on the porch and watched the boys. She was glad Ryan and Ben were having such a good time. She hadn't heard Ben laugh since the Sunday picnic before the poison ivy disaster.

She went back upstairs and called Alex and explained how much fun the boys were having. "Can Ryan stay for dinner? You're most certainly welcome too. I'm fixing one of the kids' favorites. Mac-and-cheese casserole. It's not fancy, but it's good. And there's pumpkin cake for dessert."

"That sounds great to me," Alex said, a smile in his voice. "But actually I'm trying to finish up a rush job. You're doing me a favor by feeding Ryan. Would it be okay if I came after dinner for cake?"

"Sure," Anne said. "If you have a little time, maybe we can discuss the article some more. I was able to talk to Michael and

Jen. And I ran into Kevin Kutcher at the medical clinic. Plus, I have the *Gazette* police blotters from that time period."

"You've been busy! With work being so crazy, I'm afraid I haven't been able to do anything yet."

"That's okay. I understand. Do you think you might know where your senior yearbook is? I haven't found mine yet."

"Thanks for reminding me," Alex said. "I'll take a look before I come over."

Anne boiled noodles and assembled the casserole. She made a rich, cheesy sauce but used whole wheat macaroni to give the dish more nutrition. She sprinkled extra cheese on top and put it in the oven. She had fresh green beans in the refrigerator and cleaned them up and popped them on the stove. Liddie liked to eat the long green beans as though they were french fries. Anne pulled some frozen rolls out of the oven. She'd put those in when the casserole was almost done.

She checked on Liddie, who was curled up on the couch watching an educational program on animals, and then returned to the kitchen.

Since she had about twenty minutes, she eagerly flipped open the folder with the newspaper articles. The police blotter listed local crimes. She leafed through the pages until she reached the day after the homecoming dance.

There were several listed for that night.

Graffiti on two walls of Stonebridge Elementary school, which was a small private church school.

Burglary at Dillon's Auto Parts store. At least five hundred dollars' worth of tools were stolen and several thousand dollars in damage done.

Hit-and-run accident with injuries on Larkin Road. Two victims with injuries. Police were investigating.

One DUI arrest on Woody Road.

Three juveniles picked up for being disorderly and intoxicated on Main Street.

She highlighted the incidences. For a typically quiet little town like Blue Hill, it seemed like an inordinate amount of criminal activity. And all of these could have had serious consequences.

Grace, bless her heart, had included a couple articles that mentioned the burglary and school graffiti. Anne noted that donations were collected to repaint Stonebridge Elementary, but apparently no arrests were ever made. Same with the burglary at Dillon's Auto Parts and the hit-and-run. At least arrests weren't mentioned in the news items Grace had given her. Neither were the names of the injured people mentioned anywhere.

She found a later article with a short interview with Mr. Dillon's wife, who reported that her husband had returned to the store to get some important paperwork for his appointment with their accountant the next morning and surprised the perpetrators. He never got a good look at them, but he thought they were juveniles.

She tapped her highlighter on the table. Could one of these be the crime referred to in her article? But then, there was the possibility too that the crime in question was never reported to the police or mentioned in the newspaper.

The phone rang, startling her. The caller ID indicated the call was from her parents' home in Florida.

"Anne!" her father's booming voice made her hold the phone away from her ear. "How's my baby girl?"

Anne grinned. She'd always be her father's baby, and she loved it. "Doing okay. I suppose Mom told you about the poison ivy incident."

"Yes, yes, yes. Got to watch out for stuff like that. I'd think you'd remember to avoid it," he said cheerfully.

"I should've warned them, but I didn't think about it at the time. They were off playing hide-and-seek in the woods. I didn't think they'd be rolling in the stuff." When they'd lived in Brooklyn, they hadn't worried about poisonous plants.

"Poison ivy has three leaves. Remember the phrase, 'Leaves of three, let it be?' That might help them remember."

"I remember, now that you mention it. I'll tell the kids, but you know what would be really nice? Maybe when their grandpa comes up to visit, he could take Ben and Liddie out in the woods and show them."

"Be happy to." Her father chuckled at Anne's obvious hint. "Hey, kiddo, I'm sorry for not getting back with you earlier today, but I did get that video in the mail. You should get it in a day or two."

"Oh, thank you, Dad. I hope it wasn't too much trouble to find it."

"Nah, your mother may call me a pack rat, but I'm a *neat* pack rat. A place for everything and everything in its place."

"You're super, Dad."

"Now, kiddo." His voice took on a more serious tone. "Are you going to tell me why you need it so quickly? Your mother thinks maybe you're getting interested in that boy again."

"What boy?" Anne asked and then laughed when she realized that "boy" was Alex. "No, the thought didn't even cross my mind."

Anne shook her head. Trust her mother to put a romantic spin on her renewed friendship with Alex. Anne was glad Alex was back in her life, but it was too soon to even think about another romantic tie. Maybe she'd never be ready. She'd loved Eric so much. Right now, providing a good life and future for their children was her utmost goal.

"Actually, I was just trying to remember who had been at the dance that night," Anne said.

"What's going on? Are you in any trouble?"

"No," Anne blinked, forgetting how perceptive her father could be, even over the phone. "Not yet anyway. I didn't want to worry Mom when it all could just be a prank." She took a deep breath and explained about the article. "So you see, I know Alex and I weren't directly involved in anything criminal, but I'm worried that these obscure accusations might have some truth behind them and one of my old friends might be in trouble."

"It sounds like this person who wrote the article is crying out for help."

"Do you think so?" Anne asked, not so sure about that. "I know it was a long time ago, but do you remember anything about a hit-and-run accident or a burglary that night?"

"I can't really recall anything specific, but I do vaguely remember something about an accident, and I was thankful you got home safely. I didn't really like it that you were traveling around in that tiny little car of Edie's. I always felt less stressed when you took the Buick."

Anne smiled at the memory of her father's old sedan she'd nicknamed The Tank. "The convertible worked well for the parade." But had it? The article writer had said their actions had started a domino effect that resulted in someone being harmed. Would it have really made a difference if they'd all carpooled in the same vehicle?

"Anyway, about the accident," her father continued, "I could be remembering another incident when you were driving around town. Fathers always worry." So did mothers, Anne thought as she looked out the window to check on Ben. She was glad she still had years before Ben started driving.

"It must not have involved anyone we knew, but let me ask your mom."

Anne waited while a muffled conversation ensued and then her mother came on the phone.

"I just had a thought, dear. If the accident involved someone in our church who was hospitalized, the ladies of the church would've visited them in the hospital. Maybe you should check with them."

"That's a good idea. But what are the chances they would remember too?"

"They kept records of their visits for the yearly report. The church may still have those somewhere."

Anne thanked her and they chatted a bit more as she set the table. The accident hadn't occurred very far from her neighborhood, which meant it was possible that the victims may have gone to their church. It was worth checking out.

The oven timer started beeping, so Anne took the casserole out of the oven and called the kids to the table. Ben wiggled and had trouble sitting still, saying the chair rubbed the rash on the back of his legs. Anne suggested he could eat standing at the counter.

"Can I do that too?" Ryan asked.

Anne smiled. "Sure." She cleared them a place for their plates.

"Me too." Liddie stood, ready to move her plate.

"Honey, you're too short to eat off the counter, but if you're itchy, then you can stand by the table."

Liddie considered the suggestion for a moment and flopped down on her chair with a pout. Anne sighed.

Ryan and Ben kept a conversation going about soccer, and Anne was again grateful that Ryan kept Ben distracted from his discomfort. Despite macaroni and cheese and green beans being one of Liddie's favorite meals, she ate very little. She kept looking over at the boys with a sad, worried expression that tore at Anne's heart.

What was her little girl thinking about? Liddie got along with her brother and his friends just fine. Usually she liked to be right in the middle of the action.

She tried to draw Liddie into conversation but just got mumbled replies. Liddie perked up a little when Anne served slices of cake. After they'd scraped up the last crumb from their plates, Anne suggested that they find a board game that Liddie could play. To Anne's relief, Ben and Ryan seemed okay with the idea, and the trio headed for the living room.

Anne started a pot of decaf coffee and had just loaded the dishwasher when Alex arrived. He wore jeans, and a light blue polo shirt peeked out from under a lightweight black jacket. His hair was still damp from a recent shower, and Anne caught a whiff of a mixture of soap and musky aftershave. He carried a book tucked under his arm.

He gave Anne a big smile. "Hope I'm not too late for cake."

"Nope. Perfect timing. We just finished dinner. The kids wanted seconds on the cake, but I saved us some." Anne closed the dishwasher door and got out small plates and mugs.

"My lucky day." He grinned and set the royal blue yearbook with "Blue Hill High" stamped in gold on the cover on the table and slid his jacket on the back of the chair.

"Coffee?" Anne asked as Alex took a seat. "It's decaf."

"Sure thing." He took the mug Anne offered. "I don't think I'll have any trouble sleeping tonight anyway. What a crazy day!"

Anne didn't think she'd have trouble sleeping either after being up the previous night with Liddie. She ladled caramel sauce over the cake slices and added the whipped cream. "So how did the job go? Get it done on time?"

"I'm still a day behind with a customer's shed, but I'll finish it tomorrow. The lumberyard delivered untreated lumber by mistake, so we could only get the frame up today," Alex said. "The customer is worried that bad weather will hit before she can get her new riding lawn mower under cover."

"Why doesn't she put it in her garage? Assuming she has a garage, that is," Anne asked, curious. Alex had done a superb job remodeling Aunt Edie's house, and Anne had no doubt the customer would ultimately be pleased with Alex's work.

"She does, but it's only a single. Apparently there is no room with her car in there. She bought the mower on sale, not realizing she had no place to put it. Hence the shed. With rain forecasted for the end of the week, I'd like to have the roof on."

He picked up a fork and dug into the cake. "This hits the spot. I like pumpkin." He took another big bite. "I've had this cake before somewhere."

Anne scooped up leftover caramel sauce on her plate. "It's Aunt Edie's recipe. She used to take it to church potlucks in the fall."

"That explains it then. My taste buds have excellent memory." He grinned at Anne. "Now, speaking of memories, did you uncover anything useful today?"

"I'm not sure how useful the information is, but it is interesting." Anne set her folder and notebook on the table. "Michael and Jennifer said they don't know why they are blamed in the article any more than we do, but Michael is going to do some checking on crimes the night of homecoming."

"That will help. He may have access to information the rest of us don't."

"That's what I'm hoping," Anne said. "Okay, Heather is out of town until Thursday, but I did some digging on her. Remember how she always wanted to be a concert flutist?"

Alex nodded.

"Well, it seems she was doing really well as a flutist at some major orchestras and then she just quit. Do you know why she'd give up her dream and move back to teach in Blue Hill?"

"I really don't know. I've never had a good chance to talk to her. I saw her at church a couple of times when she first came back, but I think she stopped attending."

Anne hadn't seen Heather at church either. Maybe after Heather got married she'd changed to her husband's church.

"I left a message for her to call me. And like I mentioned on the phone, I saw Kevin Kutcher at the Blue Hill Medical Clinic. He's a lab tech there. She told him about their visit.

"The thing that struck me though is that the writer of the article has to be someone who has been watching all of us. How else would he or she know Kevin was in town? The article was delivered to his parents' house and he's only been here three weeks."

Alex leaned back in his chair, forgetting his cake momentarily. "I don't like this at all."

"Me either." She glanced at the dark window. Could someone be out there watching them right now? She suppressed a shiver and focused on the folder in front of her. "Maybe if we can figure out what crime was committed, that will tell us who wrote the article. I have the police blotters from the *Blue Hill Gazette.*" She opened the file to reveal the newspaper copies. "These are the crimes recorded by the police for that night. I made a list." She pushed her notebook across the table.

Alex leaned forward and scanned the list Anne had compiled. "Busy night for Blue Hill."

"And apparently not a good one for the police, since there isn't any mention of at least three of the crimes being solved. I'm hoping Michael finds out more for us." She shared the newspaper articles with Alex, and after he'd read them, they pored over the yearbook looking for any connections between people.

Who hadn't gotten along? Who might hold a grudge?

They studied the two pages of homecoming photos but didn't note anything unusual. There was one photo of Anne and Alex as homecoming king and queen.

"We look so young!" Anne blurted out loud.

Alex grinned. "We were."

"It seems a lifetime ago."

"It was."

Anne let out a sound of exasperation. "You could at least put up a little resistance. I don't feel that much older."

Alex grinned. "I was just being agreeable."

Anne shook her head with amusement and studied the page again. None of the photos were the same as the one in the article that included Michael, Jennifer, Alex, and Heather.

In one dance shot, a short, skinny boy stood in the background behind Alex, Anne, and Jen.

"Who is that?" Anne pointed to the boy.

"Which one?"

"The one glaring at you like he wants to punch you."

"Are you sure he's not looking at you?" Alex said and then mock sighed at Anne's expression. "No sense of humor tonight."

He picked up the yearbook and tilted it into the light. "Isn't that Shaun Milhouse?"

"Shaun?" The name was familiar. He had been a scrawny little guy with spiky hair and big glasses, whose big mouth and chip on his shoulder got him picked on a lot.

"I'd forgotten he was so short compared to everyone else. You wouldn't recognize him now. He works in a body shop and is really good if you ever need some repairs done," said Alex.

An image of Shaun's' grimy fingernails holding his lunch tray flashed through her mind. "Didn't he work in an auto shop when he was in school?"

Alex nodded. "Same place he's working at now. It's off of Main Street."

Anne jotted Shaun's name down in her notebook. If anyone deserved to carry a grudge it was Shaun. He'd tried to hang with the popular crowd but went about it in the wrong way. Not that his behavior excused some members of the football team from dropping him in the dumpsters behind the cafeteria. Nor the time someone ran his small gym shorts up the flagpole.

Shaun had asked Anne out to a movie once during their senior year, and she'd been nice but declined. At least she thought she had been nice. Thankfully, she'd already made plans to go to the movies with the gang. He'd understood she was already busy, hadn't he? She could still picture his red face. Surely he didn't hold that against her.

"Is Shaun married?" she asked.

"Subject has never come up."

And Alex hadn't asked, which didn't surprise Anne. In Anne's experience, men were often slow to inquire about personal things when meeting others. Eric would run into a male friend of theirs while he was out and when Anne asked how the friend's wife or kids were doing, Eric would just shrug. The guys only talked about work or sports. Sometimes politics.

Anne turned the pages, studying the faces of friends and classmates she'd spent at least a year with. She noted life ambitions listed under their names. Anne had wanted to be a journalist. Kevin was heading to medical school. Jennifer declared her ambition as a decorator in New York, and Heather's dream was to be a concert flutist.

Anne noted that three of them had changed their minds along the way, but Alex, Heather, and Michael had reached their ambitions listed on the page. Alex wanted to go into business for himself and Michael wanted a career in criminal justice. Heather had met her goal of being a concert flutist but gave it up to come back to Blue Hill and teach.

"Sometimes life doesn't turn out the way you planned," Anne observed.

"And that's okay," Alex replied. "It's how you handle your decisions and life's challenges that matter."

She looked at her old friend. "Are you happy with your choices?"

"For the most part. What I can't change, I try not to worry about."

Anne's thoughts turned to Eric, and even with the immense heartache and being widowed so young, she'd do it all again without hesitation. Alex had taken on the job of raising his nephew and, although that must've changed his life drastically, he never complained.

She picked up her list of crimes for that night and put question marks by the burglary, graffiti incident, and hit-and-run accident. They all happened the night of homecoming. Were any of them related? And who had committed them?

She turned her attention back to the faces of her classmates. Was one of them a thief who broke into the auto parts store? Or had one of the juveniles been picked up for drinking and driving? Some of the teens liked to party, but Anne hadn't hung out with them.

She still needed to talk to Heather. Maybe she had some answers, but so far at least everyone mentioned in the article claimed to be innocent of whatever happened that night.

Unless someone came forward, how could Anne uncover the truth before it was too late?

CHAPTER NINE

Anne yawned over her breakfast of scrambled eggs and hash browns. Liddie had been restless again last night, although Anne only had to get up once with her. Liddie had been really itchy before bed, so Anne tried giving her a bath with baking soda in the water. The warm water seemed to soothe Liddie some, but she had still gone to bed more cranky than usual and hadn't wanted a bedtime story again. Anne still couldn't figure out if Liddie's uneasiness was from the rash or if there was a deeper issue.

Kids went through phases, she reminded herself. Ben used to refuse to go to bed without Anne singing a silly song to him.

She looked over at Ben, who was reading the back of a cereal box. He shifted in his seat every few seconds. There was no way he'd get through the day sitting in class without endless fidgeting. Liddie kept wanting to scratch the bumps on her face and only refrained when she caught Anne watching her. Anne sighed. It would be better if they stayed home from school another day.

She cleaned up the kitchen, applied medicine, got dressed, and hurried downstairs to get some paperwork done before she opened the library.

Wendy breezed in the front door. "Good morning, good morning! Isn't it a fabulous morning?"

"Good morning to you too," Anne said with a laugh, delighted to see her friend with her two youngest children. "And hello Ethan and Jacob. Liddie will be glad to see you."

Wendy came around the counter, taking off her denim jacket and then helping the boys take off their coats. "I was going stir-crazy at home. Cooped up in the house with a passel of itchy kids is not something I'd like to repeat. I cleaned the house on Monday and then cleaned some more and baked yesterday. I needed to get out of the house this morning. My other kids are better and went back to school, but my babies aren't ready yet. I hope you don't mind if I brought them. Their rashes are dry now, so no chance of spreading it."

"Poor little guys. Liddie and Ben are still home too. If it wasn't for the rash on the back of Ben's legs, he could've gone back today," Anne said. "Liddie still wants to scratch her face. She'll be happy to have someone to play with."

"Well good. Then bringing the kids was the right thing to do. Do you want me to do Story Time this morning? Or did you plan something?"

"I was just thinking I better pull something together. You're welcome to it," Anne said. Wendy enjoyed working in the Children's Room.

Wendy smiled and lifted a bag that had some stuffed toy bunny ears poking out. "Good. I brought some props with me."

It was almost lunchtime when Anne's cell phone rang.

"Anne?" a breathy, cheerful voice said. "This is Heather Stafford. You left a message to call you."

"I'm so glad you called. This is Anne Summers Gibson and—"

"Anne! I'm sorry. I'd forgotten your married name. Wow! It's been way too long since we've been in touch. How are you doing?"

Anne smiled. Hearing Heather's voice reminded her of how bubbly and fun her friend had been. "Doing great. I'm running the town library. How about you?"

"Just fabulous. Work is terrific, and my family is healthy and happy." She paused, obviously waiting for Anne to get to the point of her call.

"Heather, something's come up, and I really need to talk to you. Would it be possible for us to get together sometime soon?"

"Sure, I'd love to get together, but I'm having a rather hectic week after being gone for the first two days. Is this urgent?"

Anne thought about the deadline mentioned in the article. "It could be. Have you, by any chance, received an article about the night of our homecoming dance?"

"Article? No, but then I haven't gone through my mail yet."

"I'll just warn you that it's very strange. You're mentioned in it, as well as me and some others. It would be so much easier to explain in person and show you a copy. Maybe I can come by after school if you have a few moments. I'd really like to know what you think."

"Okay, now I'm really curious. Hold on, let me check my schedule." There was a long pause and then Heather said, "I teach private lessons after school today, but I'm free for lunch. Nothing on the schedule until one. Any chance you can come by here?"

"I think that will work out," Anne said thinking that if Wendy was doing Story Time, she'd probably planned on sticking around as usual until then. "How about I pick up some sandwiches for us at Coffee Joe's?"

"That would be wonderful, thank you. I'm sick of cafeteria food, and I was too rushed to bring anything from home. I'll take a tuna salad on rye. I'll provide the drinks, and we can have a picnic in my office," Heather said merrily. "We'll have more privacy there than in the teachers' lounge. Just have them call me from the office."

Anne put the phone down and went to find Wendy. She had set a variety of toy bunnies around the room and drawn a meadow scene on the chalk wall in preparation for the two o'clock Story Time for preschoolers. A Peter Rabbit book lay on the table. Liddie, Ethan, and Jacob were putting a puzzle together.

"Wendy, something's come up, and I need to run some errands."

"Sure, go ahead. I'll manage things here and watch the kids," Wendy said cheerfully. "I was planning on sticking around, and I brought our lunch."

Thanks so much. "I'll fix sandwiches for Liddie and Ben before I go." Anne hurried upstairs and fixed lunch for the kids. Seeing that she still had twenty minutes before she had to leave, she decided to do a quick search for the chest Aunt Edie had given her. She'd kept the key on her charm bracelet, but when she searched her jewelry box, she couldn't find it. She grabbed a paperclip, remembering she'd used that before to turn the lock.

Anne climbed the stairs to the attic, where she used to love to play on rainy days. As Jen had mentioned, sometimes she would come over and Aunt Edie would let them get into her old clothes trunk and try things on. Anne and Jen would also push trunks and boxes around to create forts and tunnels. The attic provided hours of fun when going outside wasn't an option. Plus it had housed Anne's treasure chest, where she kept her favorite things at Aunt Edie's.

Anne pushed the door open and surveyed the stacked boxes, chests, and trunks. Some of the boxes were from the move from New York. Her mother had also stored a few things up here when they moved to Florida and planned to retrieve them someday. And of course there were Aunt Edie's belongings.

Aunt Edie had written to Anne in New York, and in one of her letters had mentioned she'd been going through the attic and organizing, but that the attic was still jammed full. Anne just hoped her chest was still there. She circled the perimeter and finally spied her beloved chest shoved in a corner. She pulled it out into the light and brushed off the dusty cedar lid. Excitement squeezed her chest as she tugged at the latch, hoping she'd left it unlocked. She hadn't. She took the paperclip out of her pocket and tried turning the lock. It held tight. After all these years, the mechanism was probably frozen in place.

She stood, brushing the dust off her pants. Well, at least she had found it. She'd take another look for the key and if she couldn't find it, then maybe she could take it to a locksmith.

She glanced at her watch. Time to get going if she wanted to run by the auto parts store mentioned in the police blotter. She checked on Ben. He was on his bed, reading his English book, a notebook and pencil by his side

"How's it going?" Anne asked, pleased she didn't have to nag Ben about doing his assignments.

"I'm almost done with the reading," Ben said. "But Mr. Layton wants us to write a paper about what we want to be when we grow up. What if you're not sure what you want to be?"

"I imagine he just wants you to write about something that interests you."

"What if a lot of things interest me?"

"Just pick one. He doesn't expect you to know for sure, and you'll have lots of time to change your mind."

"Maybe I'll be an editor."

Just like his father, who was an editor at a New York publishing company. Anne's heart squeezed. "If that's something that you're interested in, then I think that would be something good to write about. Mrs. Pyle can help you find some books on it. She's downstairs with Liddie, Ethan, and Jacob. I'm going to run some errands for a couple hours. If you need me, call me, okay?"

Ben nodded and turned his attention back to his book. He had grown over the last year, and Anne suspected he was going to be tall like Eric. But right now he still seemed small and vulnerable. In Anne's eyes he was still her baby.

She picked up her folder, purse, and notebook and headed down the stairs and out the door. Hershey let out a bark, and Anne went over to give him a pat on the head. "Be a good dog."

Wendy had been right, the day was fabulous. Cloudless sky above the rolling hills. She took a deep breath, loving the scent of the sun warming the damp leaves.

She backed her car down the driveway and drove into town. Dillon's Auto Parts, a family-owned business, was about a half mile from the high school. According to the police blotter, the store had been broken into on homecoming night. The squat, long brick building with dusty windows looked just like her memory of it from childhood. Anne had accompanied her father to the shop a couple of times, and he'd said Mr. Dillon always gave him a fair deal.

She pushed the door open and saw a thirty-something man standing behind the counter. "Hi, I'm looking for Mr. Dillon."

"That's me." His brown eyes twinkled.

"Oh," Anne said. This man was too young to be the Mr. Dillon she remembered.

He grinned. "You're looking for my father, aren't you? I'm Pete, his son."

"Hi, Pete," Anne said with a little laugh. "Yes, I was looking for your father. I'm Anne Gibson. My dad, Dale Summers, used to come in here a lot."

Pete looked over his shoulder and shouted, "Dad, someone here to see you."

A stooped little man with a short beard and sharp blue eyes shuffled out of the back room. "Who are you?"

"Dad, behave," Pete said with a wink at Anne.

"Hello, Mr. Dillon," Anne said with a big smile. This was the man she remembered, although he hadn't used a cane back then. "I'm Anne Gibson. You probably remember my father Dale Summers. He used to come in here a lot."

His face brightened. "Summers? 1990 Buick and later a 2005 Toyota Camry."

"Yes, that's right," Anne said, amazed. "You have a good memory."

"I haven't seen Dale in years. Started going to the Auto World across town, I suppose," he said with a scowl.

"Oh no, he always said you gave him a fair deal and he would only come here. Anyway, he and my mother moved to Florida about five years ago."

"See, Dad?" Pete said. "Auto World didn't steal all our old customers."

"*Hmmph*," Mr. Dillon said as if he still believed it. "Well, how can I help you, young lady?"

"Actually I'm not here for auto parts but information," Anne said, feeling suddenly guilty that she wasn't. "This may sound odd, but I'm trying to get some information about a break-in you had seventeen years ago."

"Why would you want to know about that? You weren't involved, were you?"

"Dad!" Pete admonished again.

"What? If it weren't for those blasted kids, I wouldn't be in pain every single day of my life. But what does anyone care?" He picked up a package off the counter and stomped to the back room, muttering all the way.

"Sorry about that," Pete said with a shake of his head. "He has good days and bad ones. It's obvious which way this day is headed."

"I didn't mean to make him upset," Anne said.

"No, no, it's not your fault. He hasn't been himself since my mother passed last year. Anyway, about that night—Dad came back here to get something and surprised them. He hurt his back when he chased them out of here. Slipped a disc and was on his back for weeks. After that, he couldn't do any heavy lifting or stand on his feet too long."

"I'm sorry about your dad. That must've been terrible."

"Yeah, it was. That was the first time we were hit but not the last. We've had a couple burglaries since. Dad finally put in an alarm system and got us some insurance—Rocky." He nodded to a huge Rottweiler-mix dog snoozing on a large, plaid pillow.

Anne's hand automatically went to her heart. "Oh, I didn't see him. He's really big."

"So is his bark." Pete grinned. "But don't worry, he's a marshmallow by day. Protector of his kingdom at night. Ever since Rocky started sleeping in the store overnight, we haven't had any break-ins. So, why did you want to know about the break-in?"

"I'm doing some research on events that night. I was wondering if they ever caught whoever broke in."

"Nope, but Dad was convinced it was some local teens. They took things that didn't have much monetary value."

"Like what?" Anne asked, looking around.

"Some hood ornaments. A couple tool sets. I can't remember what else except the paint. They spray painted the walls and shelves with some touch-up paint. Made a big mess."

Anne thought about the graffiti painted on the walls of the elementary school. Surely the police would have investigated a connection between the two.

"Anyway, thanks to that night, I knew what I'd be doing for the rest of my life."

"What's that?" Anne asked, although the answer seemed obvious.

"Running this store. Dad just kept getting worse, and someone had to do it. At least we didn't have to change the name." The door opened and he looked over her shoulder. "Hey, Ralph."

Anne couldn't tell from his tone if he thought his situation was good or bad. She gave Pete a wave since he was busy with his customer and headed out the door to her car.

Maybe the article was referring to Mr. Dillon's accident. It certainly had harmed him and changed his and Pete's life. But if so, what was the connection to Anne and her friends?

* * *

Coffee Joe's was packed with the Thursday lunch crowd. Anne took her place at the back of the line and spied Michael sitting at a table. He was talking to a couple other officers, looking very professional in his blue uniform. He hadn't gotten back to her yet about any official police reports from homecoming night. Of course, it had only been a day.

Michael didn't see her as she inched forward toward the counter. Joe was behind the cash register taking orders. A young brunette was serving up food on the stainless steel counter. Anne perused the already prepared lunch items, seeing Heather's tuna salad.

"Good morning, Anne," Joe said. "What can I get you?"

"I'll take that tuna on rye and then a turkey and Swiss."

"Potato chips or veggies?"

"Give me one of each," Anne said, not sure which Heather would prefer. "It's busy in here."

"Business has been growing thanks to my daughter. She's the one who suggested we expand our lunch menu, and she had some great ideas," Joe said. "Mia, come here a sec."

A petite female version of her father approached. "This is Anne Gibson," her father said. "She was one of your grandpa's regulars."

Anne smiled. "Along with most of the high school. Nice to meet you, Mia."

"Hello," Mia said, looking a bit shy.

"Mia just graduated last spring," Joe added.

"Congratulations!" Anne smiled as she handed Joe some bills. "Do you know Bella and Remi?"

"Yep. They graduated with me."

Joe slung his arm around his daughter's shoulders. "Mia is thinking of becoming a writer, but I think she'd do great things in advertising. She was on the school newspaper staff."

"Oh? I was on the newspaper too. But I was Anne Summers then."

Mia gave a little shrug. "My teacher gets out stuff from the olden days when she wants us to write about the history of the school. I might have read one of your articles."

The *olden* days? Was Anne that old? "I was hoping to get access to some of the photos taken for the yearbook and newspaper back then. Do you know who I could talk to?"

"Mrs. Ashbury, probably." Mia handed over a white bag with the sandwiches and sides.

"Thanks. And nice meeting you, Mia." Anne turned to leave and noticed that Michael and the two other officers were getting up from their chairs. She waited as they went outside and followed them. One of the officers strolled away down the street.

"Hi, Michael. How's it going?"

He turned his head and gave her a tight smile. "Oh, hey, Anne."

"I know it's probably too soon, but I was wondering if you had a chance to check the old records yet about what we had talked about."

"No, not yet." He glanced at the other officer and then back at her. "I'm not sure when I'll be able to. I'll see you around."

"Oh, okay." Anne said, wondering if she had said something wrong. "I found some things in the police blotters that might be useful."

"Sure, we can talk about it later." He turned and walked away.

Anne walked to her car, puzzled at his coolness. Maybe this was the way Michael behaved when he was on duty. After all, he was working and didn't have time to chat.

She glanced back at them as she got in her car. The two officers didn't seem to be in any hurry to leave. Michael glanced over at her and she lifted her hand to wave, but he shifted his gaze and acted like he didn't see her.

How odd. She felt like she was in high school for a second, being ignored by the popular kids. Not that she really cared when that happened, but there were moments when it could cause self-doubt. She hoped her kids would be immune to the silly, hurtful games, but she realized that learning how to deal with it was part of growing up.

She drove to the high school. This time the parking lot was jammed with cars, but luckily there was a space in front labeled Visitor's Parking. Anne checked in through the office and met Heather in the hall.

Heather had been pretty in high school, but she had matured into a beautiful woman with tight dark curls that were captured in a ponytail at the back of her neck and cascaded down her back. Her figure was still lithe. She was dressed in black slacks, a fuzzy black sweater, and petite pumps with a silver bow over the toes. She looked artistically professional but approachable.

"Anne, how nice to see you again." Heather leaned forward for a hug. "The last time I saw you was at graduation."

"I know. I was thinking that on the way over here. How could time go by so fast?"

"I really don't know, but it happened to me too," Heather said with a chuckle. "Come this way. My office is behind the assembly room. We can cut through the cafeteria."

They went through the wide doors into the large dining area full of chatter and smells of steamy food. As they passed one of the tables, a skinny boy lobbed a spoonful of mashed potatoes at another student.

Heather cleared her throat loudly, and the boy slumped down and tried to look innocent.

When they got out of the cafeteria Anne said, "Do you remember the food fight Alex and Michael got into our junior year? Some other guy started it, but they all got in trouble."

"That was Jed Hardy. He is friends with my brother-in-law now," Heather said. "Small world, huh?"

Jed had been a grade behind them, and he and Michael didn't get along. He blamed Michael for getting him detention after the food fight. There had been other incidences too.

"So, is Jed living in Blue Hill?" Anne asked, wondering if he could possibly have anything to do with the article.

"Not now. He joined the army and lives overseas." Heather pulled a key out of her pocket, and they entered the hallway behind the stage and went into the band room. Her office was nestled in a glassed-off corner. Several chairs faced her desk and Anne chose one to sit on.

"So, what is this about an article?" Heather asked after Anne passed out the sandwiches. They decided to split the sides of veggies and chips. Heather had gotten them two bottles of lemonade.

Anne withdrew her copy from her purse. "Everyone mentioned in it got a copy. I'm assuming you did too."

Heather read it through, a worried wrinkle forming on her forehead. "Is this guy serious?"

"I don't know. Michael and Alex seem to think it's a prank but are still taking it seriously." At least Anne hoped Michael was, after his brush-off of her earlier. "The author mentioned a crime. Something happened that night that somehow he or she tied all of us into."

Heather started to take a bite of her sandwich but then set it back without taking a bite. "Something did happen that night. I haven't thought about it in years." She sighed.

Anne's heart skipped a beat as she waited for Heather to continue.

"I was at the homecoming dance, and that dumb Shaun Milhouse bumped into me and I spilled punch all over my dress. It was sticky, and I just wanted to go home rather than hang out with the others. Trudy and Mandy were with me. We stopped at a light, and there was an accident right in front of us."

"A hit-and-run?" Anne asked.

Heather raised her eyebrows. "Yeah, how did you know?"

"There was an accident mentioned in the newspaper, but there weren't any real details. What happened?"

"We were waiting for the light to change, and all of sudden a car came right though the light and sideswiped another car. He didn't hit them hard, but the other car veered off the street and smashed into a light pole. The person that hit the little car took off. Glass was everywhere. It was awful." Heather twisted the napkin in her hands. "We just sat there for the longest time and didn't know what to do."

"You were just kids," Anne said sympathetically.

"Trudy finally ran to a nearby house and had them call the police, and Mary and I went to check on the people in the other car."

"Were they hurt badly?"

"It was hard to tell. It was a man and a woman. There wasn't any blood or anything. The woman moaned a little, but they were both talking. The ambulance got there really quickly."

Her heart thumped. This had to be the same incident mentioned in the newspaper. Hit-and-run with two victims.

"Did you know who they were?"

Heather shook her head. "No, I didn't recognize them and never learned their names. They were older. The man was bald and the lady had gray hair. The police wanted to talk to us. They wanted to know about the other car. Only it all happened so fast."

"Do you remember anything about the other car?"

"I didn't get a good look. I thought the car was blue, but Mandy said it was green. Trudy just said it was a dark color. But we did agree that it was a smallish four-door sedan, possibly a Nissan. Or maybe a Toyota. I don't remember." Heather picked up her sandwich and then set it down again.

Anne felt bad that she was disturbing Heather's lunch, but they had to get to the bottom of this. "Was the person ever caught?"

"Beats me," Heather said. "I didn't even know they'd mentioned the accident in the paper. Once we were done being questioned, the police sent us home. An insurance company called later and asked the same questions the police did, but then things got busy at school. And really, it wasn't something I wanted to think about."

This was something Michael could find out, Anne thought. She wondered if he had made any progress.

"It really shook me up for a while, even though we did nothing to cause the accident," Heather said. "It was the sound of the crash and thinking that it could've been us. I had bad dreams about it for a while." Heather picked up her sandwich and this time took a bite.

"I'm sorry. I didn't want you to have to relive it," Anne said. "You called the police and did everything right. You were heroes. Just think if no one had been there, the couple might've suffered a lot more."

"Thanks. I know you're right, but I feel a little guilty about not ever trying to find out how the couple fared," Heather admitted. "So what does this have to do with the article? Do you think the accident could be related to the crime?"

"I'm not sure." Anne studied the article. Suppose this was the crime the author was referring to, then how was it connected to their group of friends? "It sounds like the crime had to have happened on homecoming night. We were all at the dance except for Kevin."

"Really? I thought I saw him there." Heather sounded puzzled.

"When?" Anne asked.

"Before the dance started." Heather reached for her drink. "I was upset with him because he said he wasn't going to be there and I got stuck with his job of taking photos until Keith got there. Mrs. Earland was breathing down my neck, so I didn't even get to dance the first half. Then Shaun spilled the punch on my dress, and, well, you know the rest. Not the best night of my life."

"So Kevin was there?" Anne repeated. Had Kevin lied to her?

Heather shrugged. "Maybe I'm mistaken. It was a long time ago."

She tapped the photo in the article. "That looks like something I might've taken before I gave the camera to Keith."

"Are the photos you took that night still around? Joe's daughter mentioned that Mrs. Ashbury might know."

"If they are, they'd be locked away in one of the cabinets in one of the storerooms. When they moved the school to the new building, most of the memorabilia got stuck in the basement. I can check on it if you'd like."

"That might be helpful. Whoever wrote the article must've been at the dance. There are too many details."

"Michael and Jennifer," said Heather, as she tapped the paper. "Michael had such a temper."

"He could get hot under the collar, but I never saw him lose his temper."

"I did. A couple times during football practice when the band was practicing on the field. He'd get really hot if things weren't going well. Threw his helmet at a guy once. Coach benched him and threatened not to let him play."

"I didn't realize," Anne said, picking up her untouched sandwich. When she hung out with Michael and Jen, he'd always seemed easygoing, except the evening of the homecoming dance. But then they'd been arguing.

"Good thing he became a cop and channeled all that dark energy into something positive." Heather smiled. "Anyway, I was sure they'd broken up for good that night. He called me."

Anne almost choked on her sandwich. "When?"

"Huh?" Heather looked up from the photo. "Oh, after the dance. After I got home. He was looking for Jennifer. I was still shook up about the accident and brushed him off."

Anne froze for a second. Jen and Michael had said they'd been together. If Michael was calling Heather, then they must've been apart for at least a little while. Why hadn't they said so? And on top of that, Michael had seemed cold toward her earlier today at Coffee Joe's.

"How's Alex doing? Are you in touch with him?" Heather asked. "I always thought the two of you would get married."

Anne felt herself blush. "We were just good friends and never that serious." At least she hadn't wanted a commitment. If she'd hurt Alex's feelings back then, it was totally unintentional.

"We were too young," Anne added. "And yes, I see him often. He repaired my great-aunt Edie's place and helped turn it into a library. Also, his nephew and my son are good friends."

"I thought that was so courageous of him taking in his sister's child. Tragic how they both died in a car accident. Poor little kid." She gave a little shiver. "So, do you like running a library?"

"Oh yes. It's an answer to prayer." Anne explained how after Eric died, Aunt Edie left the house to Anne with the stipulation that she was to convert the first floor and a portion of the second into a library and the remainder to serve as the personal living quarters for Anne and her children.

"I had never planned to come back to Blue Hill, although I'm now glad I did," Anne said. "Can I ask you something personal? Why did you come back here to live?"

"I didn't plan to either," Heather said with a smile. "I was *out of here*, if you know what I mean. I had my dream job playing with the Washington, DC, orchestra. But I came back to visit my parents at Christmas one year, and Mark was in town."

"So you gave it up for love."

"Go figure," Heather said with a smile. "And I've never been happier."

They finished lunch, and Heather walked Anne back to the office so she could sign out. Heather was turning to leave when Anne remembered something.

"Heather, before you go, I wanted to ask about Jerry Newman."

"He was bad news," Heather said and then smiled. "Oh, I know I used to be attracted to the 'bad' boys in school, but that was just a phase."

"Could he have been involved in anything that happened homecoming night?"

"Who knows? I broke up with him before homecoming and never looked back. I have no idea what happened to him after graduation," Heather said, looking at her watch. "Got to run to class. Let me know if there is anything I can do to help you."

As Anne drove toward home, she thought about what Heather had said about Michael.

If Jen and Michael weren't together after the dance, then where were they? His demeanor was very different this afternoon at the coffee shop than from the other day.

She had a hard time believing Michael would have done anything wrong, but then they were so young back then. It was so easy to let emotions rule and make mistakes. If he had been upset with Jen, could he have done something stupid? Like vandalize a store or elementary school? Could he have been involved in a hit-and-run accident? She tried to remember what Michael's car had looked like. Jennifer had done a lot of the talking when she'd visited them. Had his anger caused him to drive recklessly and get into an accident? Or some other mischief? Could Michael be covering something up? He certainly didn't seem to be in any hurry to investigate when she talked to him at Coffee Joe's. Or maybe he was investigating on his own and didn't want Anne involved. He was up for a promotion at a time when the town was cutting budgets. If the writer of the article did have something on Michael, could it damage his chances of promotion? Jen and Michael had a lot to lose if it did.

CHAPTER TEN

Anne got back to the library before Story Time started. She'd driven by the church in hopes of asking Reverend Tom if they had kept the visitation records, but he wasn't there.

Anne stowed her purse and smiled at the flow of incoming patrons. She loved seeing the little children come in with a parent or grandparent and gather around on the floor to listen with rapt attention to a story. Wendy connected exceptionally well with children. They could sense her sincerity and got caught up in her enthusiasm.

Wendy finished reading *Peter Cottontail* and then had each of the children choose a stuffed rabbit so they could reenact the story together.

Anne left the giggles and happy voices and returned to the quiet of the front desk. Ben was outside in the backyard trying to teach Hershey some tricks.

The check-in box was empty, and books waited on the cart to be put away. Anne checked the spines of the books and started off for the Fiction Room. Some librarians hated the job of filing books back into their places, but Anne had always found it soothing. She felt like she was creating order.

She shoved one of Tom Clancy's thick novels back on the shelf and then headed to the *P* section to return a James Patterson book.

Mysteries were next. She paused over Sue Grafton's latest novel displayed at the end of the shelf, wishing she had time to read it right then and there. She was tempted to check it out and take it upstairs with her, but she already had a stack of books on her nightstand.

She continued on her rounds, her mind playing over the day's events again. Heather had seen the hit-and-run that had been in the paper. Surely whoever had hit the other car had damaged their own car. She assumed that they would want to get it fixed. Surely the police had checked local body shops, but what if they had missed something? After she finished returning all the books to their homes, she returned to the counter and found the local phone book.

She flipped to the auto repair pages. Blue Hill boasted four body shops. Three of them were close by. Now, how could she tell which had been in business seventeen years ago? Two of them had taken out larger ads, and Bob's Body Shop claimed it had been serving the area since 1990, so that would be one. Fowler's Auto Repair just off Main Street sounded familiar to Anne. There was also one outside of town about five miles away and the last one was a Ford dealership.

The twins, Bella and Remi, were coming in tomorrow, so maybe Anne would have a chance to check the shops out. Body shops kept records. She just hoped they'd be willing to help her.

Children came down the stairs indicating that Story Time was over. Most of them had books to check out, which kept Anne busy. Liddie showed up hugging a little brown toy bunny. Ethan and Jacob also had rabbits tucked under their arms. Wendy came down last with a basket of even more toy rabbits.

"Cute idea with the bunnies." Anne grinned at Wendy.

"Thanks. It was fun. The grandparents used to give the kids each a stuffed rabbit at Easter, and with seven kids, pretty soon you have a zoo." She laughed. "Of course, I probably should've saved the idea for springtime and Easter."

"You can do it again with a different book."

"I could, but I have great new ideas for Story Time to make them even more interactive." Wendy started rattling off ideas about including more elaborate crafts, role-playing, and games.

Anne listened as she straightened up the counter. When Wendy got an idea, it was best to let her run with it for a while. Sometimes the process or the timing wasn't the way Anne would do it—like when Wendy had organized a library camp for kids when Anne had first arrived and was still remodeling and getting the library up and running—but the end result usually worked out wonderfully.

"I don't see why we can't try to expand Story Time a bit more," said Anne. "But we might want to consider creating a separate time slot if it gets too lengthy. We'll also have to check the budget and see if we can afford the craft items."

"I probably could get some of the mothers to donate items or take turns leading with the crafts," Wendy said. "It'll be great, you'll see. I was thinking one of the first crafts could be making cards for shut-ins or residents at the nursing home. I have a sweet little storybook at home about some kids who adopted a grandmother. I could get a list of names from the church for people who might appreciate getting some cards."

Anne nodded. "I could ask Reverend Tom. I was going to stop by the church tomorrow morning."

"Mommy, Liddie won't give me Tiny." Ethan pointed to the toy rabbit Liddie was making hop across the table.

"Ethan, we brought the bunnies to share," Wendy said as she put on her jacket.

"Liddie, honey, Ethan is getting ready to leave," Anne said.

"Liddie, you can keep Tiny until we come back tomorrow. Ethan has lots of rabbits," Wendy interjected.

Ethan blinked and looked like he was about to cry as Wendy helped Jacob with his coat.

Liddie clutched the bunny tighter, and Anne knew she wanted to keep it. Liddie looked at Ethan and then walked over and handed it to him. Ethan sniffed and gave Liddie a hug.

Wendy caught Anne's eye and smiled.

Anne smiled back and wished she could talk to Wendy about the article, but again she felt like she might be betraying one of her friends who may be in trouble. If there were secrets, they weren't hers to tell. Only to solve.

* * *

Anne sat cross-legged on her bed, her notebook in her lap and the article, newspaper copies, and Alex's yearbook spread out on the quilt. She doodled in the margins of a blank page as she thought over the tangled connections between her friends.

She turned to a fresh page and wrote "Crime" at the top. Someone had been hurt physically or damaged emotionally. Right now she knew of two physical possibilities that night. The elderly couple that was hurt in the hit-and-run and Mr. Dillon's back. Anne couldn't imagine Mr. Dillon going to the trouble to write an article when it was obvious he had no qualms about speaking his opinion out loud, but she did wonder about his son.

Pete Dillon appeared to be close to her age or perhaps a little younger. She flipped through Alex's yearbook checking the students for each year. She found his name and photo in the freshman pages. So he had been at Blue Hill High School when she attended. She stared at his portrait. Dark wavy hair. Dark eyes behind wire-rimmed glasses. Freckles on the nose. He looked vaguely familiar, but she didn't remember him. Had they ever talked? Probably not, since they most likely didn't have any classes together. He hadn't mentioned knowing her either.

But what if Pete did know them? Was he trying to exact justice for his father? That seemed a little too far-fetched. He certainly had seemed pleasant enough and didn't seem to recognize her.

The name of the couple that had been hurt in the car crash was still a mystery. If Michael had gotten the police reports, then she could learn their identities. Heather said they were elderly. Could the author of the article be related to them?

Tomorrow she could talk to Reverend Tom and see if she could figure out who had been hurt in the accident. Another long shot, but again, the person who wrote the article had to know all of them. Heather, Michael, Kevin, Jen, Alex, and she were all connected through the school and church. It had to be someone close to them all.

Now for those who could have been emotionally hurt by any of them. She shook her head. The possibilities were endless. High school was brutal. Feelings could be hurt by a failure to smile at someone at the right moment. Oh, she was so glad to be beyond those emotionally fraught years even though she'd had a relatively good experience.

Then there were the juveniles and the DUI who had been arrested for drunken disorderly. Rumors always flew around school when kids got in trouble, but Anne would have remembered if it had been any of her close friends.

She sighed and leaned back against her pillows, feeling like she was spinning her wheels in the mud—not going anywhere and everything becoming a mess.

The phone rang and Anne grabbed it, hoping the ring hadn't wakened Liddie and Ben. She thanked God they were recovering, but it was taking much longer than she had anticipated. Wendy's kids were almost recovered. Ben was looking good except for his back and legs, but Liddie's rash on her cheeks still had a ways to go.

"Hi Anne," Alex said. "Thought I'd check in and see if you've learned anything new."

Anne smiled. "It's good to hear from you. I was just sitting here trying to figure out this mess. The more I investigate, the more muddled everything seems."

"I can imagine. I keep telling myself to forget about it. It's most likely someone's idea of a bad joke to get us all worried and so that he can get the last laugh. But what if this person is serious and really thinks he can exact revenge for something that happened so many years ago? I was up on a roof today and it was like I could hear a clock ticking away. Four more days until the writer goes to the police."

"I know. It's like dreading something terrible that's going to happen," said Anne. "Anyway do you want to hear what I know or what my hunches are? My hunches, of course, could be totally wrong."

"Both."

"Well I went to see Heather today." Anne told Alex about Heather and the other girls witnessing the hit-and-run.

"That certainly qualifies as someone being harmed," Alex said, "but how do we know that is what the writer is referring to? Is she or he assuming that one of us caused the accident?"

"That crossed my mind too."

"But weren't we all accounted for after the dance?"

Anne hesitated. "Maybe not. Heather contradicted what Michael and Jen had told me about going straight home after the dance. She said Michael had called her looking for Jen. Michael and Jen's alibi is each other."

Alex sighed. "That's not good."

"I know. It worries me. Someone is lying." If she had to choose between the two women, Anne was inclined to think it would be Heather who was lying since Anne had been closer to Jen her whole life. But what reason would prompt Heather to lie to her?

"What if Heather caused the accident and then told the police it was someone else?" Alex asked.

Anne mulled that over. "That's a possibility, but their car must not have been damaged or the police would've suspected them."

They were both silent for a long moment.

"Seems like the police would've been smart enough to check that out," Alex said. "But that scenario would make a great twist to the mystery."

Anne agreed, and although the idea was far-fetched, she jotted it down. She brought up her trip to Dillon's Auto Parts.

"There was a group of kids who were always getting in trouble, remember?" Alex said after she'd relayed what Pete Dillon had told her. "I think they went out of their way to be rebellious."

"Like Jerry Newman. Heather told me she broke up with him before homecoming. Do you know whatever became of him?"

"Nope. I tried to stay out of his and his friends' way."

"I just ignored them. Now, as a mother, I realize that some of them may have been hurting and crying out silently for attention."

"Some, maybe," Alex said. "Some had no excuse other than to try to make others' lives miserable."

Anne sighed, wondering what Alex was remembering. They all carried scars, no matter how small.

"Do you remember Pete Dillon?" she asked. "He was a freshman the year we graduated."

"Little Petey?" Alex asked. "Sure. I didn't know him well, just that he hated to be called Petey or teased."

"But you called him Petey anyway?"

"Not me. At least not to his face after he got angry about it. I hardly spoke to him other than in gym class, to pass the ball or something."

"Do you think he may hold some sort of grudge?" Anne wondered. Pete had seemed so easygoing in the shop.

"He'd have reason to."

Anne picked up the photo of the dance and scanned it, looking for someone resembling Pete. Of course he wouldn't be in it if he'd taken the photo. "Do you ever feel like we lived in an alternate universe when we were in school? Things we said to each other, we'd never say today. I mean would you go up to the elder at church and call him Georgie Porgie? Or Phyllis Atmore, Phylly Cream Cheese or other such nonsense? Or tie someone's shoelaces together? Or stick a wad of gum on the pew?"

Alex let out a chuckle. "Not if I wanted to show my face there again."

Or keep his reputation, Anne mused. Alex had once said that most of his jobs came from word of mouth. Another reason, she reminded herself, that she needed to find out who was behind that article.

"How is Ryan doing?" Anne asked. "Is his rash finally gone?"

"About back to normal. What about Ben and Liddie? Can they go back to school yet?"

"I was hoping so, but Ben's rash on the back of his legs is really sore and cracking. He still can't sit. And Liddie's rash on her body has dried out so it shouldn't spread, but her face is tender."

"Next time we go out in the woods, we'll have to make sure they know what to avoid."

"My dad said the same thing," Anne said.

"Of course, who knows how good the instruction will do," Alex said with a smile in his voice. "When they are focused in on a game like that, they hardly pay attention to where they are going. They could run over a snake and not even know it. I did."

Anne gave a little shiver. "Thanks for that image."

"Sorry. I didn't call to make you feel worse."

"You didn't." Anne looked down at her list. "You helped me organize my thoughts. Thank you."

"Anytime," Alex said. "Do you want me to talk to Michael about homecoming night? I don't know that he'd tell me anything he didn't tell you, but we were pretty close once."

"If you find an opportunity, that might help. I'd like to get in touch with Jen again," Anne said, thinking how sad it was that they'd all drifted apart over the years, even if it was the natural progression of evolving lives. She realized, as she had with Alex when he thought she might've written the article, that they really didn't know each other well anymore.

She wondered about Michael and Jen the night of homecoming. What had really happened?

And if they were guilty, then why didn't they come forward now before it was made public? Why wouldn't any of them? Unless of course the author of the article was completely wrong and they were all innocent.

* * *

Anne awoke Friday feeling more refreshed than she had in days. Liddie had stayed awake until about eleven, but once she fell asleep she stayed asleep. *Sheer exhaustion*, Anne thought, after all those nights of itchy torment.

Anne picked up her devotional book and Bible that still lay on the bed beside her. She'd been reading about God's forgiveness and the text Matthew 18:22 about forgiving your brother seventy times seven, which she found totally appropriate for the thoughts running through her head. How hard it was to forgive and forget at times! She knew she had to work at it. And obviously the author of the article wasn't ready to forgive. He was seeking something. Retribution? Revenge?

Anne bowed her head. "Lord, I don't know what step I should take next to help my friends and the person who wrote to us. But You know what he or she is planning. Please help this person be able to forgive. And please be with my babies and help them feel better. Amen."

She popped out of bed, ready for the day. As she dressed in brown khakis and a soft black pullover, she searched again through her dresser and jewelry box, looking for the key to the chest upstairs. She should've asked Alex last night if he could get it open, but she hated to bother him when he was so busy. The weather forecaster last night was still predicting days of rain at the end of the week, and people who worked outside were scrambling. This reminded her that if she didn't get the leaves off the lawn, they'd be a soggy mess by this time next week.

Since there was no rush to get to school again, Anne whipped up French toast, one of Ben's favorite breakfasts. Her husband would make them French toast on Saturday mornings. He'd joked it was a man meal. A no-brainer. Actually, Eric had good skills in the kitchen, especially with his French toast—frying the bread to just the most delectable shade of brown and then sprinkling cinnamon and nutmeg on top. Just smelling the spices now conjured up Eric's smiling face, and Anne felt the familiar ache of missing him.

Ben padded into the kitchen and yawned. "Smells good."

"French toast. Get a plate, sweetheart," Anne said, feeling the ache in her chest ease at the sight of her sweet boy. He limped slightly, drawing Anne's concern.

"Are your legs hurting?"

Ben shook his head. "They just feel stiff like there's glue on them. My pajamas are sticking to them."

"Glue, huh. Maybe a shower will help."

After she served Ben his breakfast, Anne put a stack of French toast in the warm oven. She wanted Liddie to sleep as long as possible. She tidied the kitchen and took a load of laundry down to the basement. When she came back up, Liddie had awakened and wanted her breakfast. Her daughter seemed more cheerful this morning, much to Anne's relief.

After Liddie had eaten, Anne went back downstairs to open the library. Remi and Bella were due any minute. She glanced out the window and noticed a squad car parking in front of the library. Michael got out and walked up the sidewalk, carrying a large envelope.

Anne opened the door. "Good morning. Come on in."

"Good morning to you too." He stepped inside and stopped, taking a good look around. "Wow, this is amazing."

Anne smiled. "Thank you. I'm so pleased with how well it turned out. Would you like some coffee? I still have some upstairs."

"I'd love some, but I better not. I already drank more than I should, and the day is just starting."

He shifted his feet, suddenly looking uncomfortable. "Look, Anne, about yesterday...I'm sorry if I seemed rude."

"It's okay. I just assumed you were busy with work."

"Yeah, well, I didn't want to discuss our situation in front of my partner."

"I see," Anne said, although she didn't really. She waited for Michael to continue.

Michael set the large envelope on the counter. "You know I'm taking the detective's exam in the spring. I need to keep a squeaky clean record. Even if there is just a hint that I might've been involved in a crime, it could be detrimental to my job security."

"But surely you can explain that you're investigating an old case, right?"

"Well, there's another reason to be cautious. About a month ago, an officer compromised information by accessing some old records. Jeopardized a court case. So I had to be careful to follow proper procedure requesting the files from the hole."

"The hole?" Anne asked with a grin.

"That's the cellar where we've been storing the files older than ten years. Eventually everything will be on the new computer system, but for now some are in the hole. Anyway, I brought you what I found."

Anne looked at the envelope with growing excitement. "So it's okay if I look at them now?"

"Yeah, but I'm asking that you don't share any of the information with anyone outside the six of us involved. Deal?"

"Deal. And just so you know, I haven't spoken to anyone outside of our group about the article except my parents, and that's because I was asking their help in recalling events that night."

"Good." Michael smiled, looking relieved. "I haven't had a chance to go through the reports yet. I can take some time now if you're available. I thought we could go through them together."

"Sure, that would be great," Anne said, relieved to know that Michael had come through and her doubts about he and Jen and homecoming night were for naught. "I learned some things yesterday that I want to share with you too."

Michael pulled a small stack of brown files out of the envelope. "These are the reports that were filed for the night of homecoming and the next day. I also got a copy of the call log." He placed a sheet of paper on the counter with a handwritten log dated by time of phone calls coming into the department. "And—" He paused as the library door opened and Remi and Bella walked in.

"He was not flirting with me," Remi spoke to her sister in a haughty voice. "It's called talking and being friendly."

"Well he certainly wasn't being 'friendly' with me or any other girl in there. You just—" Remi caught sight of Michael and her mouth dropped open.

Bella dropped her backpack by the door and rushed forward. "Mrs. Gibson! Did something happen?"

"Are you okay?" Remi asked, on her sister's heels.

"Everything is fine," Anne hastened to say. "This is a friend of mine. Officer Banks. Michael, Remi and Bella volunteer here."

"Nice to meet you." Michael gave them a smile and the girls visibly relaxed.

"Oh, whew." Remi laughed. "I thought maybe the library had been broken into."

Bella gave Michael a shy smile. "Nice to meet you too."

Anne gathered up the files and the call logs. "I'm glad you're both here. Perfect timing. Do you mind watching the counter while I talk to Officer Banks? There are also some books to check in."

"Sure thing." Remi took off her coat as Bella retrieved her backpack.

"Why don't we sit over here," Anne suggested and led the way to the table in the corner of the History Room. She set the files on the table and flipped open the top one so both she and Michael could read it. There were only two typed sheets in it. Black lines obliterated sections of the report.

"Why are the names blacked out?" Anne asked.

"Looks like it was because the perps turned out to be juveniles."

This could mean they had gone to Blue Hill High, Anne thought as she read through the report. According to witnesses, three teenage boys were wandering down the middle of Hilltop Avenue at 1:00 a.m. Several calls came into the police station from households saying that the boys were shouting and throwing a football around and that they had set off several car alarms. They were apprehended and taken in to the station. The case was turned over to the juvenile court system.

"So we don't know what happened after that?" Anne asked.

Michael shook his head. "Their cases would've been sealed."

"Well, could something like this ruin a person's life?" Anne said, thinking of the words in the article.

"I wouldn't think so, unless it led to something else more serious or of permanent record, but I don't know how we could find that out without a court order." Michael picked up the next file.

"DUI. Frank Duke. Looks like this wasn't his first time." He lifted the top sheet.

Anne looked over his shoulder and scanned through the most recent report of the officer pulling him over and giving him a DUI test.

"Looks like Duke did some time and had his license revoked," Michael said when they reached the end of the report. "But since there's nothing new on him, either he didn't get into any more trouble or he moved out of the area."

"I can't see how he would be related to our situation, do you?"

"Afraid not."

The next file was the one on the hit-and-run. Michael pointed to a section of the report.

"Look at this! Heather, Mandy, and Trudy are listed as witnesses."

Anne nodded. "This is what I wanted to talk to you about. I saw Heather yesterday and she told me about the accident. She gave me her perspective of the accident and that night." Anne thought about what Heather had said about Michael looking for Jen. She decided to read through the report first before asking him about it.

The victims of the hit-and-run were Elmer and Millie Thomas, ages sixty-five and sixty-seven. They'd been transported to the hospital via ambulance, as Heather had said.

Michael leafed through the file. "Case was never solved. Paint was found on the Thomases' car from impact. The other car was dark blue."

"They'd be in their eighties now." Anne made a note of the Thomases' phone number and address and closed the file.

Michael pointed to a red sticker on the cover. "See, it's been tagged, but it must've been moved downstairs after the statute of limitations was up. Probably why no one had pursued it further. It just became a cold case."

Anne looked down at the last file. Stonebridge Elementary school. Graffiti and broken beer bottles were found at the scene. Never was solved.

"Wasn't the greatest night for the force," Michael said flatly.

"I agree. Isn't there a file on the burglary at Dillon's Auto Parts?"

"Auto parts store?" Michael asked, looking startled.

"Yes, it was reported in the police blotter column, and I talked to Pete Dillon yesterday. Do you remember Pete from school? Alex said people used to call him Petey, which he didn't like at all."

"Doesn't really ring a bell but then a lot of time has passed."

Anne scanned the call log page. "Here it is. Officers were dispatched at 1:22 a.m."

"Ah yes. Good eye. Don't know how I missed that," Michael said, taking a closer look. "So you went over to talk to Pete about a burglary?"

"I talked to his dad briefly too. Mr. Dillon seemed kind of bitter. He'd hurt his back that night, and it appears he still suffers from it. He walked hunched over. Poor guy."

"Did they catch the perps?"

"Not according to Pete. Whoever broke in vandalized the store and spray painted the walls. I thought it might be related to the incident at the elementary school. It'd be interesting to see if there was any connection."

"You may be on to something there. I somehow overlooked the Dillon file. Sorry," Michael said, shoving back his chair. "I'll see if I can find it when I get back to the station."

"Michael, there was one other thing." Anne took a deep breath. "Heather said you called her that night looking for Jen."

Michael froze for a second. "I can't see why she would say something like that. She must be mistaken." He resumed putting the files back in the envelope. "But you remember how Heather liked drama. She was always trying to stir things up. Wanted all the boys to like her."

Anne didn't quite remember Heather like that. She was pretty and outgoing. The boys naturally tried to get her attention. Sure, she had gone out with Jerry Newman, who had a bad reputation, but as she said, she got over that phase.

Michael tucked the envelope of files under his arm. "Did Heather say anything else?"

"Not about that."

"I'll see if I can find out more about the Thomases."

"Thanks, Michael, for coming over." She walked him to the front door and watched him leave, feeling troubled again. Either Heather was mistaken about Michael calling her that night or one of them was lying.

Chapter Eleven

R emi and Bella had things well under control at the front desk, so Anne ran upstairs. Ben had gotten out his small race cars and track, which he hadn't played with since they had moved to Blue Hill.

He had set the plastic orange tracks around the kitchen. Meanwhile, Liddie was in the process of creating a town out of blocks.

"Look, Mommy, this is our house," Liddie said, stacking red blocks. She pointed to a blue square structure. "That's Ben's house."

"So Ben lives in a different house than you and me?"

Liddie nodded. "That one is for boys, and this one is for girls."

"Makes sense to me," Anne said. "We can be neighbors with Ben."

Liddie nodded. "Ryan can live there too."

Ben let out a little sigh. Anne caught his eye and smiled, conveying she was glad he was including his little sister in his play, even if he found her a little tedious.

Ben sent a white car hurtling down the track. It didn't quite make the turn, tumbled off the track and across the floor, and then crashed into the oven. Liddie scrambled after it and drove it to one of her block structures.

"It's got to go to get fixed now," Liddie said.

"Okay, okay." Ben reached for a green Mustang, which he started off lower on the track. This time the car made the turn. Liddie declared the white car all better and gave it back to Ben.

Anne thought about the list of auto body repair shops that she had started. The police report didn't reveal anything different than what Heather had told her. If she had been involved in an accident and wanted to keep it secret, she'd probably get the car fixed out of town or wait until some time had passed. But if she relied on the car for transportation, it couldn't be out of sight for long.

She looked over the list of repair shops and wondered if there was a way to narrow down the list to those that had been open seventeen years ago. She could check with the Chamber of Commerce, but she recalled there were some old Blue Hill business directories in the library's Reference Room. Maybe they would be useful.

She opened the second floor door to the library and hurried to the Reference Room. Along the back shelf, Anne had reserved a section for local reference books.

She hunted along the shelf and found several Blue Hill Chamber of Commerce directories. They were updated every five years and provided addresses and phone numbers for utilities, government services, and businesses, and included other useful information as well. She selected the directory from 1996.

Businesses were listed in alphabetical order, and she cross-referenced the list she had. Bob's Body Shop was on the list as well as Fowler's Auto Repair. Blue Hill Ford was in business then also, but Andy's Auto was not listed. This gave her three local body shops to check.

She looked at the listing for Dillon's Auto Parts, making her wonder about Pete "Petey" Dillon and the injury to his father again. She needed to find out more about him.

"Mrs. Gibson." Remi appeared in the doorway. "There is someone downstairs looking for information on planting fall bulbs. I found a book on seasonal gardening in the catalog. It wasn't checked out, but it's not where it should be."

Anne put the booklet back on the shelf and got to her feet. "Wendy may have put it in our fall display."

"Oh, I didn't think to check out front."

Anne went downstairs with Remi and located the seasonal gardening book on the shelf. While Remi checked the book out for the patron, Anne used the computer to print out a map so she could easily find the body repair shops. Then she worked around the library until it was time to fix lunch for Ben and Liddie.

Since the kids seemed content for a while, Anne made arrangements for Remi to keep an eye on them so she could run some errands. According to the schedule, Wendy was due in at two. Anne called Wendy and left a message that she was going out.

Anne lifted her face toward the sun as she went outside to her car. Cold days were ahead, and she wanted to savor the warm rays as much as she could. She got in her car and consulted the map she had printed to the auto repairs shops she planned to visit. She knew Blue Hill very well from having grown up here, but it had expanded some. The Ford dealership was on the far end of the town, so she headed there first. She turned into the lot and drove past the colorful rows of shiny new cars. She found a parking spot right in front of the showroom door. A new Ford pickup and an SUV were centered in the large room. Several desks lined one wall. Men dressed in nice, navy suits looked up as she opened the door. One young man rose quickly from a desk to meet her halfway across the floor. "May I help you?

"Yes, I was looking for your repair department."

The eagerness in his expression dimmed. "Right this way, ma'am."

He showed her to a hallway that led back to a glassed-in office. She got in line behind a man and waited.

A middle-aged woman with a name tag identifying her as Bess sat behind the window. She too was dressed in a blue top and slacks, but her outfit was more casual than the salespeople out front.

When it was Anne's turn she stated, "I'm looking for a repair record from seventeen years ago—September, October. It's for a car that might have been involved in a hit-and-run."

Bess's hazel eyes narrowed as she scrutinized Anne. "Are you from the police?"

"No, but I am working with a police officer on it." She explained about the accident and how she was looking for a car that would've needed body work.

"Was it a Ford?"

"I don't know. It was dark and the witnesses didn't get a good look. I doubt it was reported to their insurance." If he or she had insurance.

The woman frowned and tapped on her computer keyboard. "I'm not sure I would have access to that information. That was a long time ago. I'm pretty sure I couldn't share any personal information with you even if I did."

"I understand, but it is important. If you do find something, you can contact Officer Michael Banks at the Blue Hill police department. It would be helpful."

"I'll see what I can find," the woman said. She made a note on a yellow sticky note and stuck it to a large paper pad that covered the counter in front of her, which doubled as a calendar.

Anne thanked her and left, undaunted. There was a good chance that the car wouldn't have been a Ford anyway. She sent up a prayer that if the information she needed was there that Bess would be motivated to find it.

She drove over to the next store on her list. Bob's Body Shop. She pulled into the empty parking lot. Was the store not open today? She got out of the car and went to the door.

"Gone out of business," an elderly man in worn coveralls called cheerfully as he came around the side of the building. "I've retired. You looking to buy the building?"

"No," Anne said with a smile. "I'm Anne Gibson. I run the library in town."

His pale blue eyes twinkled behind wire-rimmed glasses. "Ah yes, in that beautiful old Victorian. I'm Mr. Bob. My wife has been up there to visit the library. She used to know the woman who lived there."

"Edie Summers. She was my great-aunt. I may have met your wife if she's one of our patrons."

"You may have, but she hasn't been up there since the grand opening. I'll tell her you came by when I get home tonight."

"Have her ask for me if she comes up to the library," Anne said.

"I'll do that." Mr. Bob peered at her silver Impala. "Something wrong with your car?"

"No, I'm looking for information on a car you may have repaired seventeen years ago, in the fall. I thought perhaps you kept some records from that year."

Mr. Bob scratched the bald spot on his head. "Oh dearie, I think that's going to be near impossible to do anytime soon, but come on in." He held the door open for her and she stepped inside the shadowy garage.

"I would have the invoice if the work was done here, but do you see that stack of boxes over there?" He nodded toward a stack of file boxes five wide and four high lining the wall next to a small room that looked to have been the store's office.

"I just took two loads like that over to my storage unit. The unit is packed to the rafters, waiting for me to go through it when I have time. 'Course, that'll have to be when I'm not fishing in Florida." He gave her a wink.

Anne's expression must have shown her dismay, because he asked, "Is this very important?"

"It could be," Anne said. "But I'd hate for you to go to all that trouble of looking for it when the car may never have come in here."

"Listen, you seem sweet and my wife loves the library. I'll take a look when I go over later today."

Anne smiled. "Thank you so much."

"Oh, wait. What a numbskull I am." He slapped his palm against his forehead and took off into the office. Anne could hear several crashes and bangs as if things were being thrown around. Then there was a long silence.

"Mr. Bob?" Anne called. "Everything okay?"

He came out carrying a large stack of square, olive notebooks. "Logs!" He gave her a toothy grin. "When someone brought a car in, my wife would record when it came in, when it went out, a brief description of the job, and if it was paid. This helped the wife locate the paperwork when she did the accounting."

He flipped open the top notebook and coughed as a cloud of dust rose up. "Wrong year."

He tossed it on top of the boxes and opened the next one. "Nope." The notebook went flying. "Ah, here it is." He motioned for Anne to come over and take a look.

The information was recorded in neat columns. He flipped through the pages until he found the one he was looking for, then he ran his finger down the date column until he came to September.

"Here are the vehicles that came in for that month. This here is the invoice number, which doesn't help us none right now, but this tells the model. Where would the damage be?"

"Well, I assume it would be in the front. It sideswiped another car. The witnesses said the car was a smallish sedan. Maybe a Toyota or Nissan."

"*Hmm*, could be bumper damage, possible grill damage, a side panel." He stroked his chin and adjusted his glasses. "Okay, here's a Cadillac that came in, but that's a big car. He moved his finger down. These here are trucks. Ah, here is a Volkswagen, but it was rear-ended." He flipped the page to October.

"Mustang, painting job. Oh, I remember that. This gal wanted the car painted hot pink. Took a great muscle car and turned it all girly. I almost refused to do it. But" — he rubbed his index finger and thumb together — "money talks."

Anne returned his grin as he resumed his perusing.

"Okay, here's a Honda Civic." He peered closer. "This is my handwriting, and I can't read it. But I think it says a tree branch fell on it or maybe it was hail. But if I had one car in for hail, I probably would have had others."

They went through the rest of the list to the end of December. A Volkswagen, Kia, and another Honda were possibilities. Slight possibilities.

"Is there any way to know what color these cars were?" Anne asked.

"That would have been on the invoice since we would have had to match paint. What color are you looking for?"

"Blue."

"Light blue? Dark blue? Sky blue? "

"Dark. Or it could be a dark green," Anne said, recalling what Heather had said. "The witnesses couldn't agree on the color."

"Well, dearie, that doesn't help too much. There are a bazillion blue or green cars out there," Mr. Bob said. "Tell you what. When I take this load over, I'll take a look to see if I can find the box with the invoices. But I'm not promising anything."

Anne nodded. "I appreciate anything you can do. Let me give you my phone number." She pulled out one of her library business cards.

"I have lots of time now when I'm not fishing. Might as well help out a pretty girl."

Anne smiled. This was the second time today she'd been referred to as a girl, although Liddie meant it in generic terms.

Anne extended her hand. "It was nice meeting you. Best wishes on your retirement."

She returned to her car and headed downtown. The kindness people showed strangers in small towns amazed her. Not that she didn't meet wonderful people in New York, but in Blue Hill there was a strong feeling of unity and family.

Fowler's Auto Repair was on a side street off of Main. The business was housed in an ancient stone building that must've had some historical significance since it had never been torn down and replaced with something more modern.

Cars filled the lot in front of the building, and Anne had to drive down the street a ways before she found a spot where she could parallel park under an old oak tree. She walked back down the cracked sidewalk and cut across the parking lot, sidestepping oil spots. She went in a side door dwarfed by large garage doors that were currently shut. Inside, several cars were lined up in various stages of repair. A strong scent of paint greeted her.

"Hey there!" a woman called, coming out of a side room. She wore overalls covered with smudges of either paint or grease. Her dark hair was swept back in a ponytail. "Dropping off or picking up?"

"Neither," Anne said, returning the woman's smile. "I need some information."

The woman came closer and let out a squeal, nearly causing Anne to drop her purse.

"Anne Summers! It's me. Melissa Armstrong."

"Melissa?" Anne said, shocked. Could it be? The grease monkey in front of her was the same girl who had pursued Alex so relentlessly their senior year? As she came into the light, Anne could see that despite her grimy work clothes, she was as pretty as ever. Her dark eyes sparkled and her smile revealed the dimple in her cheek.

"Yep, it's me. Surprised?"

"That's putting it mildly."

Melissa giggled. "I get that reaction a lot from old classmates. I don't know why. I used to work on cars in high school too."

"I didn't know that," Anne said, but then she hadn't tried to get to know Melissa well either. She wondered if Alex knew she worked here. "So, you've always been interested in cars?"

"Yep, I just finished my doctorate in automotive engineering."

"Wow." Anne was impressed. "You've been busy. I'm sorry to be so clueless. I really didn't stay in close touch with anyone once I left after school. When my parents moved to Florida, I only came back a couple times to visit Aunt Edie."

"I can relate." Melissa took off her gloves, revealing neatly manicured, painted nails.

"So, is this your shop?" Anne asked.

"Nope, I'm only helping out a friend temporarily. I've applied to a big company in Detroit. I'm hoping to get into research and development. Maybe run a team someday."

"That is so cool, Melissa," Anne said with awe.

"So, what have you been up to? Are you back visiting your great-aunt?"

"I'm back to live here." Anne explained about Aunt Edie leaving her the library and why.

"My condolences, Anne." Melissa touched Anne on the arm. "That must've been rough."

"What about you? Are you married?"

"Me? No way." Melissa laughed. "Got engaged in college and rapidly learned I wasn't the commitment type. I like being free as a bird." She set her gloves down on a barrel. "So, you said you were here looking for information?"

"I'm trying to locate a car that was repaired years ago. Is Mr. Fowler around?"

Melissa shook her head. "He doesn't come in very often. Shaun Milhouse is the manager now, but he took off for the afternoon. Remember him? He's the friend I'm helping out. For a short little guy who everyone thought was a loser in high school, he sure is doing great for himself now."

"I remember Shaun. I didn't think he was a loser. I just didn't know him well."

"No one really did. But he was nice to me. I'd bring my car over here and we'd work on it. He's worked here since high school, and Mr. Fowler is going to sell the business to him."

"I'm so glad he's doing well," Anne said sincerely.

"So, what are you looking for?"

"The night of homecoming, there was an accident, and I'm trying to find the record of the car repair."

"Didn't you and Alex ride in the parade in a convertible?"

"Yes, that was my great-aunt's car, but it wasn't involved."

"Well, I can't say when Shaun will be back, but we can take a look in the office."

Anne followed Melissa into the small, crowded room. "So, if you don't mind my asking, what did you do after the homecoming dance?"

"Oh, I don't know. This and that. It was so long ago. I probably hung out with some of the football guys. I was always hanging out with them." Melissa grinned "Oh yeah, now I remember...

Melissa walked over to a wall of filing cabinets. "We stayed out late and were horsing around. Partying a little, driving around downtown with our music turned up loud." She looked over her shoulder and gave a little laugh. "Oh, that's right. You never stuck around. You were such a good girl."

Anne decided to ignore the teasing that bordered on a jibe. She had always gotten home by curfew, which had kept her out of trouble most of the time. She looked around the office. On the desk were several framed photos. She stepped closer. "Did the horsing around involve paint? Like in spray painting walls or worse? Or —" Her breath caught in her throat. In one photo on the desk, a young Shaun stood beside a small, midnight blue sports car.

Melissa turned around, her hands on her hips. "What are you getting at Anne?"

"Melissa, do you know anything about what happened homecoming night?" Anne asked softly.

Her eyes narrowed. "You tell me."

"There were several incidences including a burglary where the store owner got hurt. Did permanent damage to his back. They think teens were involved in the burglary of an auto parts store. And then there was a hit-and-run. A dark-colored car was involved. Two people were injured. They never caught the driver." Anne watched Melissa closely. Was it possible that Melissa knew something? Or was somehow involved?

She glanced back at the photo and Melissa followed her gaze. Both Melissa and Shaun had the skills to perhaps repair the body work on a car. Shaun had access to the body shop and could very well repair his car or someone else's if it was involved in an accident.

Melissa shoved the filing cabinet shut. "You know what, Anne? I think you should talk to Shaun." She walked to the door. "I have customers waiting for their cars. You know the way out."

Chapter Twelve

Anne drove back toward home, her mind racing. She'd seen the photo on the desk in the office and she just jumped to conclusions. As Mr. Bob had said, there were bazillions of blue cars out there. It wasn't like her to jump to conclusions so quickly. Usually she liked to mull things over, but ever since she'd gotten the article, her life had felt off-kilter. Her emotions were too close to the surface, like she was sixteen again with hormones raging.

The shock of seeing Melissa in circumstances she'd never imagined had thrown her too. She was guilty of stereotyping. She had always thought Melissa was just one of those giggly girls who chased football players and cared more about appearance than school. Anne had been introverted in high school, but she still felt like she had a large circle of friends. Suddenly her high school world seemed so small. What about all those kids who were wallflowers, the nerds who spent all their time in the library, or the nonconformists determined to make a statement? She had prided herself on not being in a close-knit clique. But now that she thought about it, there were a lot of people she didn't really know or who didn't fit into a neat little niche. Like Melissa and Shaun.

She turned on the street where the Thomases, the poor elderly couple in the accident, used to live and pulled up to the curb beside a gas station. She checked the address she had jotted down in her notebook. She was at the right place, only there was no longer any house. She tried the phone number that had been listed in the police report. It was a real estate office, and they had never heard of the Thomases. Obviously the information was out of date. She hoped Michael had more luck tracking them down.

She started home again, and as Anne turned the car down Church Street and passed the church, she noticed Reverend Tom's car in the parking lot. She remembered what her mother said about the church ladies and hospital visitation. She slammed on the brakes and did a quick turn. If the Thomases had gone to her church, then there should be some record of it.

She parked in the lot by the red brick building which had been constructed in the late 1800s. It had a huge stained-glass window above the front entrance and narrow stained-glass windows on both sides of the sanctuary. The original church bell still hung above the steeple.

Anne entered the quiet church. She stood in the foyer, and a feeling of peace washed over her. No matter what turmoil happened in her world, there was the constant anchor of her church. She drew strength from the fellowship and knowing they had a common goal of belonging to God.

Taking a deep breath, she walked down the passageway that connected the church to the newly added fellowship hall. Reverend Tom was sitting at his desk dressed in a T-shirt and jeans, which meant he was probably getting ready to work around the church grounds tending the landscaping. There were deacons assigned to cutting the grass and trimming hedges, but Tom liked to be out in what he referred to as God's first church—nature.

She knocked lightly on his open door.

He looked up and a smile creased his face. "Good afternoon, Anne. Great to see you. Please, have a seat." He waved her toward the two padded chairs opposite his wide oak desk.

"How are the kids doing? Feeling better?"

Anne sat down. "You heard about the poison ivy?"

"Oh yes. Four families were affected, and I feel terrible, especially since it happened at the church picnic. I was out there in the woods too, and it didn't occur to me that we'd have trouble with poison ivy this time of year, but evidently the plants are still potent, even in the fall."

"It's not your fault. I feel guilty too, but none of us thought about it," Anne said.

"I was just signing some cards to send out to the kids. I was out of town until last night. Otherwise I would've gotten to them sooner." Reverend Tom picked up two envelopes and handed them to Anne. One was addressed to Ben and the other Liddie. "There's a little puzzle in there, and if they put it together and bring it to Sunday school, I have a little something for them."

"They are going to love that!" Anne exclaimed. "Thank you." She tucked the cards in her purse.

He smiled. "Now, is there something I can do for you?"

"I was wondering if Elmer and Millie Thomas belong to our congregation."

"Thomas? It's a common name, but I don't believe we have anyone by that name." He clicked the keyboard on his desk and peered at his computer. "Let me pull up the membership list." He tapped the scroll button and shook his head. "We have the Thompsons, but no Thomases right now."

Since Reverend Tom had moved to Blue Hill after Anne graduated, he wouldn't have been there when the accident occurred. "They would have belonged awhile ago. They used to live just down the road from here," Anne said. "There's a gas station on the lot now. Seventeen years ago they were involved in a hit-and-run accident, and I'm trying to find them."

"How interesting." Reverend Tom smiled. "I'm sure there's a story behind this."

"Oh, there is," Anne said. She hadn't planned on talking about the article with her pastor, even though she knew that it would be held in strictest confidence, but the next thing she knew she was spilling out the entire story, including her encounter with Melissa.

"I just handled it wrong," Anne said. "I practically accused her of burglary or implied that she and Shaun ran into that old couple. And afterward I realized how little I knew about the people I went to school with. I feel like I was so self-centered."

Reverend Tom nodded. "I'm not saying your feelings aren't justified, but you were a teenager, a mere child compared to the mature, compassionate woman you've grown into. You can't change the past, only forgive and move forward."

Anne wiped away a tear that had slipped onto her cheek at Reverend Tom's kind words. He seemed to know just what to say to make her feel better. "I'm sorry. I didn't come to dump all this on you, but thank you."

"Would you like me to offer your troubles to God in prayer?" he asked.

"Please."

He prayed for God to forgive Anne if there was anything she had done wrong as a youth or now. He asked for guidance in her quest for the truth, and he prayed for whoever had written the article to get the help they needed and to help right any wrong.

When he finished, Anne felt a burden lift. She didn't realize how much the situation had been weighing her down.

"There's that beautiful smile," Reverend Tom said. "Now, let's see what we can do. We can check the old church records if you want. You know where they are."

Anne nodded. She'd searched the records before. "My mother mentioned that the Visiting Ladies kept records of hospital visits. Even if the Thomases weren't official members of this church, they might've received a visit, especially since they lived in the neighborhood."

"Good thinking. The ladies usually fill out a record sheet. We like to keep track of our outreach for the monthly and yearly church board reports." He led the way to the basement stairs. "Also, if the Thomas family was associated with another family of the church, the visitation committee might've sent flowers. There would be receipts kept for that week."

They reached the bottom of the stairs where there was a small foyer, along with a water fountain situated between two restrooms. Double doors led into the large meeting hall that held the Sunday school classes. One of the rooms held several metal filing cabinets where the records were kept.

Reverend Tom got her started thumbing through the pages and then went outside to finish the mowing he'd started. Anne spent about an hour going through the records and was about to give up when she came across a report that made her gasp.

Two days after homecoming, the visitation ladies delivered flowers and later took up a collection to aid with expenses for Mrs. Milhouse's parents. The Thomases were the grandparents of Shaun Milhouse.

Her mind reeled. So Shaun's grandparents had been hurt in the accident. What if Shaun had written the article in order to somehow expose the person who'd injured his grandparents? Did he know something they didn't? Like who had been driving the car?

No doubt Melissa would tell Shaun that Anne had been there snooping. If he was the author of the article, then he might think that Anne was on to him.

* * *

"Whee!" Liddie made a flying leap into a big pile of orange, yellow, and brown leaves. She giggled and rolled back and forth, making Anne long to join in her carefree fun.

Ben paused in his raking. "Mom, she's ruining my pile."

"Liddie, you can jump in the leaves, but don't roll." Anne wanted to remind Liddie what happened after she rolled in the pine needles in the woods, but she didn't want to ruin Liddie's good mood. Her child seemed happier than she'd been all week. Besides, Anne had checked the yard for poison ivy before they started.

Alex was coming over later after work. She was dying to tell him what she found out at the church. She had also left a message for Michael to call her. She knew she didn't have any real evidence about Shaun Milhouse, but it may be more than they had seventeen years ago and worth checking out.

"We need to push the piles to the curb," Anne said. They'd been at it for an hour, and Ben was doing great for a nine-year-old, but they'd barely made a dent. Her love of the large yard was faltering right now as she rubbed her aching back. Aunt Edie had hired someone to take care of the yard for the last couple decades of her life, and Anne wondered if she could squeeze hired labor into her budget.

A minivan pulled up to the curb, and Wendy and four of her kids piled out. Wendy waved at Anne and went around to the back of the van and started handing out rakes.

"What's going on?" Ben came up beside Anne. Liddie stopped her jumping and her eyes opened wide as the Pyle brood stared toward them.

"I'm not sure, but I think they're coming to help us."

Wendy marched up to Anne with her four oldest children at her heels. "Hi there. We came to help." She held up a hand. "And it's no use saying you have it under control. Of course you do. We *want* to help." She grinned. "Besides, what's the benefit of having an army of children if you can't use them to do a good deed once in a while?" She turned to her children and assigned them different sections of the yard.

As Anne continued to rake, she watched in amazement as the vast carpet of leaves was quickly reduced to small piles and then swept into a bank of leaves along the street to await pickup by the town's street sweepers. Ben chatted with Christian about a video game, and Liddie danced around the yard with Emily, excited to have someone to play with.

"This would've taken us days. Thank you," Anne said to Wendy and her children as she helped Wendy load the rakes back in her van.

"You're very welcome. See you tomorrow." Wendy jumped in and waved from the van window. As she had before, Anne thought her friend was an angel.

A car rolled up in front of the mailbox. "The mail lady is here." Ben went to meet her and came back with an armload. "We got a package from Grandpa."

Liddie jumped up and down. "Is it presents?"

"It's a video of when I was in high school."

"Can we watch it?" Liddie asked.

"Sure. After supper. Now let's go wash up," Anne said, hiking up the hill to the house. She gave Ben her rake to put away in the garage and took Hershey to the backyard.

Liddie climbed the stairs slowly. Now that the excitement of playing had worn off, Liddie was starting to drag her feet.

"Are you hungry?" Anne asked as they reached the second floor. She turned on the kitchen light. Liddie's clothes and face were grubby. "Tell you what, I'm going to draw you a bubble bath and you can soak in there until supper's ready. Doesn't that sound good?" It did to Anne. Muscles in her legs and arms that she didn't know she had were aching.

"Okay," Liddie said somewhat grudgingly. Anne ran the bath water and added some baking soda to it, since the home remedy seemed to have worked well last time. She got out a washcloth and dabbed at the dirt on Liddie's cheek.

"Ow," Liddie complained as some of the scabs came off.

"Sorry, sweetie." Anne dropped the washcloth in the tub and opened the cupboard under the sink. She brought out a small plastic basket with floatable toys.

She tidied up the bedrooms until Liddie tired of being in the tub, got her dressed, and then left her to play with her dolls. Anne returned downstairs to make dinner. Ben was playing with his cars on the tracks still strewn around the kitchen. Anne stepped over Liddie's town.

"Did you get your assignments done today?" Anne asked, opening the refrigerator door.

"Yeah. It goes much faster than when I'm in school," Ben said.

"If you have any questions let me know, okay?"

He shrugged one shoulder. "Sure."

Anne turned back to the refrigerator and pulled out ingredients for salad and also a pound of hamburger. She decided to make mini meatloaves. She combined an egg, seasoning, and bread crumbs with the meat and pressed the mixture into muffin pans. While it baked, she tore the lettuce for the salad. Her mind wandered over the day's events. Maybe she had jumped to the wrong conclusion about Shaun, but now she knew who the Thomases were.

The phone rang and she wiped her hands on a towel.

"Hello, Anne Gibson?" a deep voice said after she'd picked up. "This is Mr. Bob."

"Oh yes," Anne said, surprised. Despite his kindness, she never really expected to hear from him.

"I just wanted to let you know that I found the invoices for the year you were asking about, and nope, from September to December, there wasn't any damage to small cars like you described. The one blue car that came in was sideswiped. I ordered light blue paint for it. Sorry I couldn't have been more help."

"Oh, don't be. It was sweet of you to check," Anne said. "And it is helpful by process of elimination."

"Well, it kept bugging me, and then when I talked to the missus, she kept at me to take a look. By the way, she says she plans on getting over to yer library next week and bringing her friends."

"Tell her I'm looking forward to it," Anne said, delighted that her visit had resulted in more interest in the library.

"Take care, missy." Mr. Bob signed off, and Anne hung up the phone with a satisfied sigh. She liked the old man, and she was certain his wife would be just as amiable.

Liddie padded downstairs with her doll, and Anne dabbed more cream on Liddie's rash, which was shrinking. "You look like you're almost all better."

"Still itches."

"I know, but it doesn't itch as much, does it?"

Liddie shook her head and sat on a chair, watching Ben play. The mini meatloaves were almost done, and Anne whipped up some instant mashed potatoes to "frost" the tops. "Ben, go wash your hands."

Liddie jumped up. "Cupcakes!"

"It's meatloaf," Ben said as he got off the floor.

"I know!" Liddie stuck her tongue out at her brother, which he thankfully ignored.

When they were all gathered around the table, Anne said the blessing, thanking God for all He'd provided. Before she raised her head, she sent up a silent thank-you for her findings of the afternoon and prayed she was a few steps closer to figuring out who was behind this threat to her and her friends.

* * *

"Why do I think this is going to be embarrassing?" Alex groaned as he looked down at Ryan sitting cross-legged on Anne's living room floor with Liddie and Alex. "I want no cracks about how old things look back then or how funny our clothes or hair were. Seventeen years is not *that* long ago."

Anne slid the videotape her father had sent into the VCR and sat back on the couch with Alex. She'd popped some popcorn and passed a big bowl to the kids and set a smaller one between Alex and herself.

She hadn't watched the video since her senior year. It was a little grainy, but it was like stepping back in time. Her excitement grew as the camera panned her childhood home.

"That's my bedroom in Grandma and Grandpa's old house," Anne said to Liddie and Ben. "You know the one I showed you when we first moved here. Remember?"

On a Sunday afternoon, Anne had driven to her old neighborhood to show them her childhood home that her parents had sold when they moved to Florida. The house had been freshly painted a sunny yellow from the light blue it had been her entire life, but Anne liked it. There was a tricycle parked by the porch and flowers had been planted along the sidewalk in the neatly kept yard. It gave her a warm feeling to know that the house seemed loved and that someone got to grow up where she had happy memories.

"Mommy, you look pretty," Liddie said as Anne came into view wearing the aqua gown she and her mother had fun picking out. "I like your dress. You looked like a princess."

"Your mother was a queen that night," Alex said.

"You were?" Liddie asked with wide eyes.

"I was homecoming queen and Mr. Ochs was the king."

Ryan snorted and rolled over on his back, laughing. Ben looked at Alex and grinned.

"You think it's funny?" Alex asked, grabbing Ryan's leg and tickling him.

The camera view swung to the front door as Anne's mother opened it. Alex stood on the other side looking skinny, tall, and very young. He clutched a small white box, and Anne could tell he was nervous.

"Who's that geek?" Ryan asked.

"Who do you think?" Alex asked.

"Uh-uh," Ryan said and then grinned at his own joke. Alex poked his nephew with his foot.

Alex stepped inside the door and the video cut off. "That's when your dad interrogated me about my intentions."

"What are those?" Ben asked.

Alex looked at Anne, but she only smiled. He was on his own with that one.

"Sometimes when a young man is going to go out with a young lady, the father wants to know what future plans the man might have about his daughter."

"Why?" Ben asked.

"To keep her safe. That's what dads do." He glanced at Liddie and then Anne. "And mothers too," he added hastily. He looked at Anne with sympathy and apology in his eyes.

Anne swallowed hard, knowing Liddie's father wouldn't be around to screen her dates. Eric would've been very protective, as always.

"So? What were your intentions?" Ryan wanted to know.

Alex cleared his throat. A red flush crept up his neck. "I can't remember what I said exactly. Something about being her friend and bringing her home safely that night. Stuff like that."

"Mommy, you're walking funny," Liddie interrupted, and they turned their attention back to the video.

"That's because I almost tripped coming down the stairs. So much for making a grand entrance." Anne grimaced. "I was wearing high heels."

The next shot was of Alex awkwardly pinning on her corsage, which earned more snorts and rolling of eyes from the boys.

"You two don't have to watch this, you know," Alex said.

Ben looked at Ryan. "Want to race cars in the kitchen?"

"Sure."

They scrambled to their feet and ran off. Liddie climbed on the couch by Anne.

The next scene was the ball field shot from the stands. The roar of the crowd drowned out her father's narrative.

"Look, there's Mommy," Anne said as a red convertible entered the field and began a slow circle around the field. "That was Aunt Edie's car."

"Whatever happened to that car?" Alex asked. "It was a classic."

"I'm not sure. I think she sold it to a collector and bought a Jeep Cherokee. It did much better getting up the hill out front in the winter."

"I remember seeing her tooling around town in the Jeep." Alex leaned forward. "So, now what and who exactly are we looking for?"

"Anything unusual. In particular, Shaun Milhouse and Pete Dillon."

"Okay, I know why we're suspicious of Pete, but why am I looking for Shaun?" Alex asked.

"Well, there's a tiny chance he might have been involved in the hit-and-run accident. Did you know he had a dark blue sports car back then?"

"Nope. I don't ever remember him driving it to school."

"Well, the police report said the paint from the hit-and-run car was dark blue or green." She explained about seeing the photo in the office at the garage and jumping to conclusions.

"So, you think that Shaun may have been involved in the accident?" Alex asked, his tone skeptical.

"I did, but now I don't think so. Shaun worked at a body shop. He could've repaired the car and the police never would've known."

Anne's father zoomed in closer to the field as the band marched by. Anne paused the videotape and looked for Heather in the scene, but it was impossible to tell the identity of the flute players at that distance.

"Anyway, I was able to track down information about the couple that was hurt in the accident. Shaun Milhouse was involved, but not the way I thought. At least I hope not. I found out from the church records that his grandparents are Elmer and Millie Thomas, the couple that were hurt in the accident.

"Good detective work there," Alex said. "But I didn't realize Shaun belonged to our church. I don't remember him being in the youth group."

"I don't either. It may have just been Shaun's parents who were members. Anyway, the ladies took flowers to the hospital for his grandparents after the accident. You know, I can't help thinking that maybe Shaun wrote the article. But that just gives us the *what* but not the *who*. We still don't know who he was blaming."

Liddie tugged on Anne's shirt sleeve.

"Ready to watch the rest of this?" Anne clicked the forward button. Her father had gotten inside the gym door. Carol Rigsby was at the microphone and was announcing Alex and Anne as the homecoming king and queen. They were to lead the first dance. The music started and they stepped out.

"I was so nervous that I'd trip or stomp on your new shoes," Alex confessed.

"*You* were nervous?" Anne laughed. "I was the one in high heels, and that floor was slippery."

There were only sporadic video shots after that. One recorded Anne standing next to Jennifer at the punch bowl. She was shooting glares across the floor toward Michael. On the sidelines, Melissa tapped Alex on the shoulder and obviously was asking him to dance.

"Did you know Melissa works with Shaun now?" Anne said, not taking her eyes off the TV screen.

"Where? At Fowler's?"

"Yep. She's one of the mechanics. She has a doctorate in automotive engineering and a possible job in research. She's going places with her life."

"I had no idea," Alex said. "I saw her a couple times over the years from a distance, but we never talked much. Wow. I'm impressed. I thought she was smart, but I had no idea she was the engineer type."

"I was thinking earlier how little we really knew people from high school, even though we spent so much time with them."

"You shouldn't feel bad about that. We were just kids with our whole lives ahead of us," Alex commented.

Anne dragged her gaze away from the image of Alex dancing with Melissa and scanned the crowd. A short boy was standing next to a group of football players.

"Is that Pete?" Anne paused the video.

"Looks like him."

Suddenly Pete stumbled backward as if someone had shoved him.

"Did Michael just push him?" Anne asked.

"I couldn't tell who did it." Alex got down on one knee in front of the TV as Anne rewound it.

He shook his head. "No way to tell."

Pete appeared to be arguing with someone and then turned and stomped off.

In the background Heather came out of the girl's locker room. The front of her dress appeared wet. She'd said that Shaun had spilled the punch on her, but Anne didn't see Shaun anywhere on the dance floor or sidelines.

There were flashes from cameras as the students snapped photos of each other. The photo that had been in the article had come from the same angle that her father was shooting the video from. She caught sight of Keith, who had taken Kevin's place that night as newspaper photographer. With so many others taking photos too, it was impossible to tell who would've shot the article's photo. Besides, if the photographer shot the gym from the door where her father had stood, then they'd be out of the frame of the video anyway.

The video ended mid-dance when her father must've run out of tape. Liddie got up and went out to play with the boys. Alex looked at Anne. "Looks like we were all accounted for at the dance, except I didn't see Shaun or Kevin."

"Well, Shaun had to have been there." Anne rubbed the tension in the back of her neck. "Heather said he bumped into her and made her spill her punch all over her dress. And then about an hour after the dance, Shaun's grandparents were run off the road by someone in a blue car."

"And someone or some*ones* broke into Pete's father's auto shop. And don't forget the graffiti," Alex added.

"And whoever wrote the article believes that one or all of us is to blame in some way. But we don't even know what we're blamed for." Anne let out a long sigh. Seeing the video had been fun, but it hadn't helped with figuring out what happened that night. At least it wasn't obvious.

"I'm out of any new ideas. Maybe Shaun holds the key to whatever happened after all," Anne suggested. At least she hoped so.

"Maybe he does," Alex agreed. "But one way or another, we'll know soon. The deadline is only three days away."

Anne suppressed a shiver. Somehow she had to unlock the truth before time ran out next Tuesday morning.

CHAPTER THIRTEEN

Have a good morning, Mrs. Walinsky," Anne said as she handed over the book on crocheting scarves and hats.

"Oh, I will." Mrs. Walinsky, the only patron in the library, tucked the book in her large purse. "A rainy day like this is perfect for staying in and starting a new crochet project." She strolled to the door. The sound of rain hitting the porch roof grew louder as she stepped outside and Wendy dashed in. She stopped by the front door, dripping water on the rug, and stripped off her rain coat. The storm that had been promised all week had finally arrived with a vengeance, soaking the outside world and everyone who dared venture out.

She gave Anne a smile as she yanked off her boots and pulled a pair of flats out of her bag. "It's really coming down out there. The driveway is turning into a river."

Anne went to the window and looked out. Indeed, what water wasn't pooling on the steps and grass was flowing down the sidewalk and joining the stream on the street. If it kept up like this, nobody was going to want to be outside willingly, and they were in for a quiet day.

"I'm free for a few hours. A couple of Chad's math students are watching the kids. I think they're hoping to get into his good graces before he grades yesterday's tests."

Anne laughed. "I'm hoping to run Liddie and Ben over to the medical clinic and see if I can get an all clear for them to return to normal activities," Anne said, although she wasn't looking forward to venturing out in the storm.

Liddie had been cranky again this morning, but Anne suspected it didn't have as much to do with the remnants of her rash as it did with whatever had been plaguing her the last few days. Anne had hoped it was just a passing phase that was behind them, but it was back. She racked her brain over what it could possibly be. They had their normal routine after Alex and Ryan left. She'd let them have milk and cookies. Then she tucked Liddie in bed and read from the storybook, and Liddie had fallen asleep.

"I'm going to take a load up," Anne said to Wendy who was running her fingers through her damp hair.

Anne picked up the basket of returned children's books. Humming one of her favorite hymns, "Showers of Blessing," she climbed the stairs. She took her time putting the colorful books in their place, checking the shelves to see if there were any misplaced books. She had put a little plaque on the table asking that books not be re-shelved. Of course the youngest children couldn't read, and for some of them, taking books off the shelves and putting them back up — or not — was a fun pastime.

She found a couple of books out of place and put them away properly. She straightened the display that Wendy had created on zoo animals and deemed the room neat. She poked her head in the Reference Room. Nothing to put away in there.

She wondered how the kids were doing. She quietly opened the door to their living room. Ben had become bored with his racetracks and blocks and turned to Legos. Liddie had wanted to do play dough, and Anne had set her up at the kitchen table with the dough, cookie cutters, and a rolling pin.

Anne headed back downstairs to the first floor. A man dressed in jeans and a wet leather jacket was talking to Wendy at the counter. He looked vaguely familiar. Her heart nearly stopped.

Shaun Milhouse. And he looked angry.

"Sir, I don't know what you are talking about. What article?" Wendy asked, sounding uncharacteristically flustered. She caught sight of Anne. "Oh, here she is. Anne, there's someone here to see you."

"Shaun. How are you?" Anne forced her voice to be soft and pleasant, although her heart was racing. Why was he here? What had Melissa told him about her visit yesterday?

"Not good. Not good at all, as you should know!" Shaun's voice rose. "What did I ever do to you? You think this is some kind of game? Another way to stick it to me? You have some nerve, lady."

Wendy's eyes widened as she looked from Shaun to Anne. "Um, is there a problem here?" She placed her hand on the phone.

"You can say that," he snapped, locking eyes with Anne.

Anne took several deep breaths and prayed silently to know what to say. "Wendy, this is a classmate of mine from high school. Shaun Milhouse. Shaun works over at Fowler's Auto Repair, although I heard that Shaun will be the owner soon. Is that right?"

"Uh, yeah. I'll be taking over next year," Shaun said, his voice calmer.

"Oh! I have a friend who took her car over there," Wendy said. "She said the repair was top-notch. You couldn't even tell where her son's bicycle had dented the door. And the bill didn't break the bank. I told my husband about what my friend said, and we might bring our van over to have the rear door fixed."

Shaun's scowl softened. "Bring it on by and we'll give you an estimate. Here's my number." He pulled a wallet out of his back pocket and extracted a business card. "You'll find our rates are fair."

Wendy took the card and read it. "Thanks!"

Anne assessed him for a moment. His shoulders had relaxed some, and she decided he seemed more upset and puzzled than angry. "Shaun, I'm glad you came by. I need to talk with you about something rather urgent. That's why I stopped by your shop yesterday. How about we have a seat over there?" She nodded to the table at the far end of the History Room.

He hesitated, as though he wanted to say something more but then started in that direction. Anne looked over her shoulder at Wendy, who still had slightly worried crinkles by her eyes. She gave Wendy a reassuring nod and went to sit down across from Shaun.

Shaun blew out a breath. "So, why did you come by my place looking for trouble?"

"Is that what Melissa said? That I wanted to cause trouble?"

"Doesn't matter what she said. I should've known you couldn't let well enough alone. Why are you tormenting me again? Is this another sick joke?"

Anne stared at him. "Shaun, what are you talking about?"

"You know! This!" He pulled a wrinkled folded paper out of his pocket and slammed it down on the table. "You send me this stupid note and then come snooping around the body shop acting like I'm the one who committed a crime when it was my family that suffered!"

Anne unfolded the sheet, already guessing what it was. It was the article they'd all received. She looked up. "Shaun, I didn't send this to you. Michael and Jen, Alex, Heather, and I all got one too. We have no idea who wrote it."

And now Anne knew that Shaun hadn't either.

"You got one too?" Shaun looked genuinely puzzled.

"I came by the shop trying to find the truth," Anne said gently. "You weren't mentioned in the article, so it didn't occur to me that you got one too."

"I didn't write it, if that's what you're thinking," he said, answering the question that flitted across her mind. "I found it on my desk. Melissa said it had been shoved under the garage door."

"Melissa knows about the letter too?" Anne asked.

He nodded.

So, Melissa must've suspected all along that was why Anne had visited the shop yesterday, but she'd never said anything. Instead, she'd just let Anne go on and on about the car.

"I'm sorry about your grandparents. I didn't know about them until yesterday. What happened?"

He sighed and ran a hand over his face. "They were hurt pretty bad, although they were wearing seat belts. The hospital bills kept growing, and my grandparents were put in long-term care. My parents had to use their savings, including my brother's and my college funds, to help pay for it."

"I'm sorry, Shaun," Anne said. "I really am."

Shaun looked up and squared his shoulders. "I don't mean to whine. It is what it is. My brother ended up going to college on loans, and I've been doing well at the shop. I just... well, I always kind of figured it was my fault."

"The accident? Were you there?" Anne asked, puzzled. Why was he feeling guilty?

"No, but I could've been. My parents were at a late meeting, and my grandparents volunteered to pick me up at the school. I've always felt guilty about that."

Poor Shaun. And to think she and Alex had been out having fun and getting ice cream with Aunt Edie while this was all happening.

"I would've been very upset too," Anne said.

"I was angry, still am, especially since they never got the guy. I wanted to smash his face in." His voice rose and he immediately looked contrite.

"Sorry. Anyway, I thought I'd kind of made peace with it. I've been taking some business classes at community college. I'm on track to own the shop and everything is looking good, and then this arrived."

"Do you have any idea who might've sent it?"

He shook his head. "Nope, at least not until you showed up."

"I can assure you that I didn't write the article," Anne said. "I want to find out who did and what crime the author is referring to that night."

His eyebrows rose. "There was more than one? I just assumed it meant the car accident."

"There was a burglary and some vandalism the same night." Anne updated Shaun on the events of the night, including the DUI and the kids who were picked up for drunken behavior.

"Could the DUI be the person who hit my grandparents?"

"According to the police record, it wasn't the same kind of car."

"*Hmm.* Some guys were joking the next day about doing something crazy."

"Which guys?" Anne asked.

Shaun shrugged. "I don't remember. Some of the players. I used to try to hang out with them." He laughed. "I wasn't very smart then. Guys talk about the dumbest stuff sometimes. All I thought about was that it was pretty dumb of them to risk losing a college scholarship by getting arrested or something."

Anne stared at the article. Okay, so now she may know the *what* in terms of a crime and the *who* in terms of the victims, but she still had no idea who had written the venomous words on the page.

Logically, Shaun would be a prime suspect, since it was his life that could be considered ruined by the accident but—

"I didn't write it, if that's what you're thinking," Shaun said again. "I barely made it through English class. You were on the newspaper staff, that's why I assumed you did it." He gave her a small, apologetic smile.

Anne smiled back. Unless he was a good actor, Shaun seemed truthful. And he made a good point. Whoever had written it understood basic structure of a news column. Of course with the word processors these days, anyone could duplicate a newsletter. Writing one was a different matter.

* * *

Anne glanced at her watch and arched her back against the thinly padded vinyl chair. They'd been waiting forty-five minutes in the small exam room at the Blue Hill Medical Clinic. The nurse had checked them in and told them that Dr. Shields would see them in a few minutes. When the "few" minutes had stretched to fifteen, Anne switched on the small television in the room, which had been set to a cartoon channel.

After Shaun's visit that morning, she felt fairly confident that Shaun could be crossed off the list of suspects since he'd also gotten a copy of the article himself. But if so, then it meant that she was almost back to square one on trying to figure out who wrote it. At least she had an idea of what the life-altering event might have been. She pulled out the article from her purse.

So, if Shaun hadn't written the article, then who had? It had to be someone who had been at the homecoming dance and knew them well.

She again wondered about Melissa. Could she be involved? Shaun had insisted she wasn't, but he had stars in his eyes when he talked about her. She used to like to hang out with the cheerleaders and football players in high school. And she certainly seemed in charge of her life now. People changed. Melissa could've changed. Could she have been in the car that sideswiped the other? Was that why she was helping Shaun out? Did she feel guilty?

And then there was Pete Dillon, although she hadn't gotten a strong vibe that he was trying to avenge his father's injury. Of course maybe he harbored some resentment at having to take over the store. He hadn't seemed bitter, but his tone indicated he thought he had no choice.

The door opened and Dr. Shields walked in. He gave a big smile to Liddie and Ben. "Sorry to keep you waiting," he said to Anne as he washed his hands at the stainless steel sink. "On rainy days like this there's either nobody here or it's jammed."

"It's okay. They warned us out front it might be a while," Anne said. "The wait gave us a chance to dry out some."

He turned, wiping his hands on a paper towel. "So, how is everyone doing?"

"Better, I think," Anne said. "Their rashes are healing, but I was a little concerned about the scabbing on the back of Ben's legs, and Liddie's cheeks are still tender."

"Okay, hop up here, big guy, and lie down on your stomach." He patted the exam table.

Ben scooted up on the table and lay down.

"So, are you missing school yet?" Tony asked Ben as he checked Ben's legs and lower back.

"I'm missing school, but I don't miss it," Ben said with a grin and then flinched as Tony rubbed a spot on his leg. "I do miss soccer practice though."

"I used to play soccer a long, long time ago." Tony checked the back of Ben's neck. "So did your mom. Did you know she scored the winning goal one time?"

Ben looked over at his mother. "Really? You did?"

"Just once," Anne said.

"Ninth grade coed gym class," Tony said. "Practice game. Mr. Diller was the teacher. We were playing coed because there weren't enough guys or gals signed up for separate games."

"Wow. I'd forgotten." She looked at Tony with amazement. She could barely remember scoring the goal, let alone who was playing. "I know you always aced everyone out on science tests, but how can you remember something insignificant like that?"

"I was the goalie."

"Oh... well, then it had to have been a lucky shot."

"It wasn't that lucky. Your mother had the moves," he said to Ben.

Anne laughed. "Yeah, I moved so well, I never scored another goal. I ran track the next semester."

"Soccer's loss," Tony said as Ben sat up. "And I'm teasing your mother, Ben. I bet you're a great player."

Ben shrugged. "I do okay."

"Speaking of school, I was surprised to find that Kevin Kutcher works here. He was in my class."

"Ah yes, Kevin," Tony picked up the chart and clicked his pen. "New lab tech, right?"

Anne nodded. "He used to work on the newspaper with me. He talked about going pre-med just like you did."

"A lot of people change their minds when they realize how difficult it can be to get into medical school. You have to have good grades and recommendations. Starting off in competitive college can help." Tony made a note in the chart. "You have to be dedicated since the process can consume your whole life."

"Well, I'm glad you made it through," Anne said. "I appreciate what you've done to help us."

"You're welcome." Tony gave her a smile. "Most of my young patients hate to see me coming."

Tony washed his hands again in the sink and then turned to Liddie. "All right, little lady, let's see how you're doing."

Liddie clutched Anne's arm and shook her head.

"See what I mean?" Tony winked at Anne. He turned back to Liddie and squatted to her level. "It's okay. I'll come to you. *Hmm*, your cheeks are still a bit inflamed, but your arms look much better. The rash has dried out."

"I tried putting baking soda in her bath water," Anne said.

"It can't do any harm and it may have helped in this case," Tony said, washing his hands again. "I've ceased being surprised by the results of home remedies. Every person and every case can be different."

Ben cast Anne a look that said he still didn't want oatmeal in his bath.

Anne just smiled at her firstborn. Stubborn like his dad and just as lovable.

Tony picked up a prescription pad out of the drawer. "They're looking good and can go back to school on Monday. There are a couple spots on Ben's back that I want you to try another antibacterial cream on, just to make sure an infection hasn't started where the skin has broken up. Also, Liddie's right cheek down by the jaw line needs a little more time. It's still seeping a little." He looked at Liddie. "I bet it still itches a lot too."

Liddie nodded and lifted her hand as if to rub it and then dropped her hand with a glance at Anne. Anne wrapped her arm around Liddie. Her poor little baby.

"Unless you have any more trouble, you don't need to come back," Tony said and then shook a finger at Liddie and Ben. "And no more playing in the poison ivy, okay?"

"No, sir," Ben answered and grimaced.

"Thanks, Tony. Hope to see you around."

"Me too. Just not here. Stay well," he said with a smile.

The nurse came in the door as he went out. "All righty. Let's get you checked out." She ushered them out as another nurse ushered a mother and teen into the room.

The hallway was bustling with activity, and as Anne stood in line to get up to the counter to pay, Kevin Kutcher came down the hall dragging a cart.

He stopped when he saw Anne. "Hey there. Back again?"

"Hi, Kevin." Anne shifted her purse to her other side to let a nurse squeeze by. "We came in for a follow-up."

He glanced at the kids. "How are they doing?"

"Much better, thanks. Dr. Shields said they could go back to school on Monday. How are you doing?"

He guided the cart closer to the wall. "Same ol', same ol'."

"Well, if it wasn't so busy in here, I'd share with you what I learned so far about that article we all received."

"You're still on that?" Kevin said with a shake of the head. "I'd almost forgotten about it. It must be almost deadline time."

"Two more days," Anne said. "Is there some time today we can talk?"

Kevin waved at a nurse down the hall who had poked her head out of a room. "Be there in a minute." He sighed and said to Anne, "Working a double today, but do they appreciate it? Nope." He pushed on his cart.

"Oh, Kevin, before you go. Have you been in touch with Pete Dillon or Shaun Milhouse since you've been back? They went to school with us."

Kevin stopped and looked over his shoulder. "Nope. Didn't hang out with them when we were in school either."

"Mrs. Gibson, here is your bill," the clerk behind the deep counter said. She passed up an invoice, and Anne wrote a check as her cell phone vibrated in her pocket. She passed the check over and grabbed the phone before it went to voice mail. Jen's name was on the display.

She waited until they'd gone through the door to the outside. "Hello? Sorry to keep you waiting."

"Hey, friend! No problem. You've been on my mind all day. How about that lunch?" Jen said enthusiastically. "Feel a need for some girl talk?"

Anne smiled, feeling a sudden urge for just that. Jen's energy flowed across the satellite waves and gave her a boost. "I'd love to. I'm at the medical clinic right now with the kids."

"Oh dear. They're not sick, are they?"

"No, just having their poison ivy rashes checked. Good news. The end of this misery is in sight."

"Bring them along then. Let's make it Stella's Pizza. My treat!"

Anne covered the phone with her hand and asked her children. "Do you want pizza?"

"Oh yeah!" Ben said with a victory pump of his arm.

Liddie tugged at Anne's shirt, which she hadn't let go of since they left the exam room. "I want pizza."

"Okay, Jen. It's a date." Anne ushered the kids toward the car. She had a suspicion that this date was more than just a social call. She was hoping Jen had found out something more about homecoming night.

* * *

Stella's was a small restaurant a couple of blocks from the high school. The shop's rather shabby decor was offset by low prices and fantastic pizza that kept it in business for so many years. Anne had fond memories of hanging out there during cold winter evenings and grabbing carry-out boxes to take to the park or lake.

As she pulled up and parked in front, she noted that the outward appearance hadn't improved with age, but once inside, the familiar spicy smells sent waves of nostalgia through her. Jen was seated at a table with four patched, red vinyl padded seats and a red-and-white tablecloth. She waved them over.

"Hello, hello." Jen smiled big at Ben and Liddie. "So nice to meet you."

"Hi," Liddie said shyly as she hopped up on the chair.

"Nice to meet you too," Ben said politely.

"They're precious," Jen said to Anne. "I hope they can meet my three sometime. I didn't order yet because I wasn't sure what your favorite pizza was."

"I like just cheese," Liddie said.

Jen nodded. "My youngest likes just cheese too. Do you want it with extra cheese?"

Liddie nodded.

"And you Ben?" Jen asked.

"I like everything but anchovies and green peppers."

"I think we can handle that," Jen said with a smile.

Anne reached for one of the menus propped up between large containers of parmesan cheese and red chili flakes. Stella's had all the standard offerings.

"Want to try one of her new pizzas?" Jen asked.

"I'm up for anything," Anne said, feeling adventurous. "This was a great idea, Jen."

"Wasn't it?" Jen grinned as she perused the menu. "Just what we needed for a dreary day."

"How about the Greek Delight? The ingredients remind me of summer. Michael and I are saving for a trip to Greece. Italy too. Of course with three kids going to college someday, I'm not holding my breath for going anytime soon."

"The Greek pizza sounds perfect to me." Anne closed her menu and set it down just as a petite young woman with dark hair hanging in a long braid down her back approached the table. She wore a faded red apron and pulled a pad out of her pocket.

"Lucy?" Anne asked.

"That's me," Lucy said.

"I'm Anne Gibson. Summers was my maiden name. I used to come in here a lot when you were young." Anne let out a little laugh. "You probably hear that a lot.

Lucy smiled. "I do. Result of growing up in the family business."

"Anne used to come here with Alex Ochs a lot, and with Michael and me," Jen said. "We'd sit over there at the booth by the window."

"Oh yeah," Lucy said with a nod. "Nice to see you again. I thought you were living in Boston or Chicago or someplace like that."

"New York, but I'm living here now. You'll probably see more of me. I forgot how much I loved this place."

Lucy smiled. "Mom will be happy to hear that. She's been thinking of retiring and selling the place, but we keep telling her people would miss it too much." She took their order and then delivered their drinks, root beer for the kids and iced tea for the women. Jen and Anne chatted about Jen's volunteer work at the high school while they waited for their lunch. Jen took a sip of her tea and added a packet of sugar. "I didn't mind being on the fundraising committee, but I've been much happier being the advisor for the decorating committee."

Anne smiled. "I remember the great job you did for the homecoming dance."

"Thanks." Jen smiled. "What is considered awesome now is sure different from what we thought was cool, but it has been fun bouncing ideas around with the kids." She talked about her ideas for a Christmas dance that the school was sponsoring, and then Lucy arrived with their pizzas.

Anne bit into a hot slice, loving the sharp, salty taste of the Greek olives and the chewy texture of the artichoke hearts. "Great choice, Jen."

"It's better than I thought it'd be."

"Michael was telling me the progress you've made about...our little problem." Jen glanced at the kids who had consumed a good portion of their pizza and were slowing down. "He also mentioned that Heather had lied about him calling her that night."

Anne studied her friend for a long moment. "Why would Heather lie about something like that?"

"She always liked Michael. Maybe she's still jealous I got him," Jen suggested and then caught Anne's eye. She grimaced. "Okay, so maybe she was just mistaken." She reached for her iced tea and took a long sip.

"Mommy, can I ride the pony?" Liddie pointed to a coin-operated toy ride in the back corner where there were several brightly lit video games and a large pin ball machine similar to the one in Coffee Joe's. An antique from even before Anne's time.

"Sure." Anne reached into her purse and pulled out several quarters. "Ben, do you mind taking Liddie over there?"

Ben slid off his seat. "Okay, but can I play pinball?" he asked, knowing that Anne wouldn't let him play any of the video games that involved violence.

"Well, regardless of her motive," said Anne. "Heather's remark does bring up the possibility that maybe someone else might think Michael and you did something wrong that night, like being with the kids who broke into Dillon's Auto Parts or spray painted the school."

"What color was his parents' car?"

"Um, I don't remember," Jen said. "Black or maybe blue. Why?"

"The car involved in the hit-and-run accident that night had dark blue or green paint."

Jen's voice rose to a higher pitch. "So? I said I was with Michael, and he wasn't involved."

"Okay, but did anyone see you leave with him? Or together after that?"

"You did, right?"

Anne shook her head. "All I remember is that you were angry and going to break up with him. You wanted a ride home, but Alex and I just had the convertible."

She looked away. "Oh yeah."

"Listen Jen, I'm sorry to pry. It's none of my business except that whoever wrote that article believes that one of us did something wrong. Wrong enough to ruin someone's life. And we only have two days left to figure this out before he or she reveals it. Assuming that the threat is real, then maybe we'll have a chance to minimize the damage."

"I know. You're right." Jen reached for her iced tea again, this time her fingers trembled a little. She took another drink and set it down. "Okay, I didn't go home with Michael that night but —"

She took a deep breath. "He couldn't have been involved in anything because he showed up at my house not long after that to apologize."

"How much time are we talking about?"

"An hour maybe," Jen said. "Maybe a little more. He called and I didn't answer the phone."

"So he may have called Heather to see if he could find you."

Jen nodded, her cheeks pink. "I shouldn't have said she lied. I don't really know."

But Michael had told Anne that he hadn't called Heather. Did something happen that he didn't tell Jen about? Anne didn't want to cause trouble between them. She felt caught up in the games the kids played in high school. He said. She said. Rumors flying and the truth getting lost somewhere in the cross fire.

Oh, dear Lord, please guide me in doing what's right.

She reached across the table and squeezed Jen's cold fingers. "Hey, I didn't mean to upset you."

Jen gave her a little smile. "Oh, I know. I should've told you what really happened in the first place. It's just with Michael trying to get a promotion and the department cutting personnel, we can't afford something to sully his name or reputation. Even if it's something from the past. But then I keep thinking that if Michael didn't do anything wrong, then what does it matter if I was with him or not?"

Anne quietly waited for Jen to continue. Jen looked at her, torment in her eyes, and threw her napkin on her plate. "Oh, okay, I'm worried, very worried that he may have done something that could ruin his chances now. Michael has been a wonderful husband and father, but he also is very protective. The strong type who prides himself on taking care of his family. I'm the one who said that we were together all evening. He got perturbed with me for saying it, but really I was only trying to protect him for a change."

They sat in silence for a few moments. Anne could feel her friend's rising agitation. If Anne had been in her place and was trying to protect Eric, would she do the same thing? She'd be tempted to and was glad she was never put in a position like that.

"Jen, I have trouble believing Michael did anything wrong that night too," Anne said softly. "But is it possible he knows more than he's telling us?"

"He doesn't want to talk about it. But I do know he certainly wasn't involved in any accident that night. His parents' car was fine. No dents. Or I would've heard about it. His father would've hit the roof. He was always going on about teenagers and car accidents. It was such a relief when Michael finally got his own car."

"Glad to hear that," Anne said. "Did Michael mention the other crimes that night?"

"Not really. He just said the police reports weren't helpful," Jen said. "Why? What else happened?"

"Do you remember Pete Dillon? He was a freshman when we were seniors."

"Short, nerdy type?"

"Yes, but he's not short anymore. His father owns Dillon's Auto Parts. Pete runs the place now. The night of the homecoming dance the store was broken into. The vandals spray painted everywhere. Mr. Dillon got there as they were leaving and he believes they were teens. Then there was a graffiti incident with paint at Stonebridge Elementary too."

"Maybe that's why..." Jen rubbed her cheek. "That explains why there was a police car at football practice on Monday afternoon. I was heading over there to watch Michael practice, and a policeman was talking to a bunch of the team. He left as I was getting there. Michael said it was nothing. They were just asking questions about some kids who were partying Saturday night."

"Did he tell you what the police were looking for?"

"No, and since our relationship was still a bit shaky, I didn't ask. I had other things on my mind," Jen said. "Besides, the police were always coming around for one reason or another back then. Still do from what I hear."

Anne nodded. That was true enough. Although their school was considered a safe environment, the administration had the police officers over quite frequently to give safety talks and just to be a presence on campus as a preventative measure.

"Could Michael have known who they were and didn't turn them in, which would make him an accomplice?" Anne asked.

"I don't know, but the guys were loyal to each other, especially those on the team. I'll talk to him about it when the time is right," Jen said with a sigh.

Liddie and Ben had finished playing in the corner and came back to the table as Lucy picked up their empty plates and boxed the pizza.

Anne stood. "Jen, thank you for lunch. I'm sorry I sounded like I was interrogating you."

"It's okay. I know you just want to help us." Jen gave Anne a hug. "Oh, I don't want to go home right now. The kids aren't due back for another couple hours, and for some reason I just don't want to be alone."

Anne could understand. She felt shaky herself after confronting Jen. The article had brought uncertainty into their lives. She also had an empty feeling in her stomach. And maybe all this digging into the past brought a slight longing for those relatively carefree days before grown-up responsibilities and concerns — when the biggest worries were the chemistry test the next week and what to wear to Sarah Harding's party Saturday night. And whether Alex Ochs would sit with her at lunch. And having girlfriends to giggle with. Not that she would trade those days for now, but it was nice to remember.

"Why don't you come over and see the library? We close early on Saturdays so we'll have the place to ourselves," Anne suggested as she helped Liddie with her rain jacket.

"As long as I'm not imposing." Jen's face lit up. "I'd really like that. I haven't been in your great-aunt's house since before our graduation."

"You're not imposing at all. I'd love to show you around. Wendy Pyle, one of my volunteers, was planning on closing up the library, so we have time to 'play'."

Jen grinned. "I'm always up for that."

They made a dash for their cars, but Anne hardly noticed the driving rain. Being with a good, old friend could make the gloomiest day seem like summer.

Chapter Fourteen

"This is incredible," Jen slowly turned, surveying the ground floor of the library. "I never would've thought it could turn out so nice. When you said library, I imagined the downstairs rooms like they were before with a just few bookshelves. Who decorated?"

"Wendy Pyle and I worked on it. Alex did the repair work." Anne turned to smile at Wendy, who had just finished checking out books for a mother and her preschooler. "Wendy, this is Jennifer Banks. We went to school together. Aunt Edie would let us come over and play here sometimes. Wendy's husband is the high school football coach."

Wendy came around the counter. "It's nice to meet you, Jennifer. Haven't I seen you at some of the junior league soccer games?"

"Oh yes, I think I've seen you too. You have a son who plays, right?"

"Actually, I had two sons and a daughter playing last summer."

"So you have three kids?"

"Seven," Wendy said with a smile.

"Seven!" Jen exclaimed and then lowered her voice as an elderly man who was browsing glared over at her. "And I thought three kept me hopping. Your house must always be full of life."

"There's usually a dull roar." Wendy grinned. She turned away as the elderly man beckoned her and she went over to help him.

"Do you want to see the second floor? We turned that into the reference section and children's area."

"Sure. Love to," Jen said.

"Right this way," Anne led Jen up the sweeping staircase. "I have living quarters on part of the second floor and all of the third floor."

"Do you think anyone would notice if we slid down the banister like we did when we were kids?" Jen asked. The familiar mischievous sparkle was back in her eyes. Anne was glad. She hated that she had to interrogate her old friend back at the restaurant, but she didn't want them to get hurt by some revengeful person because Michael had an overdeveloped sense of loyalty and protectiveness. If he did know more about the crimes committed on homecoming night, she hoped he came forward before someone else did.

They toured through the Children's Room, which Jen particularly liked, and then poked their heads in the Reference Room.

"Want to hear something really cool?" Anne asked. "After I moved in, we discovered a secret room."

Jen's mouth dropped open. "Oh, how exciting! Can I see it?"

They went into the private living quarters and went up to the third floor. Jen was delighted with Anne's apartment and kept exclaiming over the great job Alex did as Anne led her to a small sitting area.

"Watch this." Anne slid back the secret door to reveal the tiny triangular room that contained a small writing desk and a simple chair. Light poured down from a four-paned window set into the ceiling.

"I can't believe this was here the whole time and we never knew it. We ran all over the house. Why didn't Aunt Edie ever tell you?"

"She had her reasons," Anne said with a smile. That was the first mystery Anne encountered when she moved into Aunt Edie's home.

"I wish I had a secret room," Jen said with a laugh. "I love my family, but sometimes I wish I could find a nice, quiet place to call all my own."

Anne smiled. "I know what you mean, but we'd miss the chaos soon enough."

"I know, but let me dream a bit."

"I should check on the kids." Anne hadn't heard a peep from them since they'd left the car, dashing through the rain to the back entrance. They went down the stairs to the second floor.

Liddie's wet coat and boots were lying in the middle of the kitchen floor. Anne picked them up.

Jen looked around the kitchen and living area.

"After seeing this, I can understand why you're so happy to be back. When I heard you had left New York, I couldn't comprehend why anyone would give up an exciting city to live in Blue Hill where nothing happens." She glanced at Anne. "Okay, almost nothing."

"I miss Brooklyn too, and I worry about the kids adjusting to small-town living, but I think we're going to be just fine. This is becoming home all over again."

"I'm glad," Jennifer said.

A clap of thunder shook the house.

"Mommy!" Liddie ran out of her bedroom and threw her arms around Anne's waist.

"That was loud, wasn't it?" Anne smoothed Liddie's hair. "But it was just thunder. It can't hurt you."

Another peal of thunder made Liddie's arms tighten around Anne.

Jen squatted so her face was level with Liddie's. "You know what your mother and I did when it was raining like this? Right in this very house?"

Liddie turned her head so she could see Jen. "What?"

"We'd play in the attic and pretend we were in a ship going to see the world."

Liddie contemplated that for a few seconds. Her grip loosened and she tilted her head up. "Can we go to the attic, Mommy?"

"Oh, maybe later, sweetie. We have a guest."

"Actually, I wouldn't mind going up there," Jen said. "I have great memories of that dusty old place."

Anne poked her head into the living room where Ben was watching baseball. "We're going up to the attic, do you want to come?"

"Why?" Ben looked perplexed as if she had asked if he wanted to fly to the moon.

"Just to look around. Mrs. Banks and Liddie are going up there with me. If you want to watch the baseball game instead, that's fine."

"Okay, I'll stay here." Ben leaned back against the couch cushions and looked relieved.

Anne opened the door to the steep stairway that went up to the attic. She flipped on the overhead light to dispel the gloom. The rain pelted overhead, but under the solid roof, it sounded cozy. The air was cool but not cold, and it smelled of old wood, dust, and a hint of lavender from the potpourri balls that Aunt Edie used to store in her boxes and trunks.

"Close the hatch, sailor," Anne said with a wink at Jen.

"Huh?" Liddie asked.

"That means close the door," Jen explained. "Aye, aye, Captain." She saluted Anne.

Liddie giggled and didn't even notice the next clap of thunder. "You're funny." She ran over to an old wooden rocking horse. She was too tall for it, but that didn't stop her from having a good time rocking back and forth.

"This looks the way I remember it," Jen said, glancing around the stuffed room.

"Are the trunks of clothes still here?" Jen turned to Liddie. "We had such fun playing dress up."

"Most likely," Anne said.

Liddie hopped off the horse. "I want to play dress up too!"

Annie smiled at her daughter. "We will someday."

"You can sometimes get quite a bit for vintage clothing," Jen said. "I was visiting a consignment shop and was amazed at the prices for some of the old designer suits and dresses."

"That's good to know," Anne said, although she wasn't ready to part with what Aunt Edie had left behind. She probably never would be. Right now, sentimental value and the family history associated with some of the items far outweighed any monetary value. Maybe she'd feel different later.

Jen stepped farther into the room. "Is the treasure chest still around here?"

"Treasure chest?" Liddie asked. "What treasure chest?'"

"That's what we used to call a trunk that Aunt Edie gave me," Anne explained. "She gave me a key and told me I could keep whatever I wanted in it. And now I can't find the key. I was thinking of getting a locksmith in or seeing if Alex can get it open."

"Didn't Edie have a spare key?" Jen asked. "I remember once when you lost the key and she opened it for you."

"That's right, she did," Anne said. "Aunt Edie kept it on a chain in her jewelry box. She left some of her jewelry to the cousins, but I saw some of the more inexpensive trinkets somewhere up here in one of the trunks. In a wooden box."

They opened the trunks, searching through contents. Liddie tried on some of the hats and pumps and looked so cute, Anne had to stop and take some photos with her cell phone camera.

Finally, after opening several trunks, Anne reached down under some dresses and her fingers hit something solid. The box. She pulled it out. "Here it is."

Liddie clapped her hands with excitement and clumped over in her heels.

Anne opened the lid. Inside was a jumbled pile of chains, pendants, several silver rings with large glass stones, and long strands of beads. She picked up the big knot of the silver and gold chains while Jen searched through the contents on the bottom of the box.

Anne's heart tripped when she uncovered a little silver key on one of the chains. "This might be it." It took her a few minutes to untangle it.

She turned to the trunk and inserted it in the lock.

"I feel like we need a drum roll," Jen said over Anne's shoulder. Anne turned the key. It stuck, but after she wiggled it, the lock turned. She lifted the lid.

"Can I see?" Liddie asked, breathing on Anne's neck.

"Sure, honey." She scooted over.

Gazing inside the chest was like stepping back in time. She lifted out a favorite childhood sweater and a stuffed giraffe that Alex had won for her at a carnival that had come to town. She handed the giraffe to Liddie. On the bottom of the chest was a stack of high school newspapers, photos, a couple of school reports she'd earned *A*'s on, and her senior class yearbook.

"This is so cool," Jen said and then gasped. "Oh my, look at the time. I better run. Michael and the kids will be back from soccer practice."

Anne shut the lid on the chest and went downstairs with Jen.

"Thanks for a great afternoon," Jen said at the door. "I'll call you later if I find out anything new from Michael. I appreciate what you're trying to do. I'm starting to feel like everything will be all right."

Anne gave her a quick hug, praying that was true.

Although the library had been closed for an hour, Wendy still puttered behind the counter. "Your friend seems fun. It must be great reconnecting with old classmates."

"It is. It's amazing how young it makes you feel to visit with people from childhood. We were upstairs, and for a moment I felt like we were twelve years old again and Aunt Edie had shooed us to the attic to play." Anne smiled, remembering the salute Jen had given her.

She just wished their visit had been under better circumstances...

"Oh, I know. If you live near someone, you age together. But then it can be a little shocking to go to a reunion and see someone from a decade ago. Like Kirby Wilson. I went to my ten-year reunion, and he had a huge beard and was totally bald. I had no idea who he was until he gave me a hug and whispered, 'It's Kirby.' Wendy giggled. "Apparently I wasn't the only one who didn't recognize him!"

"There is that risk when we go to reunions." Anne laughed. "Thank you so much for running everything down here."

"I enjoyed it. It was quiet and I got some reading done," Wendy said. "The benefit of working in a library is never running out of new stuff to read."

"That's so true," Anne said. And she was even luckier to live above one.

Wendy grabbed her coat. "I better get home and start on supper. I did all the re-shelving and pulled a couple of reserved books. Sheila Livingston will be in tomorrow to pick those up. I also left a list here of possible ideas for Story Time with a list of crafts that might work."

Anne picked up the list. "And you had time to read too? You're amazing." She often wondered what she had done to deserve such a great new friend as Wendy.

Wendy smiled. "I just like being useful." She pulled the coat hood over her head. "Now I hope I won't drown on the way home."

"Be careful!" Anne called as Wendy darted out the door into the waterfall of rain. She went to the window and waited until she saw Wendy's car pull out of the doorway and head down the street, water spraying out from behind her tires.

Anne returned to the counter and checked the weather online. It appeared the storm front would pass in a couple hours, but there were more storms lined up behind it. She was so glad they'd gotten the leaves taken care of when they did. Again she thanked God for someone like Wendy who had taken a stranger under her wing.

She checked on the kids and gave them permission to watch television and felt a little guilty about that. Normally she tried to limit their TV time, but the last week had been miserable for them. Next week they'd get back in their routine in more ways than one. The kids would be back at school, and the questions surrounding the article would be solved one way or another. Either Anne figured out what was really going on or the police and all of Blue Hill would know, assuming the author followed through on his or her threat.

Anne realized she'd left the article in her purse downstairs. She returned to the main floor, relishing the quiet. She sat behind the counter and pulled out the article and her notes. She had a feeling she was missing a vital clue.

A thump sounded at the door. Anne hurried over and unlocked it, wondering who was out in this weather. The door burst open in her hand, and a gust of wind rattled the leaves and papers on the display board. Betty Warring and her sister Nellie were arguing on the porch.

"I told you it was Saturday and the library closed at one," Nellie said to Betty.

"Oh, pooh. You are always getting the days mixed up. How was I to know you were right?" Betty replied.

"I'm sorry," Nellie said to Anne. "I'll just give you our book and we'll go."

"Oh, come. Please. You're both wet." Anne stepped back. "I don't mind at all. I was down here anyway."

Betty stepped inside and tugged at her rain bonnet, which had slid down the back of her head exposing her tight grey curls that now lay flat against her head. "For a minute there, I felt like I was out on the Sea of Galilee. Wish Jesus was in my boat today. Even the wind and rain obey Him."

Anne helped Betty with her coat and hung it on the coatrack by the door. "I'm glad to see you, but what you are doing out in this weather?"

Nellie stamped her boots on the rug. "We wouldn't be out in this monsoon if Betty hadn't insisted on getting a new book. I told her it was too late."

"I suffered through King Henry VIII, and it's my turn to pick."

Nellie blew out a breath of exasperation as they made their way into the library. She handed Anne the plastic-wrapped biography.

"I'm sorry you didn't like it." Anne unwrapped the book and set it on the counter.

"Oh, I enjoyed it," Nellie said. "Betty just didn't understand the motivation of the wives."

"I heard that," Betty said from the biography session. "Anyone who'd marry that buffoon in the first place probably deserved to be beheaded or divorced."

"Betty Warring!" her sister exclaimed. "You don't mean that."

"No, I don't. But you'd think after the first three wives were beheaded, somebody would get a clue to raise their hand when the priest asks if there is any reason for the couple not to get married."

The phone rang and Anne left them to their arguing to answer it. It was Alex.

"Hi Anne. Just calling to check on things over there. I've been getting several calls about roofs leaking. The wind is taking off shingles. Any problems at your place?"

"Not that I know of. I was in the attic earlier and I didn't see any leaks. Everything seems shipshape, thanks to you."

"Glad to hear." He paused. "Anything new about that article?"

"Just when I think I might have things figured out, there's a new twist." She glanced over at the ladies who were still good-naturedly arguing and told Alex about Shaun Milhouse's visit that morning.

"Poor guy."

"Yeah, he's had it rough," Anne said, thinking again of how self-involved they must've seemed. "It's sad, really. He was in our class and we saw him almost every day at school. How could we not know?"

"You'd think we would have heard about it at church, but then I don't think Shaun belonged to our youth group."

"Well, I did some checking, and his mother was the only listed member and she didn't attend regularly," Anne said.

"That may explain it. And we didn't hang out with Shaun much at school," Alex said. "It was a busy time for us being seniors. I feel sorry for him, but we can't help it that no one told us. If they had, we would've done something. We were always trying to help others in the youth group."

"True," Anne said, remembering the times they visited the nursing homes to sing, collected food for the needy at Christmas, and made cards for those who were sick.

"It doesn't help to feel guilty now for something we had no part in," Alex said, obviously sensing her angst and maybe some of his own.

"It changed his life. He would've gone to college if the accident hadn't happened. So that makes him an obvious suspect, but I believe him when he says he has nothing to do with it. He seemed shocked to get the article too. He also pointed out he couldn't have written it. Said he barely passed English. This, again, brings me back to thinking that there is a strong chance it has to be someone on the newspaper staff or a contributor. Could be someone on the yearbook staff too since they attended all the functions, although there wasn't much writing involved."

"Who else besides you, Heather, and Kevin contributed articles?"

"Whoever wanted to. Mr. Harrelson would put out an announcement every month that if anyone wanted to contribute, they could turn them in by the 25th of each month. He'd go through them and then give us any he thought were good enough to include. There were several who sent things in every month."

Anne thought about the newspapers up in her treasure chest. "I still have copies of the newspaper. I can go through them tonight."

"Good idea. Let me know if you find anything interesting," Alex said. "I think I'm going to call Shaun. Too little, too late, but at least he'll know that we never intended for him to go through that ordeal alone. Maybe there's something we can do now."

"I think he'd like hearing from you," Anne said. "Especially if you can refer him some repair jobs."

"That I can do," Alex said. "In my business, vehicles can take a beating."

They said good-bye, and Anne went to check on the ladies. They were debating whether to read a book on the Caesars or Chopin.

"Which do you like better?" Betty asked Anne as she moved down the aisle peering at book titles.

"I haven't read either yet," Anne said, trying to stay neutral.

"But have you heard anything about them?" Betty asked.

"Oh, Betty, what difference does it make which one we read first?" Nellie said with a wink at Anne. "We'll end up reading them both." She leaned closer to Anne and whispered, "Actually if Betty doesn't like it, she just skips to the last chapter."

"I heard that!" Betty said from down the aisle.

"Now, how come you can hear me whisper ten feet away and never hear me when I suggest you do the dishes or fold laundry?"

"Huh?" Betty said. "Did you say something?"

Nellie turned back to the bookshelf with an exasperated sigh. Betty winked at Anne.

Anne stifled a giggle and went back to the counter. The wind still howled outside, and the rain was coming down at a slant. But at least there was no lightning or thunder, or Liddie would be down here clinging to Anne's legs again. The sisters seemed to have settled on a book, although they were still discussing it.

"Would you ladies like some hot tea before you go?" Anne asked. She hated to send them back out into the rain until it let up some.

"What a nice idea. That would be mighty appreciated," Betty said.

"If it's no trouble," Nellie added.

"No trouble at all. I was thinking a cup of tea would hit the spot. Make yourselves comfortable. I'll be right back." She started toward the library's kitchen, but remembered she had carried the box of specialty teas upstairs to their private kitchen, so she detoured up the staircase.

"Ben, don't forget to do your math," Anne said as she passed through the living room.

"I won't."

Liddie had gotten out her coloring books and was surrounded by crayons on the floor. She seemed content and Anne told her she'd be downstairs for a little while more.

Anne put the kettle on and gathered up a large wooden box filled with an assortment of herbal teas and her great-aunt Edie's tea service. When the water had boiled, she poured the water into the tea server and transported the tray downstairs via the elevator.

Betty was sitting in one of the comfortable overstuffed chairs by the History Room. Nellie stood at the checkout counter reading the article that Anne had left by the phone.

Nellie looked up as Anne set the serving tray on the counter. "Sorry to be snooping. The article caught my attention."

"Nellie is always sticking her nose in where she shouldn't," Betty said with a shake of the head. "She knows better."

"It's okay. I shouldn't have left it out." Anne set the tray down on the counter.

"There's quite a threatening tone to it," Nellie said. "I hope it all got sorted out okay. Imagine someone bringing up something that happened so long ago. Sounds like someone suffered."

That was what Anne's father had said. "Yes, I think so too." She looked over at Betty. "I have Earl Grey, Cinnamon Spice, or peppermint tea.

"I'll have peppermint. Maybe it will pep me up some," Betty said.

"Would you like lemon or milk or both?" Anne asked.

"Just a touch of milk," Betty said. Nellie opted for Earl Grey with lemon. Anne served the sisters and then made herself a cup of peppermint also. She pulled out a chair for Nellie and herself and they sat in a circle sipping their tea.

"This was so nice of you," Betty said.

"So who turned out to be the bad guy in that article?"

Betty made a tsking sound. "Quit being a busybody, Nellie."

Anne smiled. "It's okay. And to answer your question, Nellie, I wish I knew."

"So it's an ongoing mystery?" A gleam glinted in Nellie's eye.

Anne nodded. "I'm afraid so."

"If this were *Murder She Wrote*, the murderer would be the least obvious suspect."

"No, it was always the famous guest star on the show that turned out to be the bad guy," Betty countered.

"Not always," Nellie said, setting her tea cup down on her knee. "But yes, that did happen a lot."

Anne smiled, enjoying the banter between the sisters.

"Looks like the rain has let up for a bit. Guess we better dash before it starts up again." Nellie rose gracefully. Anne took her teacup, and they helped Betty get to her feet and into her coat.

The sisters had decided on the Caesars book, and as Anne checked it out, she said she hoped they liked it.

"Even if we don't, we'll learn something." Nellie tapped her temple. "Always got to keep learning, or you grow old."

"Speak for yourself," Betty said as she thumped her cane to the door.

Anne escorted them outside and then locked the door. As she turned off the lights and took the tea service to the library kitchen then headed upstairs, she kept thinking of what Nellie had said. If this were a mystery TV episode, the least likely suspect was usually the culprit. In their mystery, Kevin Kutcher would be the least likely suspect since he wasn't even in town that night and was on his way to a college interview. Alex would be the next least likely suspect in her mind. She knew where he was, up until he dropped her off at home. He was involved just as much as she was.

A chill tickled the back of her neck. At least she hoped she and Alex hadn't done anything to be guilty of.

She set the tea service on the kitchen counter as her thoughts continued. The next least likely suspect in her mind would be Jen. She knew Jen and liked to think she'd know if she was lying. That left Michael and Heather. Both were out that night. Both had a lot to lose if they were accused of a crime, with Michael being in law enforcement and Heather as a school teacher, where good reputations were crucial.

Anne looked in at the kids. Liddie's array of crayons had expanded to an even greater circumference and now were mixed with piles of blocks. Ben had gotten his car tracks out again and had them draped over the couch in elaborate jumps. How they managed to create such a mess in such a short period of time never failed to astonish Anne. "Okay, guys, it looks like you had a great time, but let's get this room cleaned up."

"Aww, I just got it all set up," Ben said.

Anne was sympathetic, but she felt like it would benefit them all to get to bed earlier tonight. "You can play for fifteen more minutes, but then put it away. Did you do your math?"

Ben looked down and shook his head.

"We'll work on it after supper," Anne said. "You don't want to get any further behind."

Liddie glanced up at Anne but didn't say anything. Her eyes looked tired.

"You too, Liddie. Fifteen more minutes," Anne said and returned to the kitchen. Rain was hitting the window again. She studied the cupboard, wanting something simple but hot and filling. She decided on a quick vegetarian chili her mother used to make and cornbread from a mix. She chopped and sautéed some onion and added it to the canned beans and tomatoes in the saucepan. She sprinkled in chili powder, keeping it very mild for Liddie, and mixed up the cornbread. She set the chili to simmer on the stove and slid the cornbread in the oven.

She checked on the kids again. Ben was picking up his tracks and blocks. Liddie still colored in her book, lying on the floor, her head propped up on her hand.

"I'm going to run up to the attic. I'll be right back," she said and headed for the stairs.

A wave of cold air washed over her. The attic was much chillier now than it had been earlier in the afternoon and seemed dreary and cold instead of cozy. She flipped on the light and hurried across the room to her chest, sending a mental thank-you to Jen. If it hadn't been for her remembering about Aunt Edie having an extra key, Anne wouldn't have been able to open it today. She scooped up the pile of school newspapers and her yearbook. Underneath was a paper-wrapped package. That was odd. She didn't remember putting anything like that in there. She picked it up and shut the chest, hurrying downstairs.

Back in her warm kitchen, Anne set her armload down on the table. She curiously opened the package and gasped. It was the strand of pearls that Aunt Edie had loaned her for the homecoming dance, her prom. She picked up the note inside.

Anne,

I could think of no one who would appreciate these more.

May you have many more wonderful nights wearing these under the stars.

Love,
Aunt Edie

Tears pricked her eyes. Oh, Aunt Edie! She was still surprising Anne with her generosity.

"Mommy, what are those?"

"Aunt Edie's pearls." Anne wiped her eyes and let Liddie touch them. When had Aunt Edie put these in the chest?

"Are you going to put them on?"

"I can," Anne said. She opened the clasp and slid them around her neck. The pearls felt cool and smooth against her skin and heavier than she remembered.

"What do you think?"

"Pretty," Liddie declared.

The timer beeped on the stove. "The cornbread's done. Did you pick up your crayons? No? Hurry and go pick them up and then wash your hands."

Anne wore the pearls through dinner and while she assisted Ben with his math. He didn't need much help, but Anne lingered, enjoying the time with him.

After the homework was done, Anne reminded them of the puzzles Reverend Tom had sent in his cards. If they completed them by church time, he'd give them something.

"Can I use markers to color it?" Liddie asked after they'd cut out and assembled the pieces.

"Sure, honey," Anne said, glad to see Liddie smiling.

After they'd finished the puzzles, she gave Liddie a bath again with baking soda, so thankful that most of the rash was gone. She treated Ben's legs and back with the new ointment.

By the time she got back to Liddie's bedroom, Liddie had already crawled into bed and shut her eyes.

"Liddie, honey, do you want to say your prayers?" Liddie nodded her head but didn't move.

"Okay, do you want me to say them for you?"

Liddie sighed and nodded. Anne took Liddie's hands and said a prayer.

"Thank you, Mommy," Liddie whispered.

Anne kissed her on the forehead, hoping that Liddie was just tired and not getting sick.

Ben was lying on his stomach on his bed. A book propped up in front of him.

"Hey, kiddo." Anne sat on the edge of the bed. "How are you doing?"

"Okay. I guess."

"I know it's been a rough week, and I just wanted to say that I'm grateful about how well you behaved and helped out around here, despite being so uncomfortable."

"I yelled at Liddie," Ben blurted out.

"You did? When?"

"While you were downstairs today. She was being a brat and kept messing up my racetracks on purpose. I told her I was sorry later, but I think she's still mad at me."

"I see. I'm glad you told me, sweetheart," Anne said, wondering if that was why Liddie was so subdued this evening. "You did the right thing by telling her you were sorry. All things considered, this week could've been worse. Things will be better when you can get back to school and can be with your friends and go to soccer practice."

He nodded. "Okay." He flipped over onto his back. "Are we going to church in the morning?"

"Sure. The doctor said you could go back to school Monday, so I think church is okay."

"Good."

They said a prayer together and Anne kissed him goodnight.

She was feeling unusually tired and subdued too. Maybe it was the rain and a day without sunshine. More likely it was the knowledge that time was passing, and she still didn't know who had written that article.

She gathered up the stuff from the attic and went to her bedroom. She removed the pearls and took a hot shower. Feeling relaxed, she thought about going right to sleep, but the growing tension that they were running out of time prompted her to prop herself up against the headboard and start reading.

She started with the yearbook and skimmed through the autographs and messages from her friends.

Alex's message, *Friends forever*, warmed her heart and also made her sad. A few weeks later, they had quarreled about the future and they didn't speak again until she returned home fifteen years later, brokenhearted and trying to start a new life without Eric.

She paused over one signature. Shaun Milhouse. He'd signed it with, *To Endless Possibilities*. She didn't even remember having him sign her yearbook. She flipped back to his senior portrait. Under his name his ambition had been listed as engineer. He'd been so positive even though he must've known by then his family didn't have the money for college. She wondered if he'd tried for student loans or maybe he felt he had to work to help the family. Pete Dillon too had indicated he'd had to run the family business. She wondered if he had different dreams for his life. Those two guys, Shaun and Pete, may have had their futures altered forever that night.

Anne picked up the school newspaper, the *Blue Hill Bugle*. She'd joined the staff her sophomore year. The paper came out monthly and she'd kept every issue. She started with her senior year and decided to work backward. She skimmed the articles, jotting down names of people who had contributed. Surprisingly, there weren't as many as she had thought. It was usually the same people who sent in articles, and of course, members of the staff were required to post something monthly.

She smiled over an article Heather had done on prom dresses and shoes and how to save money. She'd interviewed several of the girls and had a tough time finding anyone who had bought or were considering buying a used prom dress. She'd never interviewed Anne, but she and her mother had taken a gown of Aunt Edie's and updated it to make a really pretty, simple styled dress. She'd worn it with Aunt Edie's pearls and cream satin pumps they'd picked up at a discount store. Anne had felt like a princess.

Anne reread one of her articles on the need to update the computer system in the library. Little did she know then that she'd be a librarian herself someday.

She paused over an article by Kevin Kutcher. He was one of the official newspaper photographers, but he also wrote an article occasionally. Her eyelids were growing really heavy by the time she came across an article by Kevin. He'd written about the wetlands at the edge of town and the proposal to turn part of it into a shopping mall.

She skimmed through the column to the end of the piece and read his closing sentence.

The actions of a few naive spectators created a domino effect that landed other creatures in harm's way.

She reread it again. Grabbing the fake article, she reread it out loud.

Excited students arrived for the game and dance afterward, not knowing they were mingling with six traitors whose thoughtless actions that night would start a domino effect that landed others in harm's way.

Domino effect? Could both pieces have been written by the same person? She squeezed her eyes shut. Maybe she was just too tired to judge. Kevin had been in another state that night.

"It's usually the least obvious suspect," Anne repeated Nellie's words, but that was only in mystery novels or movies or shows. Still…what if Kevin had stuck around longer in Blue Hill than he'd said? The author of the article had written:

Kevin Kutcher, high school newspaper photographer and reporter was assigned to record the evening's event, but he let everyone down. He had a gift for sniffing out stories and seeking justice, except when it really mattered.

Kevin had told her he was on his way to UNC. The university was a good nine-to-ten-hour drive but…could Kevin have been in town longer than he'd said?

Had Kevin attended the school dance after all? Heather had thought so. Maybe he hadn't left town until later, which meant he could've been involved in the crimes that night. The store break-in and the car accident occurred around eleven fifteen according to the police report.

There had to be a way to find out if Kevin was at the dance. An idea formed. Anne was going to need Heather's help.

Chapter Fifteen

"Welcome, Anne, Liddie, and Ben," Reverend Tom said heartily, his brown eyes warmed by his big smile. He stood in the entrance of the church to welcome members and visitors. He grasped Anne's hand. "So glad to see you this fine morning."

"Good to see you too, Reverend," Anne said, returning his smile.

Reverend Tom turned to Liddie and Ben. "So nice to see you are well enough to come today."

"Thank you for the puzzles," Ben said. "We put them together last night."

"It was fun," Liddie added. "I used markers to color mine."

Reverend Tom beamed at them. "I'm so glad you enjoyed them. Did you bring the puzzles with you?"

"I have them right here." Anne pulled the little paper puzzles out of her purse that had been in the "get well" cards from the reverend.

"Very nicely done," Reverend Tom said. "Come on over and you can collect your prize."

Liddie's eyes widened and she did a little hop as she followed Ben and Reverend Tom to a table with a pretty basket full of small items such as miniature New Testament Bibles, picture frames, coloring books, balls with Bible verses on them, and other things Anne couldn't see.

Liddie picked out a sticker book about the story of Esther, and Ben selected one of the balls. They thanked the reverend and headed toward their Sunday school rooms in the basement. Anne followed Liddie down. She said hello to her teacher and quietly explained that the rash still on Liddie's face was poison ivy but that it wasn't contagious.

Anne stifled a yawn as she found a seat in her class. She'd tried to fall asleep fairly early last night, but the phrase *domino effect* from Kevin Kutcher's article kept swirling through her mind.

Wendy waved from across the aisle as she took a seat next to her husband, Chad, a tall, stocky man in his early forties with thinning, sandy-brown hair and brown eyes. He shot her a quick smile before turning his attention to Mr. Willet, one of the church deacons, who was teaching the lesson for the day.

The lesson was on the faith of the Roman soldier and how he had such faith that Jesus would heal his child that Jesus didn't even need to go to his house. Anne hoped her faith would grow to be that strong. She enjoyed the discussion, and too soon the class was over. She entered the hallway as Liddie came out of her class with a sober expression on her face. She marched up the steps to the main sanctuary and their usual pew without a word to Anne.

"Liddie, sweetie, what's wrong?" Anne whispered, wondering if one of the other kids had said something unkind to her.

"Nothing," Liddie said.

"How was Sunday school?"

"Good," she said softly.

Mr. Willet walked up to the podium and started the announcements. Ben slid into the pew beside Liddie with a smile on his face.

"I'll be right back," Anne said to her children and she hurried back downstairs. Clara, the Sunday school teacher, was still cleaning up the room.

"Hi, Clara," Anne said, picking up a little chair that had fallen over. "How did class go?"

"Good. The kids were well behaved this week. It does my heart good when they seem to learn something. Why? Is something wrong?"

"Liddie just seemed subdued when she came out. I was wondering if you noticed anything."

"She was her usual, happy self until we were almost done. It was during the lesson time that she got quiet."

"The lesson was on the Good Shepherd, right?"

Clara nodded. "The Good Shepherd finding his lost sheep. Normally she raises her hand to answer all the questions and is one of my best singers. I thought maybe she wasn't feeling well."

"That could be. She had a rough week. She was really tired last night." Anne still wondered if it was something else, though. "Thanks, Clara, for all you do for the children."

Anne went back upstairs. The congregation was singing the opening hymn. She picked up a hymnal and turned to "Amazing Grace," although she knew almost all the verses by heart since it one of her favorite hymns of all time. Her Grandma Summers loved that song, and even now Anne could imagine her up front playing her violin, her face lit up with her love for the Lord.

After they finished singing, she sat back down and tucked an arm around Liddie, who seemed content watching Alex and Ryan sitting two pews up. Anne hoped she'd get a moment after the service to discuss with Alex what she might have discovered last night.

Reverend Tom continued the faith theme in his sermon, and the scripture was one of Anne's favorites. Jeremiah 29:11, "'For I know the plans I have for you,' declares the Lord, 'plans to prosper you and not to harm you, plans to give you hope and a future.' "

Anne noticed a couple of teenage girls, whispering until a parent silenced them by the clearing of his throat. Anne remembered those days. The youth group would crowd together on the back pews. They could sit together as long as they were quiet. Little did they or their classmates know where their lives would lead. Oh, they had big plans. One look at the ambitions listed under their names in their yearbooks confirmed that. Back then they really had no clue what was in store for them, but God did. She wondered what the outcome would be now for the author of that article or the one he accused. Would justice be served? Or only more turmoil and pain?

She bowed her head and prayed along with Reverend Tom's closing prayer that she'd trust God's plan for them.

Lord, I seem to be struggling this week and stressing too much. I feel like there's a ticking time bomb hanging over my head. I know I should have more faith. Please grant me peace and the wisdom to do what is right.

She raised her head, determined not to worry anymore. She'd do the best she could to help her friends but leave what she couldn't do in God's hands.

She shook hands with the reverend and thanked him for his sermon. Ben ran ahead down the steps to talk to some friends. Liddie waited for Anne.

Alex came out of the church, looking trim and handsome in his navy suit. He caught sight of Anne and waved.

"Good to see the kids out and about," Alex said. "Ryan has been missing Ben at soccer practice."

"I'm glad Ryan was able to come and keep Ben company. It was a long, long week in some aspects. Lightning fast in others."

Alex nodded. "I know what you mean. Crazy week, and then there was that nonsense with that article."

"I think I may have discovered something. I was going through the old school newspapers last night and —"

"Alex Ochs?" a female voice said. Alex and Anne turned to see a beautiful woman standing on the steps above them. Anne had to look twice to realize it was Melissa. She looked so different out of her overalls. Dressed in a lovely, fitted, soft blue dress and high heels that increased her height to almost that of Alex's, she looked almost as young and beautiful as she did the night of homecoming dance.

Alex stared at her. "Melissa?"

"Yes, silly. Have I changed that much?" She playfully slapped her clutch purse against his arm.

"No, I'm just surprised to see you. Anne mentioned you were back in town."

"Yep, but not for long. I just got confirmation that I got a research job in Washington."

"Congratulations," Anne said.

"Thanks." Melissa glanced at Anne. "It's what I always wanted. I don't leave for another month, so meanwhile I thought I'd catch up with old friends. I've been somewhat of a hermit working so much over at the garage."

"I was going to drop by over there sometime in the next couple weeks," Alex said. "I have a dent in my truck I wanted to get an estimate on."

"Bring it on by. Shaun will appreciate it. We do good work." She looked at Anne again. "Shaun told me he went over to talk to you. Get everything straightened out?"

"Mostly," Anne answered, keeping an eye on Liddie, who had gone down to join the boys on the grass.

"Shaun was upset about someone dredging all that stuff up concerning his grandparents," Melissa said. "He'd be really happy if the guy was finally caught."

Melissa smiled at Alex. "I told him that if anyone could get to the bottom of this, you or Michael could. You know this town better than anyone, and Michael is a cop of course."

Alex glanced at Anne and his face reddened some. "Actually, Anne has been the one really trying to get to the bottom of all this. If this situation ever gets resolved, it will be because of her."

It was Anne's turn to feel her face warm at the sincerity in Alex's voice. "It's been a group effort," she said.

"The old gang together again," Melissa said lightly, but there was something in her voice that caused Anne to wonder if Melissa had wanted to belong to their group in high school. It wasn't like they had excluded her, but she seemed to have her own friends.

Reverend Tom walked over to them. "Melissa. So glad to see you. It's been a long time. How are your folks doing? Your mother used to send me a note from Arizona every so often."

"I—I guess you didn't hear." Melissa's eyes brightened with tears. "My folks passed away last spring. They were involved in a light plane accident."

"Oh, my child, I didn't know." He placed a hand on Melissa's arm. "My condolences."

"I'm so sorry, Melissa," Anne said, and Alex echoed her sympathy.

"Thanks. I should've put a notice in the newspaper here, but they'd been in Arizona for over twelve years. I didn't think to notify anyone but a few close friends. Being the only kid and trying to finish up graduate school during all this was a bit overwhelming."

"Perfectly understandable," Reverend Tom said. "I just wish we could've been there for you."

Melissa took a deep breath. "Yeah, well, I'm doing okay. I put the old house on the market, and I'm looking forward to the move. It will be a fresh start." She squared her shoulders and gave them a bright smile. She told the pastor about her new job, a dream come true. But Anne couldn't help but notice that sadness lingered in her eyes. How awful to not be able to share her accomplishments with her parents.

"If you need anything at all, you give me a call, okay?" Reverend Tom said.

"Sure thing," Melissa said.

After Reverend Tom had gone up the steps, Anne asked, "Melissa, are you doing anything today? Would you like to come over for lunch?"

Melissa stared at her for moment as if assessing Anne's motives and then smiled. "I appreciate the invitation, but I'm meeting someone. Maybe some other time? I'll give you a call."

"Yes, let's make sure we do it before you leave town," Anne said sincerely, although somehow she doubted Melissa would call. "If you get a chance, come by the library sometime."

"I'll try." Melissa turned back to Alex. "Now about your truck, is it here?"

Anne glanced down at the lawn and caught sight of Liddie dashing across the damp lawn, mud spewing out from behind her little Mary Janes.

"I think I better get the kids home," Anne said as Liddie did a cartwheel, her skirt flying through the air. She looked at Alex, feeling her nerves tightening. She hadn't had a chance to discuss Kevin Kutcher and the article. She was both excited about the discovery but also perplexed about what to do about it.

"We can catch up later," she said to Alex and hurried down the steps. At the bottom she glanced back up. Melissa's hand rested on Alex's arm, but this time she didn't feel a twinge of jealousy like she had on homecoming night. She only felt a wave of compassion for Melissa.

She called Liddie and Ben and they scampered to the car. Liddie's eyes were bright and her face flushed from activity. She seemed like her normal high-spirited self. Anne helped Liddie buckle herself in to her booster seat and shut the back door. She turned and almost bumped into Melissa.

"Oh, hi. Did you change your mind about lunch?"

"No, but thanks. I've been thinking about what you've been doing to try to help your friends and Shaun. I didn't want to get involved in this..."

Anne waited quietly, praying that Melissa would make up her mind to share whatever it was that she was struggling with.

"But you know, after time goes by, you start thinking about what a friend really is. Shaun has always been my friend, even though I've taken him for granted. The other guys and gals I thought really cared about me didn't keep in touch. So maybe I had some misplaced loyalty. I don't know. But I'm going away and starting fresh, you know?"

Anne nodded. She knew about starting over in life.

"Anyway, I overhead the guys bragging. They act like a pretty girl has no ears or brains." She took a deep breath. "They were laughing about breaking into a store and stealing paint. They spray painted some snooty school's wall. I didn't know anyone had been hurt until you mentioned it the other day."

Anne's heart skipped a beat. "Can you tell me who was involved?"

"A couple of the football players and Chuck Bentley. Jerry Newman too," Melissa said.

Anne remembered Chuck as being a big guy who skipped class and liked to bully the freshmen. He seemed to always be in detention.

"Ralph Emerson and Speedy White made jokes about it too, but I don't know if they were actually involved."

"Have you thought about talking to the police about it?" Anne asked gently. "It would be good to close the chapter for the Dillon family."

"Ugh, I really, really don't want to talk to the police."

"What about Michael Banks? Would you feel more comfortable talking to him?"

"Michael?" She gave a little laugh. "I don't need to talk to him."

"Why?"

"Because he was there."

* * *

Anne loved Sunday afternoons. When Eric was still with them, weekends were always reserved for being with the kids and they'd always reserved those special hours after church as family time. Housework and business were put on hold. It was time to focus on God and her family.

But this Sunday she was having trouble relaxing. Not only did she have the unresolved suspicion concerning Kevin being the author of the threatening article, but there was Melissa's statement about Michael being involved in the break-in of Dillon's Auto Parts. She had encouraged Melissa to still talk to Michael or someone else in law enforcement, but when they parted company, Melissa still seemed reluctant.

Did Kevin know that Michael had been allegedly involved in the incident with Pete's grandfather getting hurt? Could that be the tragedy? A hurt back? It had altered the course of Pete's life. But then so had the car accident for Shaun Milhouse and his grandparents?

O Lord, which is it? Or am I missing something else entirely?

A snippet of the sermon text filtered through her muddled thinking. *"For I know the plans I have for you."* Okay, she'd had enough. She wasn't going to think about the article, Kevin, or the others for the rest of the afternoon. She was going to continue her usual Sunday plans of spending time with her kids. She finished putting the lunch leftovers in the fridge, gathered up their jackets, and ushered the kids and Hershey to the car. She drove them to Rosehill Park, where Anne had spent many happy hours with her parents as a young girl and later with her friends.

Hershey ran back and forth, tugging on his retractable leash as he checked out every oak and maple they came upon. They followed the path around the small pond, stopping to feed the goldfish the breadcrumbs Anne had brought along.

Hershey ran along the pond edge trying to catch fish, spraying up greenish water on Ben's jeans. Ben just laughed and did his best to restrain Hershey from going for a swim.

They left the small pond and went through a patch of woods to the rose garden. Park benches had been placed along the crisscrossing gravel paths that wound around planters. Aunt Edie had belonged to the park's garden club and helped raise funds to keep the grounds beautiful. She'd also donated rose bushes and other plants over the years.

Liddie ran ahead up the path and called back. "I found it!" She stood in front of a small brass plaque set in the planter of Japanese rosebushes that the garden club had placed in the garden after Aunt Edie's passing.

> *Dedicated to Edie Summers*
> *whose love continues to bloom here*
> *and will never fade*

Anne touched the pearls she'd forgotten to take off after church. Aunt Edie had brought beauty and grace into people's lives. Anne just hoped that she could carry on her great-aunt's legacy of the generous gift of the library to the town.

"Mommy, can I go play?" Liddie asked. The playground area lay beyond the flower garden. From where Anne stood, she could see other children climbing around the vast wooden structure in the shape of a big ship that provided slides, climbing nets, a swinging bridge, and swinging bars.

"Go ahead, I'm coming."

Ben ran past her with Hershey, their feet crunching on the gravel. Anne leisurely continued her stroll, all the while keeping an eye on the kids. Liddie had climbed up inside to the enclosed lookout on the make-believe mast. Ben was trying to get Hershey to try the slide. The chocolate dog had willingly gone up the short ladder into the ship's belly but balked at the doorway. He watched Ben slide down and then made a flying leap, all four paws hitting the slide midway, and he slid the rest of the way down.

Ben cheered and Hershey bounced around him. Anne took out her cell phone and snapped some photos. She took one of Liddie, Ben, and Hershey on the deck of the play ship and texted it to her mother.

Her mother responded, "Looks like a boatload of fun! Wish we were there to wave bon voyage."

"Wish you were here too," Anne texted back, thinking that with modern technology she felt close to her parents, even with many miles separating them.

She was putting her phone back in her pocket, when it vibrated and then rang. She clicked the answer button.

"Anne? Hi! This is Heather. I've been meaning to call you for the last couple days, but it's been crazy at school and home. Do you have a minute?"

Anne glanced at the kids, who had found a couple of playmates. "Sure. What's going on?"

"I was able to track down where the old unused yearbook and newspaper photos got stored."

"That's terrific!" Anne said.

"Maybe not so terrific. Mrs. Ashbury said they're still stored in the basement at the old high school. I got permission to go over there, but I haven't wanted to go down there alone."

Anne understood her concern. The basement, referred to as The Dungeon, was a huge, dark abyss that ran the entire length of the school and consisted of several rooms that interconnected in odd ways, as if over the many years, they'd just slapped up walls whenever they felt the need to create a new storage area. It was dark and cold, full of shadows and creepy noises.

The basement was generally off-limits to students but Anne had been down there a couple times to access the storage room, where the decorations for dances and other events were kept.

"I can come by tomorrow."

"Monday is going to be crazy too. I have a class with giggly freshmen girls who took my class to get out of gym, group flute class, four private lessons, and beginners band practice with kids who haven't figured out how to move their feet and play at the same time, plus I have to practice for a gig at the Baptist church. Want to trade jobs?"

"No thanks," Anne said with a smile. She'd take a dozen Nellies and Betties arguing about biographies any day over dealing with Heather's schedule.

"Anyway, I sometimes help the band teacher over there, and she got me permission for the janitor to meet me this evening and let me in. Do you want to come?" Anne looked over at the kids. "Yes, but we're at the park right now."

"No rush. I have tons of laundry to get done. My hubby is taking off tomorrow for New York on a business trip. How about we meet there at six?"

"That works," Anne said, thinking that she and the kids could get something to eat first. A trip to McDonalds, something they didn't do too often, would make a fun ending to the afternoon. And maybe this evening she'd find out if her hunch about the article was right.

* * *

McDonalds was across town by the highway. There was an outside seating area, and Ben took Hershey over with him to find a table while Anne ordered. The fast-food restaurant had a play area, and Liddie had barely finished her kid's meal before she was off playing again. Anne was glad Liddie was active after spending so much time indoors over the week, but she just hoped Liddie didn't overdo it. Mostly she hoped that whatever was bothering her little girl and making her unhappy would disappear with the poison ivy rash.

Ben took a deep slurp of his chocolate shake and then asked, "Can I give Hershey the rest of my french fries? He must be hungry too."

"You know we're not supposed to feed him from the table. He'll learn to beg." Anne looked down at Hershey. His soft brown eyes gazed up at her. She sighed.

"We'll compromise." Anne pulled out the rest of her chicken from her sandwich, wiped off the mayonnaise, and shredded it. She put it in the almost empty carton that held Liddie's abandoned chicken nuggets and placed it on the ground.

Hershey sat and looked from Ben to Anne. "Go ahead," Ben said. "Eat it."

Hershey stood, wagged his tail, and then gulped down the food. He looked up expectantly.

"That's all there is," Anne said.

"I'll get him some water." Ben picked up the carton and walked to the restroom.

Two policemen came out the door, carrying coffee and white bags. Anne's heart skipped a beat thinking for a second the tall officer was Michael. She thought about what Melissa had said earlier about him. Much as she dreaded it, she needed to talk to him and Jen.

She took a deep breath, praying for guidance on what to say, and called Jen and Michael's home number. Voice mail answered, and she was spared having to ask Michael if Melissa had spoken the truth. Spared for the moment anyway. She left a message for Michael to call her. They needed to talk.

Anne stared at her phone. She hated this. She didn't like confrontation, especially with people she cared about. She just wanted everyone to be happy and safe.

At the very least, Michael needed to know what Melissa had said about him and the other guys. If Michael admitted he was involved in the burglary, there may be consequences that could damage his career. If he still insisted he wasn't involved, at least he'd have some names to investigate. Somehow the truth would have to come out.

Hershey looked up from drinking his water and set his head on her leg. A wet spot seeped through her jeans, but she didn't mind. She stroked his soft ears. Hershey thrived on just giving love and being loved. Too bad human lives couldn't be as simple.

She checked her watch. It was 5:40. Time to head over to the school and see what she could find out about that fateful night fifteen years ago.

CHAPTER SIXTEEN

Anne peered down the metal steps disappearing into the abyss that was the Blue Hill Elementary School's basement. Cool air with a slight musty smell wafted over her. A groan, then a ping sounded somewhere in the dark depths. Pipes, no doubt. She looked back at Heather who'd unlocked the door.

"See why I didn't want to go down there alone?" Heather asked with a little laugh. She'd already gotten the key from the janitor and had been waiting in the parking lot for Anne to arrive. They'd entered the empty school together with Ben and Liddie tagging after them. "Jen told me once that prom committee actually suggested holding a dance down there," Anne said, holding out her hand to keep Liddie from going down the stairs without her.

"What was the theme? The dark ages?" Heather asked.

Anne laughed. "Something to do with knights and princesses, I think. The rock walls down there are supposed to be castle-like, whatever that means. Anyway it was just too much work to clean it out."

"Good thing." Heather flipped on the light switch and started down. "Can you imagine trying to get down these stairs gracefully in high heels and a gown?"

Anne told Liddie to hold her hand. They followed Heather and Ben down the long stairway. Hallways led off in different directions revealing numerous doors.

"This is awesome!" Ben's voice bounced off the rock walls. "I wanna play hide-and-seek down here."

"That would be fun. Just don't wander too far off. It's easy to get turned around in here," Anne said. "Stay in this hallway where I can see you."

Ben sighed loudly, but Liddie said, "Yes, Mommy."

Heather turned down one passage. "Mrs. Ashbury said it was in the old curriculum closet. The high school is using the space down here until they get a new storage area built off the auditorium. It's been years, but nobody seems to mind." She jangled her keys and stopped in front of a battered looking metal door. She inserted the key and the door creaked open on stiff hinges.

"I can't find the switch," Heather said, feeling along the wall. Dressed in black jeans and sweater, she vanished into the dark. Anne felt along the wall in the other direction, hoping there weren't spiders down there. She bumped into something hard and cold as the light filled the room half blinding her.

"Why anyone would put the light switch on the opposite wall from the door is beyond rational reasoning," Heather said.

An old wooden table painted blue dominated the middle of the floor. A variety of metal filing cabinets, tall and short, some green, others gray, lined two walls. Bookshelves on the other walls were filled with old English textbooks.

"Okay, Mrs. Ashbury said the filing cabinets were labeled by year," Heather said, brushing dust off her sleeve.

Anne examined the faded label on the top drawer of the nearest cabinet. 1965–1966. The next drawer down was 1962–1965. She was going in the wrong direction.

"The nineties have to be here somewhere," Heather said from the other side of the room.

Anne sidestepped down the wall. "Ah, here they are." She'd found the right drawer. She gave it a tug and it didn't move. "Yikes, this is stuck."

Heather hurried over. "Is it locked?"

"I don't know. I can't tell." Anne tried wiggling it and then reached for a lower drawer. Stuck fast too.

Heather opened some of the other cabinet drawers. "None of these are locked. Let me see if I can find something to pry it open. Maybe there's a tool in the shop." She walked back out into the hall.

Anne checked on Liddie and Ben. They were racing each other up and down the long hall. She returned to the room to peruse the bookshelves and recognized several textbooks she'd used through school. Copies of the school yearbooks lined one shelf.

She was familiar with the yearbooks from the years she attended Blue Hill High that chronicled the school lives of her and her classmates, but what had happened after she'd left for college?

Curious, she pulled out the volumes three years after her graduation. She flipped to the page with Pete Dillon. For his ambition, he stated he planned to study business in college and run his own business someday. So maybe he was happy in what he was doing—or maybe he just said that, if he already felt stuck working in the family business.

Ben walked past the door again, causing Anne to look up. He'd found a small ball and was bouncing it off the walls.

Anne glanced at her watch. Heather had been gone at least ten minutes. What was keeping her? "Mommy!" Liddie wailed. Her voice sounded far away and frightened. "Mommy! Help!"

Anne dashed out the door, her heart pounding so hard she could hardly breathe, and she smacked hard into someone big and solid. She stumbled backward, hitting the wall, and looked up at the tall, broad man standing in the hall.

Michael Banks.

"Whoa there!" Michael reached out his big, beefy hands to steady her. "What's wrong?"

"Where's Liddie?" Anne shoved herself off the wall and avoided Michael's grasp. She looked down the long hall. No Liddie or Ben. "Liddie!"

"Down here, Mom!" Ben called. Anne took off in a run in the direction of his voice. She got to the end of the hall where it turned down another passage. Ben stood, looking through a door. "She's in there. Hurry!"

Anne skidded to a stop by Ben. Michael ran up behind her. About six feet inside the doorway was a large square box with a solid top and bottom and lined with bars. Liddie stood inside the box, her face pressed up against the bars.

"Mommy," Liddie said with a quaver in her voice.

"How on earth did you get in there?" Anne asked.

"I don't know." Liddie sobbed.

"Are you hurt?" Anne reached through the bars, trying to soothe her daughter.

Liddie shook her head and sobbed louder.

"It's okay. Don't cry, sweetheart. You're okay. If you got in there, you can get out." Anne looked all over the box but couldn't find a door or hatch. How did she get in there? "Ben, see if you can find a light switch."

"It's right here," Michael said. There was a click and the room flooded with light. He hurried over to where Anne stood.

"What is this thing?" Anne asked, trying to lift the roof. It didn't budge.

Michael leaned over, examining the inside. "You know what? I think it might be a cage, like for a circus."

"It must be," Ben said. "Look there's an elephant." He pointed to a wooden cutout. Liddie sniffed and looked up, her eyes widening at the sight of the life-size pachyderm.

"This stuff must be from one of the school plays," Michael said. "We're in the old prop room."

Anne had calmed down enough where she could look around the room; it was loaded with everything from fake trees, painted background walls, racks of costumes, lampposts, benches, a couch, and cans of paint.

Michael circled the cage to the back. "Ah! Here is how she got in." Michael pushed on a section of bars and they moved apart. "These are plastic sections with elastic in the middle. Probably easier for whoever put this together than to make a door. Come out this way, little lady."

Liddie pushed her way through the bars and dashed over to Anne. She wrapped her arms around Anne's middle, burying her face in Anne's stomach.

Anne hugged her for a long moment and Liddie said, "I didn't mean to get stuck. I just wanted to play hide-and-seek."

"I told her we couldn't" — Ben held his hands out in a gesture of futility — "but she ran in here anyway."

"I tried to hide, and I fell down." Liddie rubbed her eyes and nose on Anne's shirt.

"She must've slipped through the bars in the dark." Michael had a twinkle in his eye.

"Thank you, Michael," Anne said, feeling a little guilty. When she had run into Michael in the hall, for a second she thought maybe he'd done something to Liddie. Her knees quivered a little after the surge of adrenaline and dash down the hall.

"You okay?" Michael asked, and Anne nodded.

Anne looked around for her son. "Ben!"

Ben came out from behind a rack of clothes wearing a gladiator helmet and carrying a fake sword. "This stuff is really cool, Mom."

"It is, but put it back where you found it, please."

Michael grinned. "Join the theater club when you get to high school and you'll get to play with stuff like this."

"Really?" Ben said. "Awesome!"

"There you are," Heather said from the door. "What's going on?"

"We had a little fright," Anne said, smoothing back Liddie's hair. "But everything is okay." At least she hoped so. She knew Liddie had been frightened by being trapped, but her usually rambunctious girl would have normally welcomed this as an adventure.

"Oh dear. I didn't mean to be gone so long. I finally found a tool that might work." She looked at Liddie still wrapped around Anne. "Everyone okay?"

Anne nodded, gently prying Liddie off of her waist and taking her hand. "She's okay."

"The policeman got her out of the cage." Ben looked Michael up and down.

"Good thing I let you in then, so you could be a hero." Heather gave Michael a teasing smile. "Did you find out what Anne wanted?"

"Didn't get the chance," Michael said as they all walked back out to the hallway. He looked at Anne. "I got your voice mail and was going to call later, but then on patrol I thought I saw your car in the parking lot and figured it was best to speak with you in person."

Heather held up a big screwdriver. "Okay, let's see if this thing does the trick and gets the cabinet open." After Heather hurried ahead of them, Anne turned to Michael. "Did Melissa talk to you?"

He gave her a nod, and Anne's stomach tightened at the somber look in his eyes. "I'll take care of it." He called good-bye to Heather and walked to the stairs.

Anne entered the storeroom, pondering Michael's response. Did he mean Melissa was mistaken and he'd clear it up? Or was he involved in the burglary and was going to confess?

"Got it. The drawer wasn't locked, just stuck." Heather called.

Anne pulled out chairs by the table so the kids could sit, and then she hurried over to the drawer to peer inside at the piles of photos. Anne got a tingle of excitement. There might not be anything of monetary value, but there could be something priceless in there.

Like the truth.

Heather lifted out two shoeboxes full of photos and put them on the table. The boxes were labeled "Yearbook."

Anne examined the files at the back of the drawer. "These contain photos taken for the newspaper. They are filed by month. And there are copies of all the issues."

"Glad someone was organized," Heather said, dumping out the mishmash contents from the boxes.

Ben leaned forward and picked up a photograph "Is that you, Mommy?"

Anne studied the photo of three girls locking arms together as they roller-skated. "Yep that's me. The girl in the middle is Jen, and the one on the outside is Tami Bates."

Heather studied the photo.

"Did you know that Tami took a study abroad trip and married an Irish actor?"

"No I didn't," Anne said. "That must've been fun."

"They're both working in the London theatre." Heather set the picture down.

"Incredible," Anne said, remembering how shy Tami had been. Here was another example of being surprised by how people changed. Or maybe she just hadn't known Tami as well as she thought.

Anne spied a photo of Michael and four other football players posing in front of a goal post. One of the players was Speedy White. Melissa had mentioned that he'd been making jokes about the elementary school graffiti incident. She set the photo aside and wondered again about the look in Michael's eyes when she asked him if Melissa had talked to him.

"There is so much to go through. What are we looking for specifically again?"

"Any photos from the homecoming game and dance," Anne reminded her.

Ben wanted to help, so Anne put him in charge of sorting out yearbook photos of football games and giving them to Heather. Liddie had the job of putting discarded photos back in the box. Anne went through the pile on the table with Heather and then searched the September newspaper file adding those photos from the dance to their stack. Some she'd seen already.

"Okay, that's all of them, I think," Heather said. "Thanks, guys," she said to Ben and Liddie.

Anne picked up the stack. There were several photos of Alex and her as homecoming royalty, but she was mostly interested in the group shots. She scanned the faces, searching for one in particular.

She found a couple with Pete in the background and another of Shaun standing on the sidelines, his head turned looking at Heather.

Heather looked to see what she was staring at. "Shaun had a crush on me. Would follow me around with sad, puppy dog eyes. I felt bad, but what could I do?" She shrugged.

Anne studied Shaun's unhappy face. "This was before he bumped into you and made you spill punch on your dress."

"I turned too quickly to get away when he was coming up to ask me to dance. I blamed him of course. Bad, I know," Heather admitted.

"Not trying to make you feel worse, but did you know that couple in the car that you saw get hit were Shaun's grandparents?"

Heather gasped. "No way. Really? Oh man, now I really feel guilty for being mean to him."

"If it weren't for your calling for help, his grandparents could've been worse off. He works over at Fowler's Auto Repair now and seems to be doing well."

"I'm glad," Heather said, "but I still feel awful."

So did Anne. She was sorry that old pain had been dredged up, but it couldn't be helped. They needed to find the truth before Tuesday. Two days away.

Anne returned with earnest to her search through the photos.

One outside shot captured her attention. The flash had caught several people in the parking lot. Two girls dressed in formals and a blond-headed guy were getting into a dark-colored car. The blond guy's profile was familiar but out of focus. Her heart beat faster. If she wasn't mistaken—

"Heather, take a look at this."

CHAPTER SEVENTEEN

H ow can you be sure it's Kevin Kutcher?" Alex said on the other end of the phone.

Anne circled her kitchen table, picking up the kids' milk glasses and taking them to the sink as she talked. She and Heather had gone through the rest of the photos and found two more that might contain an image of Kevin. By that time it was 7:30 and the kids were tired, bored, and restless. Heather had insisted that Anne take the photos home with her.

"I can't be sure," Anne said. "The face is blurry or teeny tiny in the background. But I think it's him. And that means—"

"It could mean he wasn't on the road to UNC when he said he was," Alex jumped in.

"Right. There is no time stamp on the photo, but his car was a dark blue like the paint they found on the other car."

"So, he may be the guilty party the article is referring to. If you're right about it being Kevin."

"If I'm right," Anne echoed, feeling a smidgeon of doubt. There had to be some way to examine the photos. It was too late in the evening to get to a photo shop, but she had another idea.

"I'm going to see if I can scan these photos and blow them up bigger on the computer."

"Good idea," Alex said. "Let me know if you need any help."

"Thanks," Anne said, glad she had confided in Alex. She'd also updated him on what Melissa had said about Michael. Alex was curious, as well, about what Michael meant when he'd said he would take care of it.

After they'd hung up, she picked up photos. Ben was in pajamas playing a computer game with Liddie sitting beside him giving her opinion on what moves he could make.

Anne told them she was going downstairs to use the library scanner and then descended the double set of stairways to the main floor.

Moonlight streamed in the window, lighting a path to the counter and the office area behind it. She turned on the lights and looked around the library with a feeling of satisfaction and gratitude at the neat rows of books holding knowledge, adventure, romance, and spiritual insight. No matter what happened in the next twenty-eight hours before the deadline or what secrets from the past were revealed, she had been truly blessed to have a family, home, friends, and a job she loved.

She lifted the lid of the printer copier and placed a photo facedown. She had to wait a few minutes for the computer to boot up, and she took a moment to sort through the mail that Wendy had placed in a basket. When the computer was ready, she scanned the photo of the car and the blond-headed guy in the parking lot and then two group photos that Heather had found, at the game and inside at the dance. After she'd scanned them all, she opened the photo software. She was familiar with the program from her time at the New York library when she had been in charge of making some brochures.

She enlarged the game photo and then the dance floor. There were several blond guys in the stands behind the band, but none she could recognize. She caught sight of Speedy White, the guy Melissa said may have been involved in the Dillon store burglary and school graffiti.

She'd saved the parking lot photo—the one she had the most hope for—for last. She focused in on the car and enlarged it. The face was still blurry, but it resembled Kevin. And half a dozen other guys.

Was that…? She zoomed in until the face filled the screen. A pinkish blur on the jawline. Kevin's birthmark?

Anne sat back, not sure what to do. She had no solid evidence other than this blurry photo in the parking lot at homecoming, which he said didn't attend. He could always revise his earlier statement so that he left before or during the dance to go to the university. But there was Heather as an eye witness plus the police report, which recorded that a car with dark blue paint hit Shaun's grandparents' vehicle.

There was also that phrase from the article that was almost the same as the one Kevin used in his last article, but maybe that was just a coincidence. Had the author of the article given them a deliberate clue pointing to Kevin?

She dropped her face into her hands, feeling weary.

Lord, I hate to think that any of my friends are involved in this mess, but please let the truth and forgiveness come out of this.

She lifted her head, knowing what she needed to do. With a surge of resolve to discover the truth, she shut down the computer, picked up the photos, and marched back upstairs.

"Okay, munchkins. Time for bed. School tomorrow," she called. She put the photos into an envelope and set it with her purse. She was going to return them to school after everything was over.

Liddie was in her bedroom sitting on the bed playing with one of her dolls. Anne smiled and picked up the bedtime storybook. "Ready to see what adventure Martha is up to tonight?"

Liddie nodded and let Anne help her snuggle under her quilt. Anne opened the book to where they'd left off and began reading.

"Martha ran down the path toward home, hoping her mother was waiting for her. She—"

Anne looked up as Liddie burst into tears and buried her face in her pillow.

"Liddie, honey, what is it?" Anne asked, rubbing the little girl's back. "You've been unhappy for days. You might as well tell me. Is it about getting stuck in that cage? I know you were frightened, but everything turned out okay." She waited for a bit and then added, "You know you can tell me anything."

Liddie looked up. "It was because I was bad!"

"What was?"

"Getting poison ivy."

"I don't understand."

Liddie's lower lip trembled. "I went way back into the woods where you told me not to go. Bad things happen when you don't obey...like Martha."

Anne looked down at the book she'd set on the bed. "But honey, everything turns out okay for Martha. She learned from her mistakes just like you have."

"But how come I got itchy and Isabelle didn't? And Ryan got better quick. Why do bad things happen to me and not other people? I got stuck in that cage and Ben didn't."

Anne took a couple of deep breaths, her mind searching for the right words to say. "Well, honey—"

"Is God mad at me?" Liddie looked at Anne, her eyes awash with more tears.

"No," Anne said firmly. "Not at all. I love you, but He loves you even more."

"Even when I'm bad?"

"Even then, and even when Ben is bad or I am bad." Anne drew Liddie close and rested her cheek on her head. "Listen, honey, I don't know why bad things happen to some people and not others. I wish I did. I wish I could see the future. But God has a plan for each of us. And Liddie, if we continue to love Him and try to do our best to be good, then everything will work out right in the end. You just have to trust Him, okay?"

After a moment, Liddie nodded.

Anne lifted Liddie's chin so she could look into her eyes and smiled. "We can talk more about this or anything else that's bothering you tomorrow or the next day or whenever you need to."

"But you might get mad if I tell you I was naughty."

"I'll try not to get angry. I worry about your safety. That's why there are rules. We will just do the best we can, okay?"

Liddie sighed, looking not entirely sure, but she nodded.

"Now, do you want me to keep reading about Martha?"

She nodded. Anne helped Liddie slide under the covers. She finished the chapter about Martha's trip to the African well and they said prayers together.

Anne tucked her in and shut off the light. She turned just outside the doorway and watched Liddie for a few minutes.

Poor little girl. She'd been hurting all week, thinking God was punishing her. What a terrible burden to carry.

Her father's words came back to her. He'd said it sounded like the author of that article was crying out for help. All these years he or she would have been carrying that burden. How sad.

Anne thought about each of her friends. Kevin, Jen, Michael, Heather, and Alex. Suddenly she smiled. If she was right, she not only knew what crime was committed but also who wrote the article.

* * *

"Why am I so nervous?" Anne said to the empty kitchen. She wiped her hands on a towel and checked the tray of cookies, cake slices, and miniature fruit tarts. She'd brewed fresh coffee and had cream and sugar on the table. There was hot water in Aunt Edie's tea server waiting on the counter. She'd even picked up a bouquet of autumn colored flowers. She was ready. She hoped.

She'd invited everyone mentioned in the article over for coffee and dessert. When some seemed to hesitate, she reminded them that the deadline the article warned about was tonight.

Except for Alex, none of them knew the others were coming. She wasn't completely sure if her conclusions about the author or crime were correct, and she wanted to leave the alternatives wide open. Only Alex knew what she suspected.

She sent the kids over to Wendy's for the evening. They would have fun over there, and besides, she didn't know what was going to happen. Not that she thought they were in any danger, but many years had passed since they were friends in high school, so there was an element of the unknown.

The buzzer rang for the back door. She pushed the intercom button. It was Alex. "Come on up." She pushed the button to release the lock. His footsteps sounded on the steps and then he was in the kitchen. He had changed from his usual work clothes into dark brown casual slacks and a long-sleeved, striped shirt.

Anne too had chosen to bolster her confidence by dressing up a bit in black slacks and one of her favorite burgundy sweaters.

Alex gave her a reassuring smile. "Ready?"

Anne put a hand over the butterflies in her stomach. "No, but I want to get this over with."

The buzzer sounded again. Michael, Jennifer, and Heather had arrived at the same time and came up the steps. Michael had come right from work and was still in his uniform. Heather wore her usual black slacks and a sweater, looking sleek and poised like a cat. Jen wore high-heeled boots, fashionable jeans, and a woven, off-the-shoulder white blouse.

"Anne, you didn't tell me that Heather was going to be here!" Jen exclaimed, giving Anne a quick hug. "This is great!"

Anne welcomed them and asked them what they'd like to drink, then invited them to help themselves to the food on the table and get comfortable in the living room. Soon they were laughing and chatting as if they were still in high school and were trying to catch up with all the weekend gossip before the bell rang.

Alex sidled over to Anne. "Where's Kevin?"

"He said he was coming," Anne said, wondering now if it had been wise to tell Kevin a slightly later time. She wanted to see his reaction when he saw everyone.

The door buzzer rang, and Anne went to the kitchen to let Kevin up.

"Hi Kevin," Anne said when he'd reached the stairs' landing. "Come on in."

He glanced down at his navy scrubs. "Sorry, I had to work overtime and didn't get home to change."

"That's perfectly fine. It's a casual evening. We're just talking in the living room."

"We?"

"Yes. You mentioned how you'd like to see the old gang. I invited them over too."

He gave her a nod. "Cool."

"Would you like coffee? Tea? There's juice or soda too."

"Coffee would be fine."

Anne poured him a cup. "Cream and sugar are on the table. Help yourself to the food."

Kevin glanced at the food on the table but didn't take any. He walked into the living room.

"Kevin!" Heather and Jen jumped up to give him a hug.

Michael stood and extended his hand. "Great to see you, bud."

"Glad to have you move back to Blue Hill," Alex added, shaking Kevin's hand after Michael did. "Where are you living?"

"At my parents' house. They haven't been doing too well."

"I'm sorry to hear that," Heather said. "They must be happy you're back."

"So they say." He gave her a small smile. He glanced at Michael again, looking uneasy.

"Please have a seat, Kevin, and make yourself comfortable," Anne said, clutching her hands together to keep them from fluttering nervously. "As you probably surmised, we all share a common problem right now. Someone is trying to slander one or all of us."

"It's ridiculous!" Jen said. "As if we'd do anything to hurt anyone intentionally."

"Yes, well, I have been looking into it." Anne glanced at Alex, who smiled at her encouragingly. She sent a quick prayer heavenward. *Please, God, let me do this right.* "And I think I know what happened the night of homecoming."

Anne pulled the article out of her pocket and unfolded it. "The tragedy the article is referring to was a hit-and-run accident that injured Shaun Milhouse's grandparents. The case was never solved, but the person who caused the accident is in this room. This person didn't mean to do it. Heather and I found some photos from that night, which prove this person was not where they said they'd be.

Then years later this person wrote an article trying to cast blame on others. But it didn't work." Her gaze circled the room and stopped on Kevin.

"Why are you looking at me?" Kevin fired at her. His gaze shifted around the room. "Why are you all looking at me?"

Anne felt Alex move fractionally closer to her. By Kevin's reaction, she knew she was right. "Kevin, if you needed help, why didn't you come to us?"

"You?" He let out a bitter laugh. "You all abandoned me, that's why."

He jumped up, his face reddening, deepening the birthmark on his jaw. Out of the corner of her eye, Anne saw Michael stiffen. His hand inched to rest on his thigh just below his holster. Anne's heart beat faster. Had she done something wrong? Surely Kevin wouldn't threaten them, would he?

"Where were you all that night?" Kevin asked and turned to Heather. "You turned me down flat about going to the game and dance together."

Heather's pretty face paled. "I–I told you I'd promised some girlfriends we'd all go together, without dates. It was a girl thing."

"Well, if you'd said yes, I would've been with you that night instead of alone. This is your fault."

He turned to Alex and Anne. "And yours too! I invited you to carpool so we could all be together, but no, you had to be high and mighty and drive that stupid convertible. I was alone! Do you know what it is to be alone?"

Alex opened his mouth as if to say something but then seemed to think better of it.

Kevin turned and waved a finger at Jennifer and Michael on the couch. "And don't think you two didn't have anything to do with this. Jen was always picking fights with Michael, making him angry. Did you know Michael cut me off that night? It was on Main Street. I almost drove up on the sidewalk."

"I didn't know," Jen glanced at Michael, who shook his head and tightened his arm around her.

"You didn't see me, but it made me so angry, thinking about how selfish you all were that night. I wasn't thinking straight and went through that stop sign.

"And no one, not even one of you, thought to offer Shaun a ride home so he wouldn't have had to call his grandparents to pick him up. The Thomases should've never been out on the road at all. Do you hear me? They shouldn't have been there! I shouldn't have been there!" he shouted and collapsed back in the chair.

He buried his face in his hands and whispered, "I shouldn't have been there." And he began to cry.

Chapter Eighteen

Anne looked at the others, a lump lodged in her throat. Heather had tears in her eyes. Jen looked at Anne and shook her head as if she couldn't believe what happened. Michael had a stoic expression, but his Adam's apple bobbed.

Alex stepped forward and put his hand on Kevin's shoulder. "Hey, man. I'm sorry we weren't there for you. I really am."

"Yeah, we never meant to make you feel alone," Heather said. "But why didn't you just come out and tell us how you felt?"

Kevin's face was still buried in his hands. He didn't answer.

Anne looked at Alex again and bit her lower lip. She didn't know what to say. She sent up a prayer for guidance and then stepped closer to Kevin. "Hey, Kev, it must've been hard coming back and dealing with your parents' health problems. That can cause a lot of stress. Plus, being home can bring back all kinds of memories. It did for me when I moved back."

Kevin sighed and nodded.

"I can see how all this would remind you about Shaun's grandparents and their health struggles. And if it were me, I'd be thinking, how did this happen to me? I've always tried to be a good person and—"

"Make one stupid mistake and ruin your life," Kevin said, looking up, with a tiny, wry smile tugging the corner of his mouth.

"And living with guilt is the worst," Michael looked at Anne. "We all have some of that."

"Regrets," Heather added.

"I think you wrote the article, Kevin," Anne said, "so that you wouldn't feel alone."

He lifted a shoulder in a shrug. "Maybe."

"I don't understand why you were still in town," Heather said. "Weren't you going to UNC for a scholarship interview?"

"I got angry that no one wanted to go to the homecoming dance with me, so I thought I'd just go to the game and then leave for North Carolina. I left too late, so I was driving too fast," Kevin said. "It was stupid, but I went to UNC anyway and got no sleep. I was afraid I was in deep trouble. I blew the interview. Blew my chances of going to the school I wanted, which led me to blowing my chances of medical school. Domino effect."

"I'm so sorry school didn't work out," Anne said. Maybe someday if this all got resolved she'd tell him that his phrase "domino effect" was one of the things that had tipped her off.

"Was your car damaged much?" Heather asked.

"Just the bumper and headlight. I got it fixed before I got home. I thought it was all over, but it never was. I don't want to live with this any longer. I need to make restitution." Kevin looked at Michael. "I'll go to jail if I have to. I've saved some money. I can hire some help for my parents. For a while anyway."

Michael got to his feet. "I think things will go easier if we go down to the station and you sign a confession."

"Okay." Kevin let out a deep breath and appeared uncertain. "I don't have anyone to go down with me or bail me out."

Anne stepped forward. "You're not going alone. Not this time."

"Nope, we're all going." Jen glanced at the others.

Heather slipped her arm under Kevin's. "I'm proud of you for wanting to do the right thing. That takes guts."

"Would it be okay if I called Reverend Tom?" Anne asked. "I think we could use his moral support."

Kevin nodded and the others agreed. They all left the house together.

* * *

Anne stood drinking her coffee, gazing out her window at the rolling hills. The house was peaceful. Too peaceful for a Tuesday morning.

Anne had been at the police station last night until after midnight, and Wendy had offered to keep Liddie and Ben overnight and take them to school. So no kids. No rush to eat breakfast and get out the door. Even Hershey was behaving in the yard. No barking or squirrel chasing. She couldn't believe she was missing the noise and stress of the previous Monday.

A pop sounded behind her. Aunt Edie's untrustworthy toaster popped up her toast, perfectly brown. She took the toast without burning her fingers, buttered it, and chewed on it halfheartedly.

This wasn't right, Anne thought, and then she laughed at herself. Here she felt out of sorts when everything was just fine.

She took another sip of coffee. Thinking of peace brought to mind another thing that happened the previous evening. At the station Michael pulled her aside and told her that after his conversation with Melissa, he decided to come clean about homecoming night. No, he hadn't been involved with the burglary, but he'd always suspected the kids involved. He lied when the police questioned him and, over time, it became easier to pretend he really didn't know anything. But he did, and he was going to see about getting restitution for Mr. Dillon. There was a slim chance it might postpone his promotion, but he said the peace of mind he felt after making the decision to come clean was worth any consequences.

The phone rang, startling her, and she almost dropped her toast. She grabbed the receiver, hoping something wasn't wrong with Liddie or Ben.

"Anne? Reverend Tom here."

"Hi, Reverend. Everything go okay for Kevin after I left?" Anne asked.

"Better than okay. Whatever you said to the captain made an impression. I think things will go all right."

"I'm so glad," Anne said. As she had paced the police waiting room last night, she kept remembering how she'd told Liddie to keep trusting God. And if Anne truly believed God had a plan for everyone's life and that sometimes He let trials happen to strengthen one's faith, then she needed to believe there was hope for Kevin. Kevin had been so full of hope and ambition, only to have his life change by a foolish split-second decision. He'd suffered all those years. She wanted him to have a chance to start over, and she went to the captain on Kevin's behalf.

"Actually the statutes of limitations on the accident have run out," Reverend Tom continued. "Shaun's folks can still sue, but I went over there this morning with Kevin and talked to them and Shaun. Kevin apologized to Shaun's parents. They're good Christian people and they forgave him. The Thomases have passed away, but Kevin offered to provide some financial assistance to Shaun's parents."

"How is Shaun taking all this?"

"He's still a little angry that it took so long for Kevin to come forward, but they shook hands. With time, I think he'll forgive Kevin. Anyway, Kevin will be getting some counseling and also will be assigned to do community service, perhaps with troubled teens, and some volunteer hours. And I hope it's okay, but I recommended some volunteer hours at the library."

"I think that's great," Anne said sincerely. Wendy would come up with all kinds of projects to keep him busy. "Thank you for all you've done for him."

"Not me, but thanks to God's grace and you and the others. Never underestimate the power of friendship."

After he hung up, Anne finished her toast and got ready to open the library. As she walked down the stairs, she thanked God that compassion and forgiveness proved to be the keys to unlocking Kevin's guilt. She hoped Kevin would find peace now.

She heard the sound of books hitting the floor and Wendy's "Oops!" She hurried down the last flight of stairs, happy with the plans that God had for her life.

About the Author

From her first introduction to the beginner readers with Dick and Jane, award-winning author Kelly Ann Riley has wanted to be a writer. She started penning tales at an early age and received special recognition for her short stories. Later, she became a reporter and the editor for her high school newspaper.

Now Kelly Ann enjoys writing romantic suspense and cozy mysteries. She lives in Alabama with her family and numerous pets. She loves visiting the East Coast and has wonderful memories of Cape Cod. Kelly Ann is an avid reader and, like Anne, enjoys spending leisurely hours reading a good book. You can contact her through her Web site at KellyAnnRiley.com.

A CONVERSATION WITH THE AUTHOR

Q. *You have written for several Guideposts series, including Patchwork Mysteries and Secrets of Mary's Bookshop. How is Blue Hill Library unique among them?*

A. As a child I fell in love with libraries, which contained the books that could transport me to any time or place in the world with characters that I hated to part with at the end of the story. When I was asked to write a book in this series I was thrilled that it included a library as wonderful and unique as Aunt's Edie's old Victorian home.

Q. *When you are not writing, what are your favorite activities?*

A. When I'm not writing, I love to read all kinds of books, particularly mysteries and suspense. I can read anywhere, but my favorite places are on the beach or by a pool. I enjoy watching TV series like *NCIS* and *Castle*, where there is a mystery to solve, and I love movies, especially those with a happy ending. I always want good to triumph over evil. I also like to travel. My family has been all over the United States and recently we went on a cruise to the Caribbean. I love scouting out new settings for books and imagining what it would be like to live in different locales. Traveling, as exciting as it can be, also gives me an appreciation for being at home in the country, where I am surrounded by our many pets.

Q. *What is the most rewarding aspect of writing for Guideposts?*

A. The most rewarding aspect of writing for Guideposts is knowing that the books are going to readers who love mystery series with small town settings as much as I do.

Q. *What advice would you give an aspiring novelist?*

A. One piece of advice that I personally found helpful as an aspiring novelist was to finish what I started. It's easy to begin novels. The excitement is high with a new project but then tends to wane when the writer hits the sagging middle. It is so tempting to start something new. Unfortunately, many novels never get finished. So, don't give up until you write "The End" no matter how badly you think the story is going. Most of good writing is rewriting, but you need to have the words down on the page before you can fix them. And remember if God has given you a talent, He expects you to use it. Never give up. Keep on writing.

Q. *Anne Gibson likes to drink her coffee without cream or sugar. What are your coffee-shop favorites?*

A. I'm a big fan of coffee drinks, particularly those offered in the holiday seasons like Pumpkin Spice and Mocha Mint. During the hot part of the year I like iced unsweetened lattes or lemonade iced tea. An occasional cappuccino is also one my favorites treats, especially when served with a piece of scrumptious cheesecake.

Recipes from the Library Guild

Anne's Pumpkin Spice Cake

4 eggs

2 cups sugar

1 cup vegetable oil

1 15-ounce can pumpkin

2 cups all-purpose flour

2 teaspoon baking powder

½ teaspoon baking soda

½ teaspoon salt

1 tablespoon pumpkin pie spice

½ cup chopped walnuts

Preheat oven to 350 degrees. Combine eggs, sugars, oil, and pumpkin in a large bowl and beat until smooth with a mixer. In a separate bowl, combine the dry ingredients—flour, baking powder, salt, and spices. Slowly mix the blended dry ingredients into the pumpkin mixture until well combined. Gently stir walnuts into batter. Spread batter in a 9 ½ × 13 ½ × 2-inch glass baking pan. Bake twenty-five to thirty minutes until lightly brown and inserted knife or toothpick comes out clean. Cool cake.

Top with whipped cream or creamed cheese frosting.

FROM THE GUIDEPOSTS ARCHIVES

*"Mystery Date" by Rebecca Keeley originally appeared in
the May/June 2001 issue of* Angels on Earth *magazine.*

Homecoming was just around the corner, and the halls of
Mountain Crest High were abuzz. Who was going with
whom? Who was wearing what? Before class started one day, the
teacher announced we had a special guest.

In walked Kirk Schroeder, the most sought-after guy in our
junior class. He was carrying a bouquet of garden roses. "I wrote
a poem to ask someone here if she will be my date to homecoming,"
he said nervously. *How romantic,* I thought.

I grew up listening to fairy tales and dreamed of turning
sixteen so a handsome prince could whisk me off to the school
dance. It never occurred to me that my cerebral palsy or
wheelchair might get in the way. But when I started high school,
I let go of fairy tales and faced the fact that I might not get asked
out.

Kirk walked down my aisle, straight toward me, and held out
the roses, saying, "I hope you'll answer yes."

"Me?" I asked, shocked. Kirk nodded. Of course I accepted,
and Kirk was my prince that magical evening. It was a fairy tale
come true.

Read on for a sneak peek of another exciting book
in *Secrets of the Blue Hill Library*!

Theft and Thanksgiving

Mommy, I don't wanna wear my coat today." Liddie Gibson scrunched her face as she looked up at her mother with eyes that never failed to melt Anne's heart. "It's too heavy, and it's hard to play."

Anne sighed. "Okay, but it's nippy out, so you'll need to wear layers." She turned to her son and smiled. "Ben, would you mind going upstairs with Liddie, in case she needs help?"

He glanced down at his feet as he shuffled them. "I don't ... "

She leveled him with one of her mom looks that she rarely used. "I really need your help, Ben."

"Sure, Mom." Ben started toward the stairs. "C'mon, Liddie. I don't want to be late for school."

Liddie shrugged out of her heavy coat and skipped along after her brother, dragging the coat behind her. Anne watched them until they disappeared from sight.

The library door opened with a *whoosh*, letting in a blast of cold air. In walked Alex Ochs, wearing a slight grin on his face. "Sorry I'm a little early, but I thought if Ben and Liddie were ready we could be at the head of the drop-off line."

She smiled. "They'll be down in a few minutes. Liddie is putting on some layers."

"Good idea. It's starting to get cold out." He leaned against the counter. "Do you have some time later this morning to go over plans for the new display case I'm building for the library? With Thanksgiving three weeks away, I need to get started soon."

Anne gave him an apologetic look and slowly shook her head. "I'm sorry I can't today. We're having our first Tea and Book Club meeting."

"Sounds interesting." He lifted an eyebrow. "What kind of tea?"

She chuckled. "Variety. As of now, it's an all-women's group, but you're welcome to join us if you like."

"All women, huh?" He folded his arms and pretended to ponder before shaking his head. "Nah, I think I'll pass on this one. But thanks."

When the children returned, Liddie glanced up at Alex and then to her mom. "Ben helped me find layers, see?" She took a half step back and opened her arms to show off her pink cardigan that clashed with her bright orange long-sleeved T-shirt that didn't quite cover the yellow undershirt beneath it. "Is this okay?"

"You can take off your sweater when you get to school." Anne nodded toward Alex, who was obviously having a difficult time keeping a smile off his lips.

He cleared his throat. "Time to go to school."

Liddie ran over to Anne and wrapped her arms around her mother's legs. "I love you, Mommy."

Anne kissed Liddie on the cheek and brushed a lock of hair from her face. "I love you too, sweetie. That sweater is fine for today, but when it gets colder, I'm afraid you'll have to wear your heavy coat."

Liddie scrunched her face again but nodded. Alex grinned as he reached for her hand. "C'mon, Liddie. We don't want to be late." He looked at Anne, winked, and focused back on Liddie. "I bought you a new booster seat so we don't have to keep moving yours back and forth between your mother's car and my truck."

"What color is it?" Before Alex had a chance to answer, Liddie asked, "Is it pink?"

"Of course it's pink." Alex smiled down at her. "What other color is there?"

Anne opened her arms and pulled Ben in for a hug. He leaned into her momentarily, but then he stiffened. When Anne let go and saw how red his face was, she felt a tightening in her chest.

Alex reached for Liddie's hand. "We can talk later about the display case, but one thing I wanted to tell you now is—"

The library phone rang, interrupting him. Anne cast an apologetic look his way as she answered.

It was Mildred Farley, one of Aunt Edie's closest friends and a dedicated library patron. She sounded frantic.

"What happened?" Anne asked.

"My friend Claire Daniels went shopping yesterday, and when she went to use her credit card, the man at the store told her it was denied."

"I'm sure there's probably just a glitch in the system," Anne said. "That kind of thing happens all the time."

"That's what I told her. But when we got back to her place, she called the credit card company and found out someone has been using it for the past couple of weeks. They've charged that thing all the way to the max."

"Do you think maybe Claire charged some things she might have forgotten about?"

"Nope. She's been home taking care of her sick husband for the past two weeks. That's why we went out. She needed a little retail therapy."

Alex held up a finger and mouthed that he'd see her later. Anne nodded and focused back on her conversation with Mildred as he left the library with Liddie and Ben.

"What did the credit card representative say?"

Mildred sighed. "They're investigating. Poor thing. Claire has been up to her elbows in taking care of other people, and the moment she tries to do something for herself, something always seems to happen to ruin it. I sure wish there were something I could do to help."

"You're being a good friend simply by listening to her."

"I know, I know. That's what Claire told me, but I also know that she has her hands full, and this will only make things worse."

"What happened to her is terrible, but I'm sure the credit card company will make things right."

"That's what the man on the phone said." Mildred let out an audible sigh. "Poor Claire."

"Are you still planning to come to the Tea and Book Club meeting today, or do you—?"

"You know I wouldn't miss it for the world."

"Good. I bought a variety of teas so everyone will have what they like."

"I love tea, but I have to stay away from the chamomile," Mildred said. "That stuff makes me sleepy, and it would be downright rude for me to start yawning right in the middle of your meeting."

Anne laughed. "Then you can have the peppermint tea. That should keep you awake."

"I'm sure it will. Well, I'd better run. Claire is probably up by now, so I need to call and check on her before she gets too involved in her busy day. Once her husband gets up, she runs nonstop making sure he gets what he needs."

"Do you think she can pull herself away for an hour or so to come for the tea?"

"I doubt it, but I can ask her." Mildred sighed. "I'm sure she'll want to be home if the guy from the credit card company calls. I better go so I can get everything done. See you later."

After Anne hung up, she rocked back on her heels and thought about her many blessings—including the fact that her aunt Edie had taken care of Anne's little family in her will and how well Anne, Ben, and Liddie had been accepted in Blue Hill.

A couple of calls came in inquiring about the Thanksgiving programs for children she'd advertised. She got another call from her friend Wendy Pyle, part-time volunteer library assistant, mother of seven, and one of the most voracious readers in town.

"I might be a little bit late today. It was rough getting the kids out of bed this morning."

"That's okay," Anne said. "We've been slow."

"Thanks! The twins are finished with breakfast now, so I need to take them to preschool. I'll be there right after I drop them off."

"Take your time." Anne couldn't imagine how difficult it had to be with so many children all going in different directions.

After Anne got off the phone with Wendy, she started toward the kitchen to set up for the tea when the phone rang again. This time it was her mother-in-law, Marlene. "Anne, dear. How is life in Blue Hill?"

"It's great. The kids and I have really settled in."

"Well then, your great-aunt obviously knew what she was doing when she left you that house."

"Yes, I agree. Are you excited about Thanksgiving? It's only three weeks away."

Eric's mother sighed. "Yes, and that leads me to why I called. You know how much I love seeing the children during the holidays."

A strange sense of foreboding washed over Anne. "Yes, and we love being with you and Byron too."

Anne heard her mother-in-law draw a deep breath. "Now I feel terrible about what I'm going to ask. Some of our friends from church purchased a cruise, but now they need to back out because their daughter was in a terrible accident. The cruise line refuses to refund their money at this late date, so we were thinking … Well, we thought it might be nice to buy the cruise from them. Byron and I haven't had a vacation, just the two of us, in a while, and it would really help … that is, if it wouldn't be too upsetting to the children. I mean, if you need us, you know we'll be there for you."

Anne knew how much the children looked forward to seeing their grandparents, but she understood. "A cruise sounds wonderful, and I want you to go! I'm sure the kids will be disappointed, but they'll understand. They know how much you and Byron love them."

"Thanks for understanding, dear. We'll send postcards during the cruise."

"Have fun and don't worry about us," Anne said. "The kids will love getting postcards."

After Anne got off the phone, she stared at the wall for a moment to regroup. For the first time in her children's lives, they wouldn't be with at least one set of grandparents for Thanksgiving. No matter how bad she felt, she was determined not to let Ben and Liddie know how disappointed she was.

She'd had her share of disappointments. Not long after Eric had passed away, she'd lost her job at the New York Public Library due to cutbacks. That had been the job of her dreams, and it upset her terribly. If it hadn't been for Aunt Edie leaving the house for Anne to convert to a library and home, she didn't know what she would have done. Thank God for family!

Anne went back into the kitchen to finish setting up for the tea. Since she didn't expect a large group, she thought it would be easiest to have it in the old library kitchen. She'd barely filled the pots with water when she heard the sound of someone behind her. She turned and grinned.

"Hi there. Looks like you've been busy."

"Hi, Mildred. Have a seat. I'll bring the tea over when it's ready."

"I'm here to help." Mildred rolled up her sleeves up as she approached the cabinet. "How many teacups do I need to set out?"

"We're expecting about half a dozen women."

Mildred nodded. "I'll rinse out a couple extras, just in case we have more."

Wendy joined them a few minutes later, carrying a platter of pastries she'd baked. "What's a tea party without goodies?" Before anyone had a chance to answer, she added, "Have you decided on a book yet?"

Anne nodded toward the stack of books on the table. "I have several possibilities. The group can decide."

"Good thinking." Wendy winked at Mildred. "That way if someone doesn't like the selection, you won't be the bad guy."

Mildred rinsed the teapots with hot water from the faucet to temper them before Anne poured the boiling water from the kettle. They put tea balls filled with loose tea in a couple of them and tea bags in the others. Wendy cut up some lemons and placed them in a bowl in the middle of the table, while Mildred filled tiny cream pitchers and sugar bowls. By the time they had everything done, all the women who had signed up to come were there.

"Help yourself to the tea and pastries," Anne said. "I'll give you a short synopsis of the books so we can decide which one we want to read first. All of these can be ordered for purchase, or if you don't want to buy one, we'll have a couple extras to check out. Before we continue, let's decide how often we should meet."

"Weekly," Wendy said.

"Too frequent." Mildred shook her head. "I think we should meet monthly."

Wendy made a face, so Anne intervened. "How about twice a month?"

Mildred turned to Wendy, who nodded. "Okay, that's fine, but since we're just getting started, why don't we meet again next week?"

Everyone looked around and nodded.

"Good, then it's settled." When people started talking, Mildred held up a finger to keep everyone's attention. "If you can spare the money, it's always a good idea to buy the books to help out the library. Every little bit helps, you know." She stopped suddenly and smiled toward the doorway, where someone must have entered. "Are you here for the Tea and Book Club meeting?"

"Y–yes ma'am." The soft voice at the door didn't sound familiar.

Anne glanced over her shoulder and spotted a woman who appeared to be around thirty, wearing faded jeans, a bank giveaway T-shirt, athletic shoes, and a baseball cap pulled down low over her forehead. Her hair sticking out of the back of it appeared mousy brown. The woman was unkempt, unlike the rest of the people in the room.

"Have a seat," Anne said. "We're trying to decide which book we want to read."

The woman slid into the chair closest to the door. She didn't look Anne in the eye. Anne tried hard not to stare at the new woman, who kept looking at Mildred but turning away when Mildred looked back. How odd!

A Note from the Editors

We hope you enjoy Secrets of the Blue Hill Library, created by the Books and Inspirational Media Division of Guideposts, a nonprofit organization that touches millions of lives every day through products and services that inspire, encourage, help you grow in your faith, and celebrate God's love in every aspect of your daily life.

Thank you for making a difference with your purchase of this book, which helps fund our many outreach programs to military personnel, prisons, hospitals, nursing homes, and educational institutions. To learn more, visit GuidepostsFoundation.org.

We also maintain many useful and uplifting online resources. Visit Guideposts.org to read true stories of hope and inspiration, access OurPrayer network, sign up for free newsletters, download free e-books, join our Facebook community, and follow our stimulating blogs.

To learn about other Guideposts publications, including the best-selling devotional *Daily Guideposts*, go to ShopGuideposts .org, call (800) 932-2145, or write to Guideposts, PO Box 5815, Harlan, Iowa 51593.